The Last Years

A humorous yet tragic story about living the dream, losing it, then going out in style!

WWW.THELASTYEARS.INFO

Copyright © 2010 by Brian Hoolahan

brianhoolahan@thelastyears.info

Cover Photographs by Eric Schlange, István Benedek & Mateusz Atroszko

Cover design B. le Ier

When The Lady Smiles © 1984 G.Kooymans/B.Hay
Life on Mars ©1971 David Bowie, Chrysalis Music, EMI, Tintoretto Music
La Grange © 1973 ZZ Top
Together © Thé Lau music&lyrics
publisher – PeerMusic/Maximan 1990/2008

The Last Years is the intellectual property of the author and registered with File-Reg International WWW.FILE-REG.COM online registration of Intellectual Property.

No part of this book may be reproduced or transmitted in any form in any manner, electronic or mechanical, including photocopying, recording or by any information system, without permission in writing from the author.

All characters in this book are the sole invention of the author and have no reference to any person, living or dead, and have no relation whatsoever to anyone bearing the same name or names.

Dedicated to Hannah and Louise Hoolahan

ACKNOWLEDGEMENTS

Thanks to a meeting with two musicians in a recording studio, one famous and one not so famous, whereby an incident occurred that sparked my imagination for this story. Read more at: www.TheLastYears/about.htm

Also thanks to Danny Honig whose sharp eye and expertise made this book readable. Thé Lau for contacting me about the correct verses of his song 'Together'. Alastair Campbell whose wit and clever remarks make me laugh daily and can be found among the pages. Alejandra Saldaña for her endless encouragement, love and strength, and Arlene for pestering me to get her name into this book while writing in a pub in Sligo, Ireland... it worked!

About the author

Brian Hoolahan was born in Ireland and has worked as a producer for various broadcast companies. He lives roughly 30 kilometers south of Amsterdam.

The Last Years

Chapter one

Rick crouched in the entrance of the department store, pulling his legs up to his chest in order to conserve warmth. The weather reminded him of the Britain he left behind long ago. It had rained three days non-stop. Years ago he would have laughed about getting a bath and washing his clothes at the same time. Right now all his joints hurt, and his cough was getting worse. This was no joke. This was a nightmare, especially now, in the dead of night in the middle of New York City.

The old German army coat he found six months ago in a rubbish dump was soaked through and weighing him down. Even if he wanted to stand up he didn't think he would make it. He had no idea of the time; daylight seemed an eternity away.

Rick remembered something, and smiled. His eyes twinkled. A bright light was at the end of the tunnel and he was the only one who knew it. He patted different parts of the coat, knowing what he wanted was well within reach. If only he could find the right pocket. His hand dug deep into one of the gaping breaches in his jacket. It turned out to be just another hole. He tried another. A smaller hole. And another. Yes.

Gripping the aluminum cap between his thumb and forefinger Rick pulled out a half empty bottle of fifteen year old Scottish malt whiskey. With a quick twist the cap was off and he hoisted the bottle high. His throat lit up. He followed the surge of the fire as it went deep into his chest, first warming then burning from the whiskey. Like petrol thrown on a dying fire: no drug in the world could have such an effect. The blazing sensation of alcohol seeped into his blood and spread gently through his body. Rick followed it with his mind, aware of every tingle, every nerve. Ecstasy. He savored it like a man inhaling the essence of his last cigarette. Good whiskey at a time such as this came at a price, and he was determined to savor it to the last drop. Especially since this was the last bottle, and hours before he could acquire the next.

From the near-total darkness of the damp corner where he resided, a searing white light suddenly blinded his eyes. He turned, crouched, and covered his eyes with his arms to avoid the stinging brightness. Without warning a deafening sound of clamoring metal came at him from all sides. Something pulled on his back and left arm. What? No matter where he turned to, everything seemed to be rising, a rippling feeling pulling on his coat.

What the fuck was in that drink? That was no cheap stuff. He might live on the streets like a tramp but he didn't have to drink like one.

"Please God, Jesus, Mary, and the rest of the family," he prayed quickly. "Please, let me live. Don't take me now. I won't let you down this time."

The metal shutters continued to rise. Squinting his eyes to avoid the painful light, he opened them a fraction to try and see what exactly was going on. Another light, appearing from a different angle flashed in his face. He turned to avoid the blinding beam, yet this light seemed to follow him wherever he turned his head. Rick tried to focus on the ground, but the only thing his eyes could see was an occupied pair of highly polished black boots on the wet concrete directly in front of him. Unless Hitler had made it to New York this had to be a security guard. By the look of the shine it was definitely the kick-ass, no questions type. No doubt supporting a haircut so tight it would put a marine recruit to shame.

"On your feet, scum bag," the guard growled. "You can get your beauty sleep elsewhere."

Rick was right. This was the kind who after army life found the police unprofessional, civilian life unbearable, yet addicted to a uniform and needed to work within the rules of a regime.

Massive hands reached down, grabbed his water-logged shoulder padding and pulled him up out of the doorway.

Rick twisted and pulled away. "Pisssss off," he screamed, followed by a shower of spittle, most of it landing on the spotless black uniform directly in front of him. The guard immediately let go of Rick and took a quick step backwards.

"I know how to stand up. Been doing it for years," Rick moaned while trying to push himself up.

Now that the security guard had got a better look at him, and more importantly a scent of his very personal body odor, he knew he would never beat him up. The fear that hobos carried all sorts of diseases like the plague, Black Death, yellow fever, AIDS, would keep him at a distance. He was probably sorry he soiled his hands on his soggy stinking coat.

"Thanks for the bed and breakfast," Rick chuckled.

"Get the hell out of here," the guard said.

"I'm going, keep your hair on," Rick replied, then chuckled once again as he eyed the marine styled haircut of the guard.

Holding his whiskey bottle tight in one hand and eyes locked on the security guard, Rick carefully maneuvered around the human bulwark and backed out onto the street. Landing in a water-filled pot hole, he turned and swayed down the street in the rain, making a mental note of the warehouse. With its shutters all raised, the window lights shimmered off the wet pavement, brightening up the cold dark streets. The next time the ape might overcome his fear and beat him to death. This was not a place to come back to.

An hour later the sun broke through the clouds. Somewhere along the way he had lost the bottle, and much to his disappointment, he was sobering up. But things were looking rosy. With a little luck breakfast was just up the street in the form of Smiler's, his favorite diner. A cup of coffee would be welcome, but then again he might get really lucky with a donut or fried egg on toast. Rick slapped his hands together and rubbed them enthusiastically. "Yes," he said in a wheezed cackle, "breakfast coming up," then quickened his pace towards the diner.

Standing outside the diner he shaded the glare by cupping his hands around his eyes and peered in through the window.

Jenny had been on her feet since four that morning. It had been quiet, just the way she liked it. Joking factory workers coming off the night shift. Worn out truck drivers drowning themselves in coffee in order to stay awake so they could get in as many runs as possible. Prostitutes resting their feet while spending their small change on coffee and breakfast. The type of clientele she preferred. Too tired to complain about the food or service, and not busy enough to run her off her feet and mix up the orders. Out of the corner of her eye she saw Rick peering through the window.

"Christ," she moaned, "trouble," and her shoulders sank. "Hey Jack," she shouted towards the kitchen, "The old man is back. What'll I do?" Normally she didn't mind the hobos turning up for a cup of coffee, but she held to three commandments: Don't stink; don't bother the customers; and keep your hands off the waitresses. This one usually broke the first one the moment he set foot in the door. The second five minutes later, and the third was something you could see he was waiting to do for a long time, but she never gave him the chance. However, something about this hobo that set him apart from the rest, yet she couldn't put her finger on it. He was smarter than most and had a way with women which although at times crude, was also charming. She wanted to turn him away but felt guilty. Jack on the other hand spared no feelings for any of the customers and always knew what to do.

"Just give him coffee and send him away." He shouted back.

Outside, Rick smiled and waved when he noticed her watching him, then hastily headed for the door. It was the only diner for miles around that would have him. Rick was convinced it was because of Jenny. Once, she single-handily broke up an argument between him and a truck driver who had had enough of his stories of days gone by. She calmed the confrontation within minutes and negotiated a compromise that left Rick and the driver leaving the diner like old buddies. She had tact, charm, and when she smiled his heart melted. What was she doing working in a dump like this?

Rick shuffled hurriedly into the diner. The warmth and the sweet smell of fresh donuts made him smile as he headed towards his usual stool at the counter, the only spot in the entire diner where he could still get a look at her when she disappeared into the kitchen. Rick greeted her with a warm smile as she placed the mug of coffee in front of him. At this very moment, soaking wet and shivering, she was more than a welcome sight. Jenny poured the remains of a pot of coffee she had made more than an hour ago into a large cup and placed it in front of him.

"Oh you're wonderful," he said, giving her his best smile.

"Just one, and that's it." She said sharply.

"Ah," he said as he slurped in a mouthful. "You're a beauty. Give us a kiss." He reached out to her over the counter. Jenny bolted back.

"Keep your hands to yourself," Jenny ordered, threatening him with the empty coffee pot.

Rick cackled. The white of her eyes lit up around her incredibly dark pupils, and her nostrils flared like a pony in heat, right now she was the sexiest thing he could imagine.

"Don't worry. You're safe with me," he said smiling.

"I think I'd be safer in a snake pit." Jenny said, immediately turning on her heel and disappearing into the kitchen.

Rick settled back in his stool, wrapped his fingers around the hot cup and took a deep slurp. If only he had some whiskey to add to it, then it would be twice as good. He scanned the clientele. All of them strangers. The moment he entered they sneered and turned away in disgust. Those near to him left the counter to take a seat elsewhere. He knew he stunk, but he didn't care.

Rick sipped the coffee as slowly as possible. With any luck it would take the best part of an hour to finish the cup. Maybe his last remark did not go down well and he didn't want to push his luck by asking for seconds. Jenny seemed a little touchy this morning. Definitely not her usual cheerful self. Had someone been ruffling her feathers? Unfortunately he could see no one to categorize as being suspicious or troublesome. They all seemed reasonably quiet and respectable citizens. He looked up at the clock. Another fifty minutes and Jenny should be finishing her shift. Maybe he could get a fresh cup from her replacement.

Outside it had turned daylight and another rain cloud broke and lashed the city streets.

Chapter two

Three and a half thousand miles away, on the edge of a desert in Utah, Preston had been walking for most of the night. His right leg was stiffer than ever. A walking stick helped ease the discomfort but what he really needed was a lift out of this hell hole. Back in the sixties hitching rides, jumping trains, and finding places to stay came a lot easier. People these days were not as friendly as back then. A seventy-five year-old busker did not fit into this world of young, glitter, hip-hop and instant fame.

Dawn broke and the temperature was now approaching 77° Fahrenheit. By mid-day it would be 104° or above and he would have to take cover in the shade of some rocks. Lie down between a couple of boulders out of the sun and get a quick nap. If there were none he could use the neck of his guitar and his jacket to create a small tent for shade.

He felt a slight tingle in his left ear. A noise, low in tone and constant, drew closer. He turned up his hearing aid to full strength. No mistake, that was an automobile.

Automatically he shot out his thumb, then turned to see a red open-top sports Mercedes coming at him at high speed. He did a quick hop and a shuffle to one side as the Mercedes roared past. The back draft turned up a huge cloud of dust that covered him completely. He raised his stick above the choking cloud. "Fuck you too, goddamn fascist." He screamed.

Like an aging ghost Preston continued to walk through the cloud of dust, cursing the driver with each step.

"Stupid bastard," he moaned through gritted teeth. "Stupid fucking bastard. Assholes like you should be fucking shot. Fucking maniac."

After ten minutes the dust finally settled. His parched mouth felt as if he had been sucking sandpaper. In the distance he could just make out a pole with a Texaco sign towering above a small service station.

The gas station was one of those that for no reason seemed to sit in the middle of nowhere. Probably started life as a resting post for stagecoaches and pilgrims on their way to better places. Stops like these sometimes developed into small towns. In this dry inhospitable wilderness this station would remain an anonymous watering hole in the middle of nowhere. Preston paced himself. The nap would come later. Right now his only concern was fresh water. His much used Perrier bottle was half full, but the water was stale, soiled and reeked of plastic. He finally reached the looming sign above the shaded canopy of the garage.

The red Mercedes was parked outside. In the back seat was a guitar. Not like the thirty-dollar instrument he was carrying, this one resembled the owner's automobile; expensive and beautifully trimmed. An issue of Rolling Stone in the passenger seat showed a picture of a young pop star dressed in denims and leaning on an electric guitar.

The headline read. 'PETE GARRET BREAKS ALL RECORDS! PASSES MILLION SALES IN TWO DAYS.'

In the stinking men's room Pete Garret washed his hands. The urinals had not been cleaned for a month. Parched excrement that had missed its mark lined the sides of the cracked ceramic bowl. Garret finally kicked open the door, and now out in the open sucked in a breath of fresh air. He looked up to see Preston standing next to his Mercedes browsing through the magazine.

"Hey you," Garret shouted. "Put that down and step back from the car."

Preston turned back to the cover of the magazine and studied the photo covering the entire front page. Same kid except now he was dressed in a black leader jacket with a black silk shirt, black leather pants and crocodile skin boots. Garret quickened his pace.

"So you're the new pop star," he said as Garret came closer, and then stopped, keeping a distance.

"That's me, and I said get away from the car old man."

Preston cleared his throat, and spit out a mixture of phlegm and dust next to the tire. "Why didn't you pick me up back there?"

"Was that you?"

"See anyone else with a walking stick and a guitar?"

"I'm not going in the same direction." Garret said resolutely.

Preston raised his solid oak hand-carved walking stick, and pointed north were the road disappeared into infinity.

"You were going that way weren't you?"

"So what."

"Me too." He shouted as he slammed his stick down on the hood of the car. Splinters of red paint shot into the air. Garret's mouth dropped open and he staggered back in disbelief. The stick left a deep impression in the hood of the Mercedes.

"The same direction." Preston slammed his stick down a second time. "With a bad leg." He slammed again. "In this hell hole." And again.

"Why you..." Garret ran at him.

"And a fellow musician..." With perfect timing Preston took a step back and swung the stick to the left, and smashed it over Garret's head. The long legged musician hit the dust face down like a slaughtered bull, and lay motionless. The oil-covered attendant looking on from the inside of the garage picked up the phone.

In the coolness of the police cell Preston strummed away on his guitar. During the last ten years Preston was regularly in and out of jail. Mostly one-night stands for getting into fights or drunkenness. Not enough to make the papers or serious enough to warrant extra attention from a judge. But this was different. He had just felled one of the top names in the music business. When the ambulance took him away he was still unconscious.

The police refused to give Preston any information regarding the state of the young faced pop idol. Maybe he suffered brain damage? Maybe he died?

Preston wondered if he had landed in one of those states who took pride and joy in carrying out the death sentence. Or, if lucky, he could probably spend the rest of his life in jail. No pride followed the thought, although at this moment in life the comfort of sleeping on a mattress and getting regular meals seemed like a fair trade.

The only comfort he really appreciated in this jail was the fact they let him keep his guitar. Strictly against the rules, he knew, but after pleading with the sheriff's deputy's for more than an hour non-stop they relented. In a state prison he didn't imagine they would be so lenient, but maybe because of his age they would be more compassionate.

His cell had no air-conditioning but it was definitely cooler than a lonely road cutting through the desert. He felt a new song coming on. He quickly tuned the guitar and gave the instrument a reasonable tone. His old friend Woody would have been proud. As a musician traveling the length and breadth of the country he had composed some of the finest and most enduring songs of the century. By the time he died of Huntington's Chorea in New York, his songs had inspired thousands of songwriters around the world. From an early age Preston had decided to follow in Guthrie's footsteps. It lasted until success, money, wives, children and the comfort of success had slowed him down, then eventually took him off the road completely. But now he was back on the right path, on the road. Living and breathing the earth; a true Bohemian.

Preston lost the melody line and started on another. Nearly a year had passed since he wrote a complete song. He sung it to a group of tramps at a campsite north of San Francisco, where he received his last round of applause to date. Since then he drifted, turning up in cities and one-horse towns busking for money to pay for a meal. Unfortunately the sight of an old man whose clothes had disintegrated, held together simply because he never removed them, scored no public sympathy. His boots were those of a true tramp. Split at the top and soles with one hole that ran from toe to heel. Since a pair were stolen while sleeping on the beach in San Diego, Preston never removed these. Tramps had a habit of stealing each other's shoes. Forever looking for a better fit, or good enough to sell for a dollar or two. Whatever the reason, he never saw them again. Maybe in five or ten years when they had gone full circle he would probably meet up with them again, worn to shreds by every other tramp in the land. He'd vowed never to get caught out like that again.

What did gain him sympathy was his ability as an old man to play the guitar and sing long-forgotten songs. As Preston studied the fingering for F sharp he noticed someone standing on the other side of the bars. He glanced up to see sheriff Pat Connelly with a large beer gut staring down at him.

"If you're going to stand there and enjoy my music you gotta pay. I don't give free concerts to anyone."

Connelly smiled and rattled the keys. "Well I can give you something concert tickets can't buy, freedom. Charges have been dropped," he said cheerfully.

Preston did not seem to care one way or the other. He found another chord to suit the melody line and continued to strum.

Connelly unlocked the jail, then leaned against the wall to support his gross overweight.

"I used to listen to your music when I was growing up. I always wondered where you got to."

Preston continued to strum the guitar.

"We don't normally allow instruments like that in the cell," Connelly continued, "but when I heard it was you..."

Preston stopped.

"Don't let me disturb you," Connelly said apologetically. "You just carry on playing. People could use the strings of the guitar to hang or damage themselves in some way. That's why we normally remove them. But not you. I know things like that."

Preston stood up and walked out of the unlocked jail. When people began to show pity it was always the best time to make an exit.

"You don't have to leave right away, it's a scorcher outside," Connelly said as Preston walked past him. "You can wait until sundown. It'll be cooler then."

The jail led out to a small office where two deputies sat at a desk across from each other. Connelly followed him into the office, quickly removing a notebook from his breast pocket. "I don't normally ask this type of thing but I'd surely appreciate it if I could have your autograph."

Preston hesitated, then turned to face Connelly. For the first time their eyes met. Connelly stood like a little boy with pen and notebook in hand.

He took them with his blackened hands and long filthy fingernails and signed. His scribble had changed only slightly since the first time he was asked for an autograph. And that was the first and only time he felt embarrassed by giving it. After that he signed, or denied, without feeling or afterthought. Suddenly, much to his surprise, he felt his face glow.

Connelly could never have noticed it; Preston's beard and scraggy hair covered most of his face. The rest could not be seen through a blackened layer of dirt. He could not understand why he was blushing. Preston was both surprised and confused. Two deputies sitting at a desk across stared dumbfounded at their sheriff. Preston returned the notebook and pen and watched

Connelly study the signature. People always inspected it as if to verify that they had actually met their hero.

"Didn't think you were into collecting hobo autographs Sheriff?" The deputy remarked, and they both laughed.

'Haven't you got work to do?" Connelly barked. Their smiles disappeared.

"Yes sir."

Preston turned and quickly went out the door without uttering another word.

"Well get your butts outta here and do it."

With speed reserved for a major catastrophe they left the office through the back door.

Judging by the sun he figured it to be about three or four in the afternoon. He felt rested, relaxed. A long time had passed since he had slept in a proper bed. Not that he missed it, but at his age his bones could do with some comfort once in a while. Maybe he should have stayed for the day. Connelly had been kind. He'd kept his distance and did not ask personal questions. But it wouldn't have lasted long. Within no time the two of them would be sitting around his creaking desk like two buddies drinking beer and talking about times gone by. A pig was always a pig, even one looking for an autograph. You didn't associate with the pigs unless there was a definite purpose. Menial comfort could never be a purpose, and he couldn't think of anything else.

Chapter three

These days Rick thrived mostly on booze. Years ago it was a different story. Money, music, parties, and so many women he often visioned death by drowning blissfully between their naked bodies. It was all part of the scene, but things were different now.
No more music. No more parties.
He had just enough money to survive from day to day, and women did their very best to avoid him. He couldn't remember the last time he had sex. Most memories had faded into a blurred haze. He had long forgotten birthday dates of his children; he even had difficulty trying to picture their faces.
A while had passed since he was down in the demolished warehouse patch near the old harbor. He hoped they'd still be there. Not that they were the best company but they laughed at his jokes and more importantly enjoyed listening for hours around the campfire to tales of pop concerts and wild parties in Japan, Europe and all over the USA. Forever questioning him to a point of interrogation on the famous names he knew. Did he know Sinatra, The Beatles, Gershwin, Tammy Wynette, Britney Spears, Paris Hilton, Whitney Houston, in fact every name in the celebrity magazines they found on the road. They had all heard about his band though no one ever mentioned they liked the music. They were only interested in the names. When anyone new joined the group the questions would start all over again, and then Rick would once again recount the days of fame and glory. They knew David was his best friend, but talking to him about his past brought total silence.

New faces used to turn up while the old and trusted friends disappeared into thin air. For a while he found it difficult to accept that people he befriended vanished without any explanation. He once talked to the police about it, even tried to push the weight of his name to get some answers, but none existed. He was convinced of a conspiracy. Tramps being snatched from the streets and vanishing without trace. It could be big news in the hands of the right people. A few years ago Rick decided to take it to the New York Times. He never got past the security guards. A price he paid for being a hobo, a bum.

The old derelict harbor was familiar territory. For years the homeless had ruled that patch of the big apple. But they, like everyone else, were getting older, and it was becoming more difficult to fend off territory. In the distance, a group of old hobos sat in thick layers of aged and worn out clothes around an open fire. All in their late sixties or seventy plus, he recognized them all. Barney, the smallest and the fattest of the lot with his typical Smokey the Bear hat. Stanley, still wearing his three piece suit and the expensive overcoat he unsuccessfully tried to keep clean. Rick was surprised he was still with the group. Two months ago, the last time Rick visited Stanley was in a severe emotional state. Constantly crying and talking about his children. Rick thought he would be in a home by now. Harry, the one to watch out for, was also there. He was the most intelligent of the group but could be nasty and snap at you without any warning.

Sitting on the ground next to Barney he saw the reason why he came back to this haunt; his old mate David. Rick threaded carefully across the rubble filled landscape. A snapped ankle was nothing to look forward to.

Barney spotted him first. "Hey look. Rick's back," he said in a troubled voice.

Harry buried his head in his hand. "Rick the mouth. Oh God. If he starts going on about the old days again I'll shove my fist down his throat." Harry spat into the fire. The burning wood cracked. Harry didn't like Rick; none of them did.

Stanley jumped to his feet. He could just make out Rick maneuvering his way around piles of rubbish lay strewn around the grounds. Stanley squinted his eyes, trying to bring Rick into focus.

"Did he bring any booze?" Barney asked, warming up his hands on the fire.

Stanly made a drinking gesture. Rick reached into his deep pockets and with both hands pulled out two bottles of whiskey.

Stanley leaned forward and squinted his eyes tighter. "He did, the old bugger, he didn't forget us." Stanley laughed, revealing his toothless gums. He shook his hands like a little child. Tears flooded his eyes.

Stanley was the newest member of the group. A year previous he had landed on the streets after his wife threw him out of the house for being too childish and emotional. She couldn't leave the house or go shopping without him getting upset. After thirty-eight years of marriage she had had enough. She never realized he was suffering from Alzheimer's.

"I knew we could count on your buddy," Barney shouted, then reached down and shook the old man sitting next to him whose stare was fixed blankly on the fire.

"David. Can you hear me David? It's your old pal Rick." He shook him again." David did not react. Barney then shook David aggressively. "Snap out of it, will you? It's the man himself and he's come back for you. Got some booze as well."

When Rick got closer Barney was quick to let go and back away. Rick went straight to David and knelt down in front of him.

"Hey David, it's me, I'm back." David remained silent. His stare never left the crackling wood in the fire.

Rick knew it had been more than twenty years since David had touched drugs, yet he looked stoned out of his mind.

"You all right pal?" He said shaking him gently. There was no reaction.

"You lot haven't slipped him something, have you?"

"You accusing us?" Harry snarled. "Do you think if we had some stuff we'd be giving it to him? The only thing he does is just sit there and eat our food. He won't even help search for wood anymore."

Rick leaned close and sniffed. No scent of alcohol. He crouched down in front of him and cupped David's head in his hands. His dark brown pupils were blank. Void of any recognition of Rick staring in his face.

"What's wrong with him," Rick asked.

"I dunno," Barney replied. "I didn't touch him either. He's been like that for the last couple of days. In a world of his own. Mutters to himself sometimes. Can't understand a word of it."

Rick tilted David's head back to get a better look at his eyes.

"He should be in a home." Stanley said. "We should all be."

Barney pulled himself closer to the fire. "You're not putting walls around me, I'd go mad. Living within four walls can be dangerous. You can be killed by walls. Goddamn earthquakes pull the things down on your head. That's why women always try to keep you behind the walls. They use them as jails then try to kill you with them. That's what she did. She tried to kill me."

The group fell silent. Barney never talked about his past. In fact none of them did, except Rick. He took a whiskey bottle out of his pocket, uncapped it, and held it out. Barney grabbed it before any of the others and guzzled down at least a quart before Harry wrenched it away, then lay back in the rubble preventing others from grabbing the bottle back.

"Don't want you to get into trouble by drinking it all down yourself." Harry snarled, and took a quick swig of the whiskey.

"Give yourself alcoholic poisoning," he said with a laugh. "Isn't that right, Rick?"

"You're a better lie down loser then a stand up fucking comedian." Rick said sharply. "Don't give up the day job."

"And I always thought you were the comedian, Ricky lad. After all you've performed in front of millions. At least that's what you tell us."

Rick ignored him. If he said anything else Harry would just keep coming at him. Other times it brought them to the edge of a fight, blocked only by the others jumping in to stop the brawl at the last minute. David was always the first to intervene. He knew Rick more than anyone and what would happen if it got out of hand.

Stanley dried his eyes and waited patiently for the bottle to come his way.

Rick took out a second bottle. He moved in closer to David, put his arm around his slumped shoulders and put the bottle to his lips. The whiskey flowed down the side of his mouth and onto his coat.

"Go on pal. Do you good." David's gaze remained fixed on the blazing fire. Rick pulled him in closer, resting his head against his. "What's wrong old son. You got the flu? Lots of it going about these days. You'll be all right. I'll look after you," he said as he patted him gently on the back.

Chapter four

Preston had managed to hitch a ride on a rig going north. No questions, no small talk, no intrusions. The perfect journey. Maybe the driver recognized him but didn't show it. Or maybe he just recognized another loner. He had a long black beard and piercing blue eyes that scanned the road. Preston had never seen a driver who drove with such concentration. Like someone on a divine mission. He leaned forward over the steering wheel and held it like a demon: and he was the one in control. The truck gave no indication of its load. He could have been carrying nuclear warheads, or a million Barbie dolls. It was of no importance. What did matter was Preston's appreciation of the ride, and the silence.

Throughout the journey the trucker constantly kept up the pace, slowing only in accordance to the regulatory speed limits of the many towns they drove through. Time passed, the mileage clocked up, and the arid countryside gradually changed from burning parched earth to lush green. They passed through small, rundown, and forgotten towns where Preston witnessed the small-town scenes of middle America where preachers gave sermons on sidewalks and fat-ass husbands escorted fat-ass wives. Police drawing guns to make arrests. Everything seemed to float by like a film without dialogue, just the music. He saw whores picking up clients. Mothers and fathers escorting their children to church, winos begging for a buck, women scouting the window sales, old men reminiscing war stories on pavement porches, dogs pissing on hubcaps, babies crying because of melting ice creams, thugs weighing up their next hit, politicians shouting for votes. A collage of pictures, mixed with a thousand songs went through his head. He wished he could take it all in then spit it all out in one mind-blowing song, just like he used to. The world was at his feet then. At least half of his generation had memorized the words to his songs, while everyone knew a chorus or part of the tune. After a time scholars began to analyze every word in every song. Universities introduced a number of them into social studies curriculum. But that was more than thirty years ago. Now he was long forgotten.

He never saw the name of the town where they finally departed company. Preston thanked the driver and told him he had enjoyed the ride. The bearded man just smiled and nodded, shifted gear, then revved the engine. A cloud of black diesel fumes blasted into the sky as the truck took off.

Preston watched him go down main street then turn left into an industrial complex. Maybe he would pick him up again sometime, he would like that.

Although it was only three in the afternoon Preston searched the town for a place to rest for the night. The small park at the back of city hall would do just fine, right out of everyone's way. Within minutes he found a secluded patch under a tree. Preston always stayed clear of park benches. Local bums usually regarded them as their own personal property. Occupying them would probably end up in a midnight brawl, and then it would take the rest of the night to scour the city for a new and safe place to sleep. His biggest worry was his guitar. He couldn't count the times they tried to steal it.

The ground was soft and not too moist under a gigantic oak in a quiet corner at the southern end of the park. He used to carry around a length of tarpaulin that protected him from the damp but as with most of his other possessions it was stolen. Preston spent ten minutes tuning the guitar he found in a trash dump a year ago. Not the greatest quality but it still produced a clear sound. A busker's delight.

His old guitar had been smashed in a brawl over a bottle of vodka on the outskirts of San Francisco. He woke up to an alcoholic standing next to him gulping down the last of his vodka. Without a sound Preston rose and slammed his guitar into the face of the unsuspecting tramp. The wood shattered and splintered in all directions. The strings sprung and cut into his hands holding the neck. The tramp hit the ground with the bottle wedged firmly in his throat. Preston stared in shock at the sight of his guitar; the only precious thing he had left in the world. It was worse than losing an arm. Devastated and helpless, Preston never looked to see if the alcoholic was dead or alive. The only thing he could recall after the incident was drifting into the darkness and cursing his loss.

Preston ran his thumb gently down the strings. It was now tuned and would probably stay that way for at least a half an hour. By then he would have collected more than enough. On a good day he usually averaged twenty to thirty dollars. Enough to get him a decent meal and possibly a couple of spare strings.

He left the park and took up position on the corner of Main and Dale Street. He felt in good shape and planned on playing the many songs going through his mind during the last few days. As usual he began with an old Guthrie favorite, 'This land is your land'. He sung with gut and feeling. He had met many musicians who lacked any expression or feeling in their songs. Singing the same tunes over and over again. They cut corners on emotion and played on auto-pilot. They collected the least. Preston gave it all he could.

An hour later he looked down at his pickings. The grubby handkerchief in front of him was empty, and he was hungry. He could pick another place to play but decided against it. He had found his spot and was sticking to it. When the town hall bells rang an hour later there was only fifty cents in front of him. Places always existed were the takings were mean. Either they had seen too many buskers or they were not used to having them around. This was humiliating. The positive feeling he had after leaving the trucker and finding a decent place to sleep had vanished. His playing began to reflect his mood, bitter and hard. He sang about the America he hated. Self-centered, bureaucratic, and hypocritically conservative. He sang about people who strangled his sense of freedom, of thought, of living. The people in favor of Vietnam, the Cold War, invading Iraq and nuking whoever got in the way. They were for white domination, and no benefits for the unemployed. He suddenly felt that all the things he had fought against for most of his life lived in this town.

The truck driver had done him a favor by dropping him in a place he believed had long vanished, the very heart of conservative America. At the same time he felt betrayed. Years of songs, demonstrations, and general understanding had brought around a positive change of mentality throughout the United States. But not here. This town had armored itself against such a change. It brewed conservatism so deep nothing in the world could root it out. This was the town of his nightmare.

Preston gritted his teeth and changed to another protest song. One more bitter than the previous. His fingers came down heavily on the strings, and he shouted his protest words at people walking past. Their paces quickened. As more rushed by he grew increasingly harsh and irritated. His anger swelled to breaking point. A string snapped through the force of his playing. Finishing one song and quickly moving to the next with no recognition, no applause, his anger exploded. Still playing, he swung the neck of the guitar at anyone who came within striking distance. Then the public began to stop at a distance and stare at the troubled musician. A shop owner wearing a bright blue apron suddenly appeared in front of him.

"That's enough. You're frightening the customers. Move along or I'll call the police."

Preston turned abruptly, smashing the neck of the guitar into his face. The tuning knobs cut deep into the shopkeepers face cheek. Blood spattered onto his apron.

"I can sing anywhere I like. I got a right," he shouted as he repeatedly slammed the shocked middle aged man with the guitar. Another string snapped. Preston rammed the man in the belly with the neck of the guitar. The bloodied man crumbled. Preston turned and ran down the street, still hanging on to his battered guitar.

"It's all your fault," he bellowed in all directions. Shocked pedestrians jumped out of his way to avoid him. "It's all your fault. You're the ones who started it. You started the wars."

Like a madman being chased by the devil, he ran three blocks until he could run no more. In the distance he heard the shrieking sound of police and ambulance sirens. Preston turned into an alley and came face to face with a local street gang. They were all dressed in leader jackets, t-shirts and jeans. The tallest one had a tattoo on his neck that read 'Made in America.' Preston shook of his guitar at them.

"You're all polluted with shit. You don't listen any more. You don't listen to the words. It goes into your head but your shit for brains can't get the message." Preston took a pitiful swing at two of the gang members.

The tallest gang member hastily removed his jacket. "Let's see whose full of shit, paps." He grabbed Preston by his coat and dragged him screaming, deeper into the alley. A gang member landed a punch on Preston's head, while another kicked him in the ribs. Preston keeled over. His head hit the ground hard. The last thing he remembered was a flurry of boots coming at him from all directions.

Chapter five

Just after sunset in New York, the campfire cinders were slowly dying. No one was sober enough to throw an extra piece of wood on the fire. Only Rick and David remained upright, although Rick was finding it difficult to keep his eyes open. The others had fallen asleep around them. Rick rolled a cigarette slowly and leaned in towards David.

"What are you thinking about mate?" Rick's speech was slurred, his British accent was more pronounced. He shook David, then knocked him gently on the forehead with his knuckles.

"Go on, tell me what's going on up there. Remember that concert in Tokyo in eighty-eight?" Rick said, chuckling at the thought. "I don't know why but that concert always stuck in my mind. The crowd screaming their heads off and we hadn't a clue what they were screaming at. I thought you lot were pulling faces behind my back. No one told me my pants had ripped and my prick was hanging out. I had drunk so much sake I didn't know what the fuck was going on." Rick laughed and lit up his cigarette. He inhaled deeply. A piece of tobacco caught in his windpipe, and he started to cough incessantly. David put his hands to his head as if trying to block out the sound, then keeled over. Rick grabbed David and tried to pull him upright.

"What's wrong, pal. You sick?" Rick shook him vigorously, but he just slumped to one side, unconscious.

"David?" Rick shouted, and gasped for breath between coughs. "You're not going to give up on me now are you?" Still coughing uncontrollably Rick tried to pull him upright but David slumped once again to one side. Rick climbed to his feet. "Hold on there pal. I'm onto it. Just wait, don't move. I'll go and get an ambulance."

Rick ran, stumbling over rubbish bags and abandoned building materials. Totally out of breath he made it to the edge of the road, then had another fit of coughing. The cough tore at his lungs, forcing him to double over. In the distance he could just make out a set of headlights. Rick tried to signal the approaching truck. He staggered onto the middle of the road and then his legs went. Rick sank to all fours. He looked up as the driver switched to full beam and the blinding lights burned deep into the back of his skull. The horn of the truck blared, shaking him into a state of alert. He tried to crawl away but his legs had turned to blocks of concrete, he couldn't move. Rick tried to wave his arms. The lights were upon him. Suddenly everything went black.

The door to Rick's hospital bedroom opened gently. Cautiously, a gray haired man wearing a white t-shirt and white pants entered, carrying a mop and a bucket of water. Rick was connected to a cardiac monitor, respirator and IV drips. The orderly gently closed the door behind him, then turned and stopped for a moment to stare at Rick, who had remained unconscious since he arrived at St. Ann's the day before. He delicately placed his bucked of water on the floor, trying not to make any noise. Slowly and steadily he mopped around Rick, taking great care not to knock against the bed, while making sure not to leave any area untouched. Every now and again he glanced up at him. The hospital staff had trimmed back his scraggy beard and cut out the matted parts of his unkempt hair. They had cleaned him up good. The orderly finished up around Rick's bed, careful to leave a narrow dry path towards the door. He put his bucket and mop to one side, pulled up a chair, then gently sat himself down next to Rick.

"I didn't think I'd ever see you in here," he said, gently patting Rick's hand that lay rested above the covers. "You were stinking when they brought you in, you know that? They threw your socks and underwear into the incinerator." The orderly said and laughed gently. "Nearly blew up the damn thing." He leaned in close to Rick. "Two beautiful nurses gave you the greatest bed bath you ever had in your life," he whispered, "and you missed it. If I was you I'd wake up in a hurry Rick. You'll never know what they'll do to you next." He chuckled, got out of the chair, then grabbed his mop, re-doing a drying patch next to the bed.

"First sign of madness, Chris." A voice said. Chris turned to see Dr. Forest standing behind him.

Chris swallowed. "What?"

"Talking to yourself. They say it's the first sign of madness."

"I was talking to an old pal."

"You know this old tramp?"

Chris looked down at Rick. Even with the cleanup he still looked like a tramp.

"He wasn't always an old tramp. He and his friend used to be in a band in the past."

"Him?" Forest said in surprise. I could never imagine him being anything else then a flea ridden alcoholic lying in the gutter. How did a guy like you get to know a person like that?"

"I used to play a little myself."

"Really? I didn't know."

"When you get to my age you don't like to brag about it, besides no one believes you anyway."

Chris studied the monitors connected up to Rick. "What are his chances?"

"Poor. I doubt if he'll ever regain consciousness."

"He was always a great fighter. He'll pull through," Chris said as a matter of fact.

Forest turned to the door. "You know I'm not one to be pessimistic but I'll give him two days at the most." Forest left.

Chris felt very alone in the room with Rick. The sound of the cardiac monitor was faint but rhythmic. For years he had watched people of all ages, beliefs, and sicknesses cling to life with the help of the best drugs, the best equipment, and the knowledge of great doctors. At night when no one was around he would study the cases of those on the floor he was assigned to clean. Over the years he had studied hundreds of cases. With the help of medical books from the library he acquired enough knowledge about diseases and ailments of the body to pass any medical exam thrown at him, and he was aware of Rick's chances. Forest was right. He was extremely weak and the infection in his lungs was a strain that killed most people half his age. He could imagine his liver, bloated and diseased after years of drowning in whiskey, vodka, gin and beer, were only just functioning, and poisoning his body.

"Are you going to die Rick? Think of the old times. The book's not closed yet my friend." Chris leaned in close. "We all got to go sometime, but not like this," he whispered.

Looking at his vital signs on the monitors he shook his head. He knew Rick probably wouldn't last another forty-eight hours. Chris replaced the chair and checked Rick's drips. The nurses had done a good job. Everything looked secure. He carefully straightened the bed linen and pulled the covers gently up around his chest. He looked at the monitors one last time then quietly left the room.

Chapter six

When Preston finally opened his eyes in the alley it was daylight. There was no sign of the gang who beat him up. With difficulty he tried to support himself against the wall as he climbed to his feet. His badly bruised face was covered in dried blood. After the first few blows he could not remember anything, and had no idea how long he had been lying unconscious amongst the rubbish. He could still feel the boots coming down on his face and chest. His left knee hurt bad. Probably smashed it on the concrete when he fell. The pain was excruciating when he put some weight on it.

He searched for his guitar and stick. Within minutes he found them under a pile of garbage. His stick was cracked in the middle. If he bent it far enough it would snap completely. His guitar was unrecognizable. Preston screamed and smashed the remaining pieces of the guitar against the wall. When he settled down he tried to repair his stick by placing a splint along the two halves, then tying it together with a couple of strings from the guitar. He tested his weight on the stick. It held, but only just. With great effort Preston limped out of the alley.

Like many of the people gathered on the sidewalk, Preston was drawn to the sound of cheers and what seemed to be a well-staged spectacle. A man in his late forties, with too dark a sun tan, and dressed in an expensive Italian cut suit, stood in front of a small crowd gathered outside the opening of the Markwell store. Above him a banner pinned to the building above him read 'Opening by Senator Houghton'.

The store was not a store for cheap discounts and year-round sales. Here the plush carpets were at least an inch thick and personnel wore haute couture uniforms. It was obvious to Preston that most of the people in the crowd were loyal supporters. More than likely contributors to his election campaigns, defending him on issues deemed controversial and right wing. This was no ordinary shop opening. The senator had to give them something for their money today. The large press contingent was here for a reason.

The senator took to the platform and quickly glanced through his notes. The television cameras and people present were rewarded with generous statements about the state of the country and a candid remark about sitting behind the desk in the Oval office. The crowds cheered.

The speech ended with applause, cheers and over excessive banner and flag waving. As he stepped down from the platform he was handed the oversize scissors by the store director. The crowd cheered on cue when he held the scissors above his head, then he turned towards the director now holding the ribbon for him to cut.

"It gives me great pleasure to open this store for a well-deserved community."

"And what community would that be?" Preston shouted from the middle of the crowd. "The worthy, well-paid, well-oiled politicians and crooked businessmen who only care for their own kind? How many stores have you opened for the people who *really* need them?"

Senator Houghton looked around but was unable to locate the person shouting amongst the crowd. "Anyone who wants to shop here can," the senator said.

"Of course," Preston shouted back. "That's what democracy is all about. Prices so high the average man of the people can't afford them." From the back of the crowd Preston broke through the bewildered multitude of guests and passers-by, then came face to face with the startled Senator. Security guards standing at the edge of the crowd pushed their way towards Preston from either side. The senator held up his hand and shook his head for them to wait.

"When was the last time you did something for the common man? When was the last time you did something for a guy like me?" Preston turned and shouted towards the surprised crowd, "When was the last time you really did something for real people," he said sneeringly.

Haughton studied the crowd for a showing of sympathy. They were his people. Well dressed, suits and quality casual wear. They were there for him, his personality, and of course the big party afterwards.

"These are real people my friend. People who work hard, pay taxes, and come here to celebrate the freedom we have in this great country."

"They just came along for the ride." Preston screamed into his face. "Somewhere to show off their fancy clothes and jewelry," he said gesturing to the people around him. "Spending too much money on designer jeans and designer handbags and too stupid to realize they're listening to someone who's full of it."

"That's enough." The senator pushed Preston to one side and turned back to the ribbon. Security guards closed in. Preston quickly grabbed Haughton's coat collar and pulled hard. The senator turned and Preston caught him squarely under the jaw with a heavyweight uppercut. As the senator shot backwards and went down Preston was pounced upon by two security guards and a police officer. They quickly removed his walking stick then grappled him to the ground face down. Handcuffs clicked around his wrists. He turned to his left to see the senator lying next to him, while shop personnel did their best to revive him.

A police car and ambulance pulled up. Preston watched the medics attend the recovering senator as he was maneuvered into the back seat of the police car. Heading away, Preston could see the senator with a bruised chin climb shakily to his feet and wave enthusiastically to a cheering crowd. Like a true war hero he shrugged off the assault and continued with the opening.

Chapter seven

Chris wheeled a television into the room. Three days had passed since they brought Rick in. He was still unconscious, and his organs seemed to be shutting down. During the course of the early morning his heartbeat had become erratic. Twice his monitors lit up screaming of a heart attack, and twice the cardiac crew came charging in with enough equipment to revive an army. Yet each time his heartbeat reverted back to its normal rhythm without medical assistance. After a consultation with student doctors on tour around the wards with dr. Forest, the students concluded that a pacemaker could clear up the problem but the patient was far too weak to have one installed. However, Doctor Forest believed the patient would not be around long enough to get the pacemaker fitted. The students agreed.

Chris positioned the television at the foot of the bed. "This is my own," he said quietly. "I thought you might want to watch it when you wake up. It can get very boring in a room all alone. They were going to put you in with some of the other patients but rumor has it you are an agitator. I wouldn't listen to them if I were you Rick."

Chris plugged in the television and flicked through a number of channels. He stopped at MTV and adjusted the volume. At that moment the sound of a cardiograph beep changed abruptly to a single tone. All of the monitors' alarms went off. Rick's heart had stopped. No need to turn and look; Chris had heard it a thousand times. He didn't think of trying to revive him. Not everyone had the luxury of dying in their sleep or in an unconscious state. Reviving him would only prolong the pain and suffering.

Chris lowered his head. "May you rest in peace," he said quietly. With his head bowed, he turned slowly to look up at the bed.

Rick was sitting up holding the electrodes in his hand. "What do you mean peace," he said angrily. "A man can't get a minute's peace in here."

"You're not.....?"

"You must be joking." Rick screamed with laughter.

A doctor and two nurses rushed into the room with a defibrillator. They stopped in their tracks at the sight of Rick sitting up in his bed with a big smile.

'False alarm folks. But I think I just blew a fuse somewhere." Rick whirled the wires above his head like a lasso, then flung them to one side. "Why don't you all go and have a nice cup of coffee, it's my round. Take the weight off your feet." He threw his head back and laughed. "I haven't had so much fun in years."

"Call doctor Forest," The doctor ordered. Tell him to get down here right away." They turned and left the room. Chris went to the side of the bed.

"Jesus Rick, you frightened the life out of me. I thought you were dead."

"Don't be silly. You know as well as I do that when my lights go out they go out with a bang. I'm not going to give up in a place like this."

"I don't think the doctor was pleased."

"I wouldn't worry too much about him. It'll give him something to talk about over coffee."

"They were near to sending you down to the morgue yesterday. They weren't giving you a chance in hell."

"They never do. You wouldn't believe how many doctors are waiting for their fifteen minutes of fame by signing their name on my death certificate. They're all the bloody same. And what was all that rest in peace shit," Rick said, pointing his finger at Chris. "And I don't like any of that prayer stuff. If you try that when I do kick the bucket I'll reach out of my grave and choke you to death."

Rick opened his arms wide. "But it's great to see you anyway. Now come here and give me a hug." The old men wrapped arms around each other. Rick wiped away the moisture building up in his eyes before Chris could notice.

'Glad you made it, Rick," Chris said with his head buried deep in Rick's shoulder. Finally they released one another.

"You're the last person I expected to see. I hardly recognized you in that white uniform. I thought you were here to wheel me to the crematorium." Rick took a good look at Chris. "Jesus you're looking well."

"I keep fit." Chris replied, standing proudly. "Gave up the cigs and drink years ago, and I eat all the right food."

"And I bet you've never been so bored in all your life."

"Can I get you something? Coffee or juice?"

"You trying to make me sick? A very expensive cognac would be the right thing for now. Something to celebrate after meeting an old friend."

"I wouldn't drink anymore alcohol if I was you Rick."

"What's wrong with it. Been doing it for years and I've never had a problem with it," Rick said scratching his beard and leaning towards Chris. "Did you know." He said in a hushed voice, "that alcohol is the best preservative known to mankind, It's when I stop," pointing his finger at Chris, he shouts, "that'll be the death of me."

"The doctor said you had a diseased liver because of the drink. As big as a basketball he said."

"Don't be ridiculous. Who is this idiot? A doctor or one of the dream team? What the hell does it matter anyway. If I don't die from the drink I'll die from a heart attack. And if I don't die from that I'll die from cancer, or brain hemorrhage, or a bullet, or pneumonia. What's the fucking difference?"

Chris knew he was right. That was always the problem with Rick, he was always right, and that pissed off a lot of people.

"David's here," Chris said.

Rick's face lit up. "Jesus Christ, I nearly forgot about him. Is he all right?"

'He's not that great. In fact he's in pretty bad shape. He's had a brain hemorrhage. They don't think he'll be able to talk again, and he's paralyzed down his left side."

"I guessed as much." Rick said. "I should have taken David to the hospital the moment I saw him. But the urge to avoid the hospitals, doctors, and needles put me off a bit."

"Things are not going well, are they?" Chris said as he slowly pulled up a chair.

"Not really, no. Definitely not the way I planned it. We are all supposed to go out holding our heads up. The band playing and the crowds cheering," Rick said, sounding more irritated with each word. "Where's the fun in dying hooked up to machines that go beep beep beep. I want to be hooked up to machines that go BANG BANG BOOM," he shouts at the top of his voice.

Chris calmly ignored him and went to the door. "If you mess around with those machines again your wish will be granted. I got to get back to work. I'll come in and visit you later."

"Why did they put me in a room of my own?" Rick asked.

'It seems you have a reputation of starting arguments and driving other patients crazy."

"And now look at the positive side of that," Rick said laughingly. "I get a nice clean room all to myself."

Chris smiled and shook his head as he went out the door. "Some things never change," he muttered as he closed the door gently.

Rick spent five minutes watching MTV before he fell into a deep sleep.

That evening Rick was still asleep when Chris paid him another visit. The doctors had replaced the electrodes on his chest and hooked him up to a new drip. A meal brought in earlier lay untouched on the table next to him.

When Chris returned at ten the following morning, Rick was awake and zapping through all the channels on the television. Once again Rick had removed his electrodes, but not before switching off the alarms in the monitors. Chris had brought a bunch of magazines and a newspaper.

"Take a look at this," Chris said as he laid a local newspaper on the bedcovers, then sat down on the edge of the bed.

Rick squinted and read the headlines aloud, "Vagabond pop star assaults senator." Rick threw his head back with laughter. "Hey Preston me old mate."

"It's a lot more serious than that. The day before he nearly killed a shopkeeper. Beat him up with his guitar."

"Bloody hell," Rick said, trying to dim his laughter.

"He needs help and a lot more than you."

"Sorry for laughing. You're right. But there is fuck all I can do lying around here. And I'm not joking. There is fuck all I can do, period."

"And that's the way it's going to stay for the next couple of weeks." Doctor Forest said as he entered the room. He gathered up the electrodes and re-placed them on Rick's chest. "Do not remove these again." Forest said, trying to sound serious.

"What are you up to?" Rick asked. "For starters, why the private room. All that bullshit about being a troublemaker. I'm well used to sharing hospital rooms with the best trash of the city, and was never accused of causing trouble in a hospital. "So?" Rick said as he grabbed all the wires connected to the electrodes and tugged on them gently. "What's with the royal treatment. And if you don't tell me you're going to have to get in an electrician to put all these back together again."

"You used to be quite famous didn't you?" Forest said with an air of feigned casualness.

Rick waved his liver spotted hand. "Bullshit. You've been hearing stories. None of it's true. Someone with the same name that's all. Thousands of fools have fallen for that one. Everywhere I go I get mistaken for someone else." Rick slapped Chris hard on the knee. "Isn't that right, Chris?"

"Dead right, Rick."

"I have been doing a little reading. You're the same one all right."

Rick could imagine him looking up his old records and studying them with wonderment. He probably called in other doctors to verify his incredible find and congratulate him on his discovery. But suddenly Rick was not in the mood in keeping up the charade. He never did it with those he met on the street, but all others he shied away from. He could never change who he really was, and his medical records confirmed it.

"That was then, this is now," he finally said.

"How did you end up in the gutter?" Forest asked.

Rick leaned back and stared up at the ceiling. "Can't you think of something more original?"

"Have to start somewhere." Forest replied.

Although he enjoyed telling stories to the boys he met on the road about times gone by he never had the urge to reflect on them. He enjoyed a laugh at the expense of their amusement but that was enough. His days of analyzing the mess he got himself into were long gone.

"Don't know," he said shaking his head. "Could have been the women, the drink, the lawyers, the expenses, the drugs, the parties, the divorces, more women, more drink, things like that."

"I could see all that by analyzing your liver. But there must have been more to it than that."

"It's a long and boring story. Why don't you just wait for the book." Rick said with an air of finality.

Forest looked down at the newspaper on the bed, pointing to the photograph of Preston. 'He was a singer like you."

"Yeah, and the old fart is still arguing with the rest of the world. I gave that up years ago. It suddenly dawned on me that I was only arguing with myself. Life is too short to argue with the world. If everybody minded their own business and kept their damn mouths shut no one would argue anymore" Rick shook his head. "Besides Preston was always frustrated by the world and everyone around him. Had he been born the luckiest person on the planet he'd still have found something to moan about. Most people mellow as the years go by. No chance in hell Preston could do something like that."

"True." Forest said. "I thought you were supposed to sing about your troubles with a guitar not beat a man to death with it,"

With much physical effort Rick pulled himself up in the bed. "Sometimes the anger becomes just too much. When singers start off they have a lot to shout about. But when the money rolls in you tend to forget the injustice, the hunger, and ugliness of the world. Then after years of living in luxury it takes you by the scruff of the neck and kicks you back onto the street. Suddenly you're confronted by the nightmares you started singing about forty or fifty years before. Except they're now more fucking depressing than you ever imagined. Besides, who wants to listen to an old man? That's why they build homes to shut them up and hope they die quickly, saving the taxpayer a bundle." Rick sunk back into his pillow, his energy drained. He never felt so sick and miserable in all his life.

"A man gets thirsty going on like that. Is there anything to drink in a place like this?" Rick said.

"Here" Chris quickly opened the small cabinet next to Rick's bed and took out a bottle of orange juice. Ricks' hands trembled as he drank the juice, gulping it down in seconds.

"Another?" Chris asked.

"No thanks. Too much of that stuff will finish me off completely."

Forest removed his stethoscope from around his neck, put it in his pocked, then pulled up a chair and sat down next to Chris at the bed.

"How many of you are like this?" Forest asked Rick.

"What do you mean? Arguing or sitting around in comfy beds like this?"

"You know what I mean. Down and out. In the gutter."

"I don't know. I'm not keeping records. We were never the type to put something away for our old age. We all did our best to spend it on the spot." Rick said as Chris chuckled.

"Don't get me wrong doc, "Rick continued. "We were never supposed to last this long. We should have all kicked the almighty bucked when we were still on stage. Become coffin heroes like young Jimmy Morrison, Hendrix, or lovely Janis. There was never any time or room in our lives to work out a pension plan. When you're a hard-living, free-loving rolling stone like me that's not the sort of thing that keeps you lying awake at night. "

"The point is," Forest explained, "we have been swamped with letters and donations to cover your hospital bills." Rick stared at him in disbelief. "What? Jesus Christ. How the fuck did anyone know I was in here? I thought I had the right to a bit of privacy in a place like this." He said, pointing a threatening finger at Forest. "If I wanted to attract attention I would have put an advertisement in the Goddamn New York Times inviting them all around for a piss up."

"They still love you out there Rick," Chris said.

"They don't love me." Rick said, pointing his finger at his chest. "The stupid buggers feel sorry for me. They think I'm on my last legs with hardly a puff left in my body." Rick leaned towards Forest. "Out on the road they ran in the opposite direction when they saw I was in trouble." He fell again back into the cushions. "Now I'm on my back like a wounded animal they're reaching for their handkerchiefs." He took a deep breath and stared up at the ceiling. "Make you sick," he sighed.

Forest sat in the chair next to the bed. "They're not feeling sorry for you." Forest said. "They care for you. There's a big difference."

"Sure there is." Rick said, still staring at the ceiling.

Forest pulled an envelope out of his pocket and handed it to Rick. "I received this. But it's actually for you." The quality cream colored envelope with Dr. Forest's name typed neatly in the center had a watermark embedded on the bottom left-hand side. Whoever the sender was they both had taste and money. There were no other markings on the envelope. Rick looked at it suspiciously.

"What is it," he said as he put the envelope to his nose. "Smells like someone with too much money."

"A request from a concert promoter willing to put together a benefit concert to help you and people like you. There is even talk of an old folks home."

Rick pressed the recline button on the side of the bed, and slowly sank back to a lying position, and gazed piously at the ceiling. "Holy Mary Mother of Jesus and all the family, what did I fuckin' tell you. I was right. We're dying in our beds they are still trying to put us into a home."

"It's not just a home." Forest quickly replied.

"Oh I get it. Isn't that what they call God's waiting room these days."

"You've got it all wrong. The idea is a special home for retired musicians."

Rick's head shot up. "What? Retired?" Rick shouted at Forest. Rick pushed the remote button and rose again to a sitting position. "You're as mad as the idiot who wrote this," he said, shaking the envelope under Forests' nose. "Musicians like us don't retire. Did Johnny Cash retire? James Brown, Bo Diddley or John Lee Hooker? No way. They all went on to the bloody end. We never ever retire. You got that?"

"Yes I've got that," Forest replied with slight grin.

"Right, at least your listening. Now, apart from that," Rick continued, "you could never get ten of us into the same house for more than a month. There would be murder."

Forest got up out of his chair. "Maybe we can talk about this later." He walked over to the door and turned. "I've got rounds to do and you need a lot more rest. Normally I'd prescribe tranquilizers but I think you've had more than your fair share over the years." Forest left the room.

Rick glanced at the envelope and threw it onto the empty chair.

Chris knew about the letter and told Dr. Forest Rick would never agree to it. Everybody had their pride and Rick was no exception. But there was hope; he didn't tear it up.

Rick pressed a button on the side of the bed and rose again to sitting upright.

"Where's David? I want to see him."

"I'll take you to see him tonight. If the doctors see me pushing you around in the state you're in I'll get fired. You're supposed to be dead."

"No chance." Rick pressed another button and began to recline. "Although I do like this bed." He closed his eyes and fell into a deep sleep.

At eleven that night the hospital had calmed down considerably. The only sound to be heard on the fifth floor was Rick complaining about Chris's pace as he was being pushed towards David's room.

"Is this as fast as you can go? What's the matter with you man. Got a gammy leg?'

Chris had rigged up a wheelchair so that he could get Rick with all his drips and tubes into it in one go. He had dismantled the drip stand from its undercarriage and taped the remainder to the wheelchair. The only thing he regretted was not taping Rick's mouth.

"Shhhhhh quiet. You'll wake everybody up."

"Must be something wrong with the patients if they're asleep at this hour. This ain't a loony hospital, is it?" Rick said, trying to peer through the glass windows along the way. "Or somewhere where everybody gets a shot at the end of the day so they sleep like elephants. Then the nurses finally get the chance to screw the doctors without any interruptions."

"This is just an ordinary hospital. There's nothing wrong with it. In fact it was the only hospital willing to take you in that night."

"Is that right."

"Yes that's right!" Chris retorted.

"So they knew who we were right from the start?" Rick tried to turn to get a good look at Chris.

"I don't know." Chris said stern-faced.

"Someone must have told them. I've been in and out of hospitals before and never been recognized. And I never gave real names either. I wonder how they found us out this time."

"I never said a word."

"You sure?"

"Of course I'm sure."

"Must have been one of the blokes down at the harbor."

"No idea." Chris replied, then took a turn so sharp Rick nearly fell out of the wheelchair.

"Sure?" Rick asked, grabbing the armrests tightly.

"Of course I'm sure. What is this, the Spanish inquisition or something?"

"Just checking."

Chris made a sign of the cross behind Rick.

"You know, back in the sixties," Chris said, trying to change the subject. "I saw your band play their first US gig. It was tremendous. I had never seen a band so wild and uncompromising, but totally in charge of the music and public."

"Don't know about that," Rick replied. "We were pretty stoned or drunk for most of that trip."

"You shocked the establishment to the bone, breaking with the two-piece suit culture that dominated the time. After that one concert I became one of your biggest fans."

"Thanks for that Chris. Could you give it a rest now before I drown in your bleeding sentiment."

Chris came to a stop in the middle of the corridor. Rick looked around in bewilderment. "What's wrong? What are we stopping for?"

"This is where David's at." Chris said, as he leaned over to open the door next to the wheelchair.

Rick grabbed Chris's arm before he reached the handle.

"Hold on a sec. What's he like. Has he got wires and tubes and everything coming out of him?"

"He's not so bad."

"They operated didn't they? He's probably all bruised with bandages full of blood and everything."

"Nothing like that. David looks all right." Chris said calmly.

He released his arm. "Okay then." Rick felt the sudden rush of panic subside and relaxed back into the chair. "I just want to remember him the way he was. Not some motionless body looking as if he had been tackled by a football team."

"Yeah right." Chris muttered under his breath.

The door swung open and Chris wheeled Rick gently into the room. The lights were dimmed but bright enough to make out a figure lying in the bed. David was connected up to an array of monitors, and three different types of drips. He was not on a respirator, and the rest of the equipment was similar to what he had been hooked up to the last week. Chris was right: David didn't look so bad after all. The bandage around his head was so neat and tidy it resembled an oversized Jewish skull cap. His face bore no hint of his long graying beard. David was clean shaven, which revealed smooth pink skin with not a rimple in sight. He looked twenty years younger and had the appearance of taking a quiet nap.

Chris pushed the wheelchair slowly to the side of the bed. Rick reached for David's hand and gently took hold of it.

"I'm sorry I didn't get you to hospital earlier pal," Rick said. "I didn't realize. I really didn't. But the doctors fixed you up good. They said you are going to be up on your feet in no time." Rick studied all the equipment connected to David.

"We've had a lot more equipment connected up to us in our day." Rick continued. "You'll beat this lot. I know you will." He shook David's hand gently. David looked serene and rested: not a sign of the hardship of sleeping rough for years on end. "The old boy doesn't look his age, does he?"

"How old is he?" Chris asked.

"No idea." Rick replied.

"We'd better get back," Chris said as he turned to open the door. Rick released David's hand.

"Hang on in there, mate. We still have a few years to go. We're not finished yet."

In silence Chris wheeled Rick back to his room. Rick knew he could never leave him again. He realized he had a duty to care for him and would be doing that for the rest of his days.

"Why now?" Rick asked, resting his head on a freshly puffed up pillow Chris had just put down. "We were sick now and again. The odd cold or flu but nothing like this." He looked up at the ceiling and shook his fist in anger. "Tried to kill two birds with one stone didn't you. Well it didn't work."

"There is no point in arguing with him." Chris said. "It's life on the street. That's where the problem is."

"We've been doin' all right 'till now." Rick replied.

"Okay, but you're not forty, fifty or even seventy for that matter and you've got to accept that. Out there its survival of the fittest. When you get to your age you're dead meat. I think it's time you came in from the cold."

"Going to lecture me now are you?"

"You've had your day, Rick. Relax. Take it easy." Chris picked up the envelope that lay on the dresser, and placed it in front of Rick. "At least read the letter."

Five minutes later Rick was alone in his room with the lights dimmed. The only sound was the humming of his monitors.

He stared at the expensive envelope for at least an hour. He knew what was in it. Some big shot was going to offer them the commercial opportunity of a lifetime. They could retire with a healthy sum in the bank, and never have to worry about a thing, only the big shot followed by a bunch of cronies walks away with his pockets bursting at the seams.

Rick weighed up the choices. Going back to the street would probably finish him off within a couple of months. The other option was an old folk's home where staff automatically assumed deafness and dementia if you were over sixty and shouted the most simple instructions at you all day long. David would probably never walk or talk again. He would end up in a home being cared for by a bunch of people who didn't give a shit. He was a vegetable, and would be treated like a vegetable. His past meant nothing to them. The knot in his stomach tightened. Rick felt miserable. Why are the last years of life wrought with sickness and ill health in the first place? Cancer, heart and liver decease, blood vessels bursting in the brain, leaking bladders, doctors, needles, bags of medicine, and a slow deterioration into oblivion. No glory, no fanfare, only complete and utter humiliation before death. There should be a better end. After rearing a family, working hard and doing your best to be a better person, life should end in a climax. The crowning of achievements. Whatever happened to the old fairy tale ending of living happily ever after? You've gone the distance, made a name for yourself and now you should be able to rise to the occasion.

Rick clenched his fists and slammed down on the bed. "Why?" He shouted. For the first time in many years he let tears flow freely down his face. He now realized why Hemingway had blown his brains out. He had foreseen the degradation of old age and decided to desist at a sensible age before it got him. He should have done the same years ago, but now it was too late. He could never leave David to fend for himself. He took the bedspread in his hands and wiped his eyes dry, then blew his nose in the linen sheet. The release of tension that had built up since he arrived in the hospital found an outlet, and he felt relieved. A burden had been lifted from his shoulders. For once in his life he knew exactly what he should do, yet at the same time he felt ashamed. He had to open the letter, and when he did the road downhill to humiliation and ridicule would start there and then. Swallowing a sword would be a lot easier than swallowing his pride, but right now doing the right thing had the upper hand.

The following morning Chris sat in a chair next to Rick as he tore the envelope open and took out a neatly typed letter. Chris moved the letter back and forward before his eyes trying to bring the small letters into focus.

"I've got reading glasses if you want?" Chris said as he reached into his breast pocket.

"Fuck off with your glasses." Rick said abruptly. "Ehh.. no offence," he followed quickly.

"Dear Sir. It's been years since anyone addressed me as sir." Rick mused. "Whoever wrote this must be going senile. *It has come to our attention that many rock stars like yourself have not had the benefit of a proper retirement."* Jesus. The asshole is trying to sell me an insurance policy." Rick said, shaking his

head. "*I have no wish to go into the specifics of this matter since I believe the past has no bearing on the present. What I do believe is that elderly musicians like yourself have a right to a decent retirement regardless their background.* Would he say that if he knew what I'd been up to the last few years? Wouldn't touch me with a ten foot pole. *Our company organizes some of the largest rock concerts in the world. Last year our company grossed $340 million.* So fucking what." Rick shrugged his shoulders and sighed deeply.

"*We are in a position to organize a concert for the benefit of aging musicians.* Really. How kind. *The proceeds will go to setting up a special home for retired musicians.* Yep, what did I tell you? An old folk's home. Gather up all the old rockers and put them somewhere where they wouldn't get up to too much mischief. *This of course is nothing new, yet we believe the home we have in mind would fill the direct needs of all those who would live there.* Does that mean doctors turn up when you really need them? Or we get to bonk the nurses? How the fuck does he know what an old rockers direct needs are. The letter was signed with an illegible scribble. Under that an address of a suite in the famous Rand building downtown New York.

"I think," Chris said, "you have to ask yourself what to do now. Is it worth going after or not? But I think you know the answers to that."

Rick massaged his temples. His head hurt. He couldn't think any further. He lay the letter on the dresser and relaxed into the cushions. "Let me think about it ok?"

"No problem. Take all the time you need. Chris left, leaving Rick staring at the shadows on the ceiling until he fell asleep.

For the next few days the letter lay open on his dresser for all to see. David's condition only improved slightly. The doctors used that unquestionable statement "critical but stable," which Rick referred to as neither living nor dead. David was now officially a bloody vegetable, and here he was, lying comfortably in a room just up the hall and unable to do a thing to help.

Each passing day Rick grew stronger. With Chris's help he took his first few steps around the bed. Two days later he ventured out into the corridor at a snail's pace, while holding onto the safety rail as if his life depended on it. It did. Rick was surprised it had taken so long to get his strength back. Maybe the doctors were right after all. Maybe he really was ill this time.

Chapter eight

The cloud that blurred David's mind passed slowly. He opened his eyes to stare at a fluorescent light in a white ceiling. He was lying in an unusually warm and comfortable bed. How did he get there? He could remember being down at the docklands with a few of the boys but that was it.

His nose itched. He tried to scratch it but his arm would not respond. He tried to move his legs; nothing. Were straps holding him down? He tried to look but his head would not respond either. Was this some kind of prison? It smelled like a hospital. A prison hospital? If he shouted maybe someone would come and let him loose. He tried to shout for help but only managed to make a noise that sounded nothing like the word he wanted to shout. He tried once again.

"Aawwaar". The sound was barely audible. David tried to look for whatever was holding him down and finally realized there were no straps or other restraints. He could get up and move around if he wanted to, but it was impossible. He tried to remember if he had been in an accident, but could not recall anything. Then why was he unable to move? Finally it dawned on him. At seventy-four his father had had a stroke. A strong man, who continued to work long past retirement. Not for the lack of money, since his son played in the world's best-paid R & B band and catered for all his financial needs, but the word retirement sounded like an affliction, so he worked right up until the day he had the stroke. The paralysis affected his left side and his speech. After eight months of therapy he had learned to talk again, but everyone except his therapists and close family had trouble understanding him. Six months later his situation improved tremendously. He regained partial use of his left arm and leg, and his speech was nearly back to normal. The therapists' hopes had exceeded all expectations. A week before his seventy-fifth birthday he suffered a second hemorrhage and died. Was he now in the same predicament as his father? He felt an incredible emptiness in the lonely room.

The nurse surprised him by walking briskly into the room without knocking. She immediately proceeded to check the drip and needles embedded in David's arms. He tried to turn and look at her but his head refused to move. If he could just look at her and get her attention everything would be all right. He tried to turn his eyes towards her but the strain was too much. Trying to shout earlier had drained him of all energy, and now he was encased in a torso unable to scream, shout, move, laugh, or die. The ultimate prison. His view of the ceiling blurred from the swelling of moisture in both eyes. Then everything went black in his left eye, then his right. He opened his eyes once again and everything was back in focus. The face of a nurse with a warm smile and holding a tissue she just used to wipe the tears from his eyes hovered above him. She finally noticed.

The doctors pricked and jabbed David for a full hour. He had no feeling at all in his left side, however his right arm and leg, although extremely weak, showed some reaction. An hour after the doctors left he noticed the door opening in the corner of his eye. Suddenly he was confronted by the sight of someone who looked like Rick hovering over him with a big smile and waving like a little kid. His hair was cut short and he was clean shaven.

"Hey David, me old mate, it's me." Rick said. "I'm staying here as well. Don't worry old son, we'll be out of here in no time."

David tried to speak but only managed a slight grunt.

When Rick stepped back he recognized Chris immediately. This was a real surprise. He never expected to see him again in this life, or the next. Why Chris was standing next to Rick after all these years was a total mystery.

"You remember Chris don't you?" Rick said with a kiddish grin on his face. "He works here. Looks like a bleedin' doctor don't he. Maybe he can get us some stuff and a couple of nurses. Get the old pecker going," Rick prodded David in the crotch. "You're the lucky one. You wouldn't have to do anything except lie there. She'd just climb on top and do all the work."

David didn't move. There was no expression in his face. Rick shook David. "Can you hear me? You're still there aren't you mate? I'm sorry I wasn't there when you needed me. I shouldn't have left you alone with that lot." Rick said, leaning in closer to David. "They're not like you and me. They're not musicians." Rick said as a tear fell from his left eye. "I'm sticking to you from now on. They're going to get you into therapy so within no time you'll be back on your feet, just like your old dad, God rest his soul."

Chris put his hand on Rick's shoulder. "Let him rest. He needs it."

"Yeah sure, of course," Rick said trying to hold back more tears. "I'll be off lad. We'll be back to see you soon." They left the room as David closed his eyes.

Days later they disconnected David's drip then moved him out of the hospital to a rehabilitation clinic.

Rick spent the following two weeks recuperating and playing a cat-and-mouse game with hoards of journalists and elderly fans turning up at the hospital to wish him well.

Because of his objection to security the staff had to move Rick to different rooms every couple of days to keep anyone from finding him. They were not used to having such a celebrity in house although Rick enjoyed being the center of the circus.

Resting in his room in the evenings Rick spent many hours watching television programs recounting his past life. Offers of money and places to stay came in from every corner of the world. None of his old friends or family had called, sent a card or flowers. He wouldn't have turned them away if they had come through the door, yet at the same time he was happy they didn't.

At the time of his discharge Chris offered him a room in his apartment. Rejecting it would be the insult of a lifetime. Here was a man he trusted, and had come to care for deeply. He could never refuse. Rick lay on a stretcher in his dressing gown in a quiet room on the ground floor of the hospital, eating a hamburger. His face, except his eyes and mouth was covered in bandages. He stuffed the remainder of the burger into his mouth, then picked up a bottle of ketchup next to him and squirted it onto his left hand. Carefully he dabbed the ketchup onto the bandages just above his left eye and jaw. Rick cleaned his hands then rapped on the door. Chris and two medics entered the room.
"Finished your meal?" Chris asked.
"Ready," he mumbled through his stuffed mouth. "I just added some special effects to cheer them up outside. It'll help to keep them off my trail."
"You'll give this hospital a bad name." Chris moaned.
Under the very eyes of the journalists who set up camp at the front and rear of the hospital they wheeled Rick out the emergency entrance to a waiting ambulance. Passing the waiting journalists and photographers Rick leaned over on the stretcher and groaned loudly. The remains of the burger spewed out of his mouth and landed at their feet. Much to the delight of Rick, two journalists were physically sick as the orderlies rolled him towards the waiting ambulance. With lights flashing and sirens wailing they made a spectacular getaway through the rush-hour traffic of downtown Brooklyn. When the lights and siren were

turned off Chris and the medics removed the bandages. Under his gown he emerged wearing a dark pin-striped suit.

"This is not from the Salvation Army I hope? " Rick asked.

"Don't insult me." Chris replied. "It's brand new."

Chris's apartment was in a respectable middle-class area and better than Rick had imagined. He lived on the ground floor, with two bedrooms and a decent-sized living room. The annexed kitchen was modern and clean. Chris lived with few luxuries; a reflection of his orderly's salary, but didn't seem bad at all. Chris quickly removed some newspapers on the sofa and puffed up the beige cushions.

"Nice place," Rick said, as he settled onto the comfortable sofa.

"It's enough. I don't need much at my age."

"Neighbors all right?"

"Nice and quiet. A friendly bunch." Chris said and pointed to the door at the back. "If you want to take a shower it's just through that door. I'm going to go out to get some groceries. I'll be back in about twenty minutes."

When Rick finished his shower Chris had already returned and putting together a lunch in the kitchen. The sound of Vivaldi's four seasons filled the room. Rick stared objectively at the modest stereo unit. "You don't have anything stronger then that do you?"

"I don't have any beer in the house if that's what you mean. Anyway you're not supposed to be drinking."

"Not that. It's the music that needs pumping up. Haven't you got something with a beat? This stuff will drive you senile."

"I never listen to any of the pop stations any more. They give me a headache."

"You're sicker than I am."

Chris put a tray of coffee and salad sandwiches on the small table then went to change the station. "I'll see what I can find."

"No don't please." Rick said shaking his head. "This is your house. I shouldn't interfere."

Chris hesitated at the radio. "Are you sure? It's no problem."

"Of course I'm sure. I've just got to learn to keep my big mouth shut. Leave the music on, it's fine. Sit down and let's eat. Wish I hadn't dumped the burger, although the effect was fucking brilliant."

Chris sat in the armchair and took a bite out of his sandwich. Rick dug into his, washing it down with coffee.

"A good change after all that hospital grub," Rick said as he patted his belly.

Chris settled back and relaxed in the sofa. He raised his right hand and began to conduct it to the orchestration of the music.

"This is Vivaldi's Four Seasons. He wrote it while..."

"Hold on a sec," Rick snapped. "Hold on right there. I'll listen to the music but don't push it, okay?"

"Sorry." Chris said apologetically. "Won't happen again."

Rick shook his head, "Wait a minute. What am I doing here? No, I'm sorry," Rick said, sounding apologetic. "I don't mean to be so pushy. It's your house."

"Don't worry. It's all right. I've known you longer than today. Just let's relax and enjoy the sandwiches."

Chris was long gone when Rick awoke in the spare bedroom the next morning. There was a note and a key on the kitchen table. "Home from work at about five and will cook dinner," Rick read aloud. "Help yourself to anything in the kitchen, and explore the neighborhood if you feel up to it."

The first thing Rick did was raid the kitchen for breakfast. He was famished. No more hospital breakfasts; now he could go for the real thing while he still had the chance. A pot of coffee, two fried eggs, two sausages, four slices of toast. He finished it all in the living room watching re-runs of MASH on TV. It made him finally feel at home.

After a shower he rummaged through his old clothes the hospital had packed into two plastic bags. His old army coat smelled musty, and the rest of his clothes smelled of urine. After going through all the pockets and holes in the coat he finally found what he was searching for: his bank card was still in one piece. During the time he spent in hospital more than enough money had accumulated on the account for a booze up with the boys down at the harbor. He trashed the clothes, put on an overcoat and left the apartment.

Outside the air was cool and fresh. He found an ATM two blocks away in a local shopping mall. The incredible amount of three thousand dollars flashed at him from the screen. The temptation to withdraw it all and spend it at the nearest bar was more than inviting. He stood still for a while, staring at the amount on the screen. How much would he withdraw? He used to take out all the money at the start of the month but quit doing it after he was mugged and all his money was stolen. Three weeks without a cent in your pocket and too much pride to beg made life unbearable. He stayed clear of the Salvation Army or any charitable organization where all the street bums congregated. He would always pay for his own food and drink, and when the weather got really bad he rented a room in a cheap hotel. Right now he yearned for the taste of 15 year old malt whiskey or some good French wine. He pushed the button on the ATM. Rick withdrew a hundred dollars. The mental fight on whether to start drinking again proved tougher then he imagined. Shortly after, Rick stood outside a liquor store gazing at the bottles of whiskey and brandy in the window. He could feel sweat breaking out on his forehead. His breathing became irregular, and he began to feel dizzy. He turned and walked a block to calm his nerves. Finally, Rick went back to the apartment and waited for Chris to come home.

The Rand building was a monumental white sandstone high rise built in the twenties by a long extinct oil company. Rick and Chris stood on the opposite side of the street and stared up.
"Did you ever meet this guy?" Rick asked.
"No," Chris replied, as his gaze rested on the windows of the top floor.
"I don't know about this," Rick said.
"What do you want Rick? This is not only about you. Are you going to turn around and walk away? This is about the lives of the people we care about. If we don't cross the street now not only your life but David's is going down the plughole. There is too much at stake. You both deserve better."
Chris looked away, took a deep breath, then turned back to Rick. "I've asked around." Chris said. "From what I've heard he's pretty straight." To avoid Rick's penetrating eyes Chris kept his stare on the building in front of them.
"A straight promoter?" Rick raised his arms and looked up to heaven in utter disbelief. "Are you kidding? A straight promoter? That's a non-existent species." Rick said with sounding assurance.
Chris turned to Rick and looked him straight in the eye.
"The business has changed since your time, Rick. Computers run the business all the way from A to Z, and controlled by so many people there is no chance of fiddling the books. The IRS sit on these guys twenty-four hours a day."
"The business has changed?" Rick said astonished. "You're stark raving mad. I don't know why I'm letting you lead me around like this. I'm definitely going to regret it."

"Then shut up and lets go," Chris said tugging on Ricks' arm as he stepped out to cross the street. "Come on, or we'll be late for our appointment. "

At the top floor they were greeted with a smile by a beautiful dark Latin secretary. "Mr. Kronin is expecting you," she said as she put down the phone after announcing their arrival.
"If you would just follow me, gentlemen," the long-legged dream glided effortlessly from behind her desk and guided them down a corridor towards Kronin's office.
"She wants me," Rick whispered to Chris, nudging him in the ribs.
"You wish," Chris whispered back.
"Did you see that look? She'd love to bed me right this minute."
"Will you shut up." Chris said, trying not to show too much irritation. "We haven't been here five minutes and already I've got the feeling we'll be thrown from the goddamn roof."
The secretary opened the double doors to an immense office. The first thing to hit Rick and Chris was the tremendous view of the city. Peaks of towering skyscrapers rose up to meet them through the mass of concrete below, as if soaking up the sun, warmth, and energy to grow even further. The same sun shone through the tinted windows and a heavenly glow filled the entire suite.
"Whoever he is he's got class." Rick muttered as he slowly stepped into the room which was designed to impress, and it did. The lush carpet was a wave of magnificent color with irregular blobs of red, blue, bright green and yellow running into one another to give the effect of walking on multi-colored clouds. This in turn was stunningly reflected off a metal-like ceiling that seemed to reflect all the colors in the room. The lights embedded into the walls were gigantic works of art. Dark metal columns

rose impressively from the floor to the ceiling, looking as if they were taken from the set of Ridley Scott's film Alien. Between the columns, the office walls were lined with photographs of contemporary pop stars. Many with personal messages signed to "Jim" and all the great things he did to help them with their career.

"Mister Kronin will be here shortly," The secretary said before closing the double doors and leaving Rick and Chris alone in the expanse of the incredible office.

"Not a bad office," Chris whispered. Rick nodded in silence as he casually walked along the row of photographs.

"That's the talent of today," Chris said. "Some of these guys make more in a month than you used to in a whole year."

"Money isn't everything," Rick replied.

"No, but it sure as hell helps. You recognize any of them?" Chris asked.

"Not one." Rick replied.

In the middle of the wall between the enormous photographs Rick stopped before a very impressive stereo system. He pressed a button and the CD tray glided out.

"Will you leave that alone." Chris said in panic. "You'll break something."

"Don't be silly. I've handled more complicated equipment than this in my day. This is kids' stuff. It's like my first stereo. You can't go wrong with it."

He removed a CD box from the rack, opened it effortlessly, swiftly placed the CD in the holder, then pressed another button, the tray disappeared back into the system.

The first track showed up on the display. Rick pressed the play button. Silence. The CD was playing but no sound came out of the speakers. He turned up the volume. Still nothing. He scanned the system for the right button to patch the CD player to the amplifier. The lettering on the controls was minuscule. Rick squinted, trying to focus the miniature type under the array of knobs and buttons. It was hopeless. He didn't like to admit it but he needed glasses. He leaned in close and scanned the stereo.

"You need glasses, Rick."

"Bugger off. I can see everything." His finger shot up to a switch on the right hand side. "Got it."

Rick and Chris were hit with a blast of sound that nearly knocked them off their feet.

Chris made a panic dive at the stereo. "Where's that button," he shouted, pressing every button and switch in sight.

"Told you there was nothing wrong with my eyes," Rick shouted back as Chris frantically continued his search.

Rick leaned over and with his face just centimeters from the panel pressed a button. Everything went dead. Silence.

"Jesus, Rick," Chris raged. "Don't ever do that again."

"What's with the panic? I knew exactly what I was doing."

"I see you've found the stereo," a voice said from directly behind them. Rick and Chris turned to face James Kronin. Late forties, well built, looked fit, expensive suit and holding a large cigar, Kronin introduced two subdued men standing to each side of him. On the left was Henry Mallow, Kronin's personal assistant, and on the right Bill Lever, his lawyer. Kronin pointed to the giant photographs on the wall.

"Have you met any of your contemporaries. Justin Timberlake, Duffy, Britney Spears, among others."

"Never heard of them." Rick said, shaking his head. "Mind you, they probably never heard of me neither."

"I wouldn't say that," Kronin replied. "Many of these kids parents still have your records on the shelves."

"You mean grandparents." Rick quipped. "And the last thing kids want to listen to are granddads records."

"One of Kronin's assistants pressed a button on a remote control he held in his hand, and a wall slid back to reveal a conference room, and at least fifty seats around the longest table he had seen in years.

"Must have been a hell of job getting that table up here," Rick muttered under his breath.

Kronin, holding his cigar aloft, gestured to the table. "Please gentlemen, take a seat."

Rick and Chris sat next to one another in the middle of the table. Kronin, Lever, and Mallow sat directly opposite. As if on cue two long legged brunettes entered. One was pushing a trolley full of coffee cakes and sandwiches, the other a trolley full of whiskey, gin, vodka, and beer. They were not as beautiful and elegant as the secretary, but just as sexy. The trolleys were parked to each side of Rick and Chris.

With a broad smile Kronin gestured to the food and drink. "Please, gentlemen, help yourselves."

"First we would like to know exactly what you have in mind for us." Rick stated.

Kronin settled back into his chair and took a deep puff from his cigar. He blew the smoke over the polished wood of the table.

"When we all heard about you and David's situation we were deeply shocked and want to do something about it. Our idea is to organize a concert given by the top artists of today. Their services will be free of course, and all the proceeds will go to creating a special retirement home for elderly musicians and artists like yourself. The concert will be big. One of the biggest ever for this type of benefit. We believe we can raise millions, enough in any case for you to relax in the company of friends and fellow musicians, and enjoy your old age."

"What makes you think I haven't been enjoying my OLD age?" Rick said.

Chris closed his eyes. "Oh God," he whispered.

"Your doctor's report," Kronin replied. "You escaped death by the skin of your teeth. If you go back to living on the streets you won't last until Christmas."

Kronin got up from the desk.

"You don't have to roam the streets anymore. We are here to help you," Kronin said as he walked over to the large cloth-covered canvas in the corner of the room. "The home we were thinking about is something like this." Rick leaned towards Chris and whispered. "Must have been practicing that speech for a week."

Kronin pulled away the cloth, revealing an artist's impression of a large mansion with extensive grounds.

Rick was impressed, but he tried his best to hide it.

"This is Mount Merrian," Kronin said. "It has room for at least a hundred and fifty musicians from all over the country. There will be staff, nurses, the works. You won't have to worry about a thing for the rest of your days."

Rick finally managed to close his jaw to say something. "You mean one hundred and fifty patients."

"No. I really mean musicians. This is a house, not a hospice."

"And what do you get out of this?" Rick asked.

"Oh I've already got it. Look around you. The music industry has been good to me and this is my way of paying it back."

The industry had indeed been good to Kronin. Just as it had been good to Rick a long time ago. He got up out of the chair and stepped up to take a closer look at the mansion. He could remember when he had a mansion just like it and twice as much grounds. He never missed the luxuries, but looking at this stirred something within him. Children running around on the front lawn. Friends and other musicians coming around for jam sessions. All night parties. Wives coming in through the front door, girlfriends sneaking out the back.

"Well, what do you say?" Kronin asked.

Rick did not know what to say. He would love to tell Kronin to shove it. If he was on the street again tomorrow he wouldn't give a shit. The pain and the hassle of living rough was temporarily forgotten. His batteries were charged and he could do it all again. But at the same time he knew he was kidding himself. The first cold night would probably kill him off. He would die alone in the gutter and probably be buried as a John Doe. What would become of David he didn't dare to imagine.

"I have to think about it." Rick said hesitantly.

"I thought you might," Kronin said, then puffed long and heavy on his cigar. "In a way of proving our sincerity I want you to meet someone," Kronin said.

Mallow opened the double doors to another office. Preston stood in the middle of the room. His gray beard and hair were scraggier then Rick's had ever been. The lines of his face engraved by years of anger were deeper and more bitter. This gave him the look of having a permanent frown on his face. He looked subdued. Must have cost them a box of valium to get him up here, Rick thought.

"Hello Rick, Chris." Preston said, sounding hesitant. "It's been a long time…." His words faded. Preston turned back to staring at the floor. Kronin quickly picked up. "We bailed him out and we mean to take care of him. The same goes for your friend David."

Rick walked over to Preston and took him in his arms and hugged him. His tired blue eyes were glazed and distant and only seemed to be held in place by the mass of wrinkles surrounding them.

"Good to see you man." Rick whispered in his ear as he patted him on the back.

"Come gentlemen. Let's sit down." Kronin said as the two female assistants returned and guided Preston out of the room. Rick tried to say something to Preston before he left, but it was impossible. Preston looked so out of it he might as well have been on another galaxy.

After seeing those newspaper reports about Preston beating up the shopkeeper and senator maybe it was better this way. But now he felt he had an extra burden. Not only did he have David to look after, they had Preston thrown in for good measure. Kronin had pulled off a good one.

Rick's sense of responsibility had suddenly grown an extra dimension and he was not enjoying it. The pressure grew by the minute; everyone was waiting for an answer. He knew Chris wanted him to do this very badly. The look on his face urging him on mentally, yet fearing the worst.

They could put it together without him, but without Rick's endorsement they could never raise enough money to get the mansion in the picture. Rick wished he had a week to think about it, or preferably a year. Looking around at the expectant faces staring at him he knew his time was up.

"All right. I'll do it."

Kronin clenched his fist and shook it at his colleagues. "Gentlemen, I think it's time we got this ball rolling."

Chapter nine

The following day the news was already worldwide. Luckily the reporters never managed to track down Chris's apartment. But what seemed like a handful of reporters at the hospital grew into a battalion outside the Rand office block. The phones rang continuously, requesting exclusive interviews or recent photographs of all the musicians connected to the event.

Kronin's organization ran like a well-oiled wheel. Within days he was dragging Rick all over the country in his private jet to promote the benefit concert. They were the host of all the talk shows. For Kronin it was just another day at the office. For Rick, too much like hard work. His nerves didn't help either. Nearly twenty years had passed since he willingly stood in front of a television camera; now they were touring all the major chat shows. Rick could remember Letterman from years back with his pencil flicking and the sarcastic smile he used as a backdrop for his jokes. So many years later nothing had changed. Oprah was still going strong too although in different pastures. Kronin told him she had dropped an interview with Mike Tyson in order to plug the charity gig on time. It turned out to be the first program where Rick felt composed and at home. Her program was more relaxed than others and he got the chance to talk in depth about his life on the road, although he avoided questions on how it had all come about.

After three weeks Kronin called a short break. On a rainy afternoon they once again boarded his private jet and flew East. From the atmosphere on the jet Rick knew Kronin had another surprise up his sleeve. He hoped it was a visit to David whom he had not seen in nearly a month. Kronin kept insisting he should concentrate on the publicity for the concert. Five minutes into the flight Rick knew they were not on their way to see David.

 The New Orleans Superdome was impressive. Outside it looked like a giant spaceship, inside it looked just as spectacular, with seating for up to 120,000. Rick knew the venue; he had played there many years ago. They stood in the center of the magnificent stadium.

 "As I said earlier," Kronin said, "we could probably fill it but the gamble would be too great. We're going for at least a quarter. We are not making any money out of the benefit but at the same time we're not prepared to lose any. We have to limit our liabilities."

 "Of course," Rick said, faking interest as best he could.

 "The people will come," Kronin continued, "no way they would they let down the greatest R & B band in the world."

 Rick looked around the stadium and realized for the first time the concert was definitely going to take place. The first stages of a concert floor were being laid down at the top end of the stadium. Two towers of scaffolding were slowly being built up either side of the stage to accommodate the speakers. Rick walked across the grass and studied the work in progress. He had seen stages being built a thousand times but it never ceased to amaze him how the puzzle was put together. Hundreds of lights, miles of cable, and enough speakers to make the sound travel over a distance of sixty miles. All connected up to a series of computers which ran the show like clockwork. He thought he had forgotten how it all worked, but it all came back to him within seconds.

Chapter ten

Robbie quietly searched through his eight million dollar house in Beverly Hills looking for anything he might need for his journey. At seven in the morning everybody was still asleep, and he knew that none of the twelve to sixteen people who occupied his house would rise before noon.

He gently opened the door to the second of his six bedrooms. Two people lay on the floor at the foot of the bed, while four others occupied the bed itself. As far as he could make out it was one male, probably Quinten, and three females. None of whom he recognized. The young male and female entwined on the floor were wrapped in a quilt from one of the other bedrooms. He didn't recognize them. Robbie carefully closed the door. Any search would be futile. The last thing he wanted to do was wake any of them. The small black leader knapsack he picked up earlier was large enough for one change of clothing and the necessary toiletries. He would have to do without the larger bag he was actually looking for.

In the kitchen, while putting together a simple breakfast, he wondered whether or not to leave behind a note. If he didn't they'd probably send out a search party. He would end up hiding like a wanted man. They'd probably do the same even with the note. Everybody knew he had reached that cycle in his life when change was due. He had talked about it often enough with anyone who still had the patience to listen to an elderly man. With any luck they just might leave him alone. The only one who probably would cry over his leaving was his lawyer. A die hard who should have retired years ago but was still trying to hang on to the few remaining celebrities he represented.

Robbie would have relished seeing the look on his face when the letter arrived announcing his decision to take his business elsewhere.

In fact the only thing he had done was get a cab from Beverly Hills to West Hollywood, walk into the local legal cooperative and ask them to witness his will. They knew who he was, yet reacted as if he was just another client. Although the look on their faces was priceless after he handed them a check for one-and-a-half-million dollars in advance for any future legal work. The only condition of this gesture was they should never bother him again on any of his legal matters. From now on they would take care of everything. Holding onto a small personal account he transferred control of his worldly possessions to the charity trust he had set up twenty years previous. With a pleasing sense of renewal Robbie cheerfully stepped out of the stuffy office and into the sunshine. The only thing that actually bothered him was how to get to New Orleans. Plane, train, or something completely different?

At seventy-two Robbie looked twenty years younger. He had not only kept his hair but it had more or less retained its natural color. More importantly, he kept trim and fit.

He threw a leather knapsack over his shoulder and walked briskly in the direction of highway 101, a distance of ten miles. Along the way he found a piece of cardboard, cut it down to size with his Swiss army knife, and wrote on it in large letters 'New Orleans'.

The traffic leading onto the junction was heavy. Cars and trucks sped past. Robbie held the board up and stuck out his thumb for more than an hour before the first truck slowed to a halt. The driver was heading for Phoenix. Robbie climbed in, and the truck pulled away. By the end of the day he had completed the first quarter of the journey.

Chapter eleven

Just back in Los Angeles Rick and Kronin were rushed off to the other side of the city by helicopter, for a guest appearance in the tonight show with Jay Leno. Rick was furious. The visit to the stadium was interesting, but now his head throbbed, his back ached and his feet were on fire. The only place he wanted to be was in a nice comfortable bed being fed by a beautiful young nurse. Instead, he waited in the wings of the stage and watched his introduction on the monitor.

"My head is killing me," Rick said as he produced a small bottle of whiskey out of his back pocket and took three hard swills, finishing the last of what was left in the bottle.

"There is paracetamol you know." Kronin replied.

"This whiskey works better than a box of paracetamol. Tastes better too,"

"It's cheaper."

"True, but 15 year old paracetamol isn't any good." Rick said as he tucked away the bottle while Jay announced him to the audience.

"My first guest tonight is a legend in rock music who had everything a man could wish for," Leno announced. "A family, big cars, houses on every continent and a bank balance that even I could only dream of. But then his world came tumbling down and he lost it all. For more than twenty years he roamed the streets as a forgotten man, looking for a place to sleep and a bite to eat. With him the man who is going to change all that by organizing the greatest benefit concert you or I could imagine for retired musicians."

Standing next to him and watching Leno on the monitor it suddenly dawned on Rick that everywhere he went Kronin was at his side. The whole world knew who Rick Macken was, once the greatest Rock and Roll musician in the world and smiled at the thought. At least he had achieved more than most. No one could take that away; it might as well be written in stone. But right now Kronin was making sure his name would be synonymous to his. Rick felt a bitter taste in his mouth. The crowd cheered as Jay called out Rick's name. Kronin placed his hand on his shoulder and guided him towards the waiting chairs.

The applause was long, hard and honest. Leno left his chair to greet them half way and shook Rick's hand vigorously. Like old friends he hugged Kronin, and guided them to their seats. Rick sat in the single armchair next to Leno while Kronin sat to his right.

"It's great to see you, it really is," Leno said to Rick. "But before we start," Leno announced to the crowd, "I just want to say that Rick has been running around the country for the last few months and tomorrow, the twenty-sixth, he turns seventy-five years of age." The band broke into a rock version of "Happy Birthday." Rick totally forgot his birthday. For more than fifteen years he refused to celebrate it. Memories of his ex-wife, children and close friends sitting around the dining room table wishing him the best for many years to come were too depressing.

He watched as balloons and confetti released from the ceiling descended into the studio.

"Happy birthday my friend." Leno said as the crowd cheered. The entire audience rose to give him a standing ovation.

"If there is anything we can get you." Leno continued.

"A bloody stiff drink to straighten out my nerves should do the trick." Rick replied. The crowd and Leno laughed.

"After the show we'll have one together. That's a promise."

"If you don't," Rick said, pointing his finger at Leno. "I'll send around a couple of my old mates."

"Talking about old mates, we realize you haven't had the time to check up on old friends so we arranged this little surprise." The curtain at the other end of the stage opened up.

"Here he is, alive and kicking, your old pal David."

The crowd cheered as David was wheeled out onto the center of the floor by Chris. Rick and Kronin stood and applauded. David waved briefly to the public with his right arm as Chris rolled him towards Leno. When they finally reached the other side of the stage Rick reached down and hugged his old friend.

"Glad you could make it, pal," Rick said in his ear.
His eyes focused on Rick, but seemed dazed, drugged up. David nodded sheepishly, yet he looked better and more alert then a month ago. "You're looking well." Rick said, trying to hold in his emotions.

There was no smile or feeling returned, just the blankness of two dark marbles staring at something that seemed to be a million miles away. David smiled and briefly patted Rick on the shoulder with his hand.

The audience broke into song. "For he's a jolly good fellow, for he's a jolly good fellow..."

When they finally finished Leno raised his hands in the air, "Hip hip." The audience screamed in unison, "Hooray." Rick held onto David's hand as Jay roused the audience into giving them three large cheers. At long last the crowd settled down.

"It must be good to see your old pal again." Leno said to Rick.

Rick tried to swallow the lump that had reared up and stuck in his larynx. "It is. He's looking better than ever."

Rick raised David's left hand slightly, then let it slip. David's hand fell loosely to the side of the wheelchair. Rick stared in shock at David's dangling arm and at the unmoving gaze that seemed to go on forever.

Leno quickly turned back to the crowd as if nothing had happened. "We have a count on the number of homeless musicians tracked down by the authorities." Leno continued. "Not all so famous as our guests, but just like our friends here they fell into difficult times and so far we have forty-three, and the number is still growing. We are determined to bring these people in off the streets and help them every way we can."

The crowd cheered. The curtain rose and forty three aging men and women appeared on the stage. Some dressed in obvious ill-fitting second-hand clothes while others looked as if they were dragged in from the streets just five minutes previous. When the applause died down and the curtain closed, they were led away.

Jay turned his attention to Kronin, "Who exactly is going to be playing at the benefit."

"Put it this way. We have asked all the top names and not one refused. We have got John Durham, Harvey Monk, The Brown Brothers, The Surge, and a special guest star whose name will be kept under wraps until the night of the concert itself. This is going to be the concert of the decade.

Leno shouted to the crowd. "And we are all going to be there aren't we." The crowd clapped and screamed.

"We've delved into the archives and came up with a number of high points of your musical career." Jay turned Rick around to see a large screen light up behind him. They showed a number of clips from the early days in the sixties, including one of his last concerts in Brazil with the band, six months before his world fell apart. Although David was always a constant companion a tear came to his eye watching the complete band. Chad the drummer who had the highest IQ of anyone he ever met and Farno whose guitar riffs were legendry yet his extravagance and weirdness often outdid his. He wasn't surprised by the fact that they didn't appear in the program, he messed it up all those years ago big time. He knew they would never want to see him again. When the video finished the stage curtain parted to a celebrity band who would play at the benefit concert. Rick tapped his foot and clapped along with the beat, but thought the music was the worst he ever heard. When the band finished the number the crowd cheered and the curtain closed.

"That was great." Leno said. "Just a small taste of what's to come." Jay turned to Kronin. "How many people are you expecting at the gig,"

"We've sold out," Kronin replied. "It's absolutely incredible. The response has been great."

"Are any of the older musicians going to play?" Jay asked.

"I don't think so. Kronin replied. "Most of them gave up their instruments years ago due to ill health or whatever. We can't ask them to perform. Those days are definitely over."

Rick felt as if a knife had been rammed into his gut. Although he had not sung on stage for many years, he never thought he would never sing again. He felt Kronin closed a door he never really wanted to shut, and it hurt deeply.

More than three thousand miles away on the east coast, Eva sat in her favorite chair in the leisure room of St. Brigit's retirement home and watched the Jay Leno show. The room was damp and run down. Just out of sight in the top left-hand corner the wallpaper was peeling at the edges, helped by dampness seeping in from the outside wall. The people around her stared in silence at the floor or sat in their chairs, rocking endlessly. This was an average night, and these average nights were repeated seven days a week, fifty-two weeks of the year. It was the most depressing sight Eva had ever witnessed. To imagine the lives these people had had in their forties or thirties depressed her even more. Full of life with mortgages to pay, young mouths to feed, and careers steaming along at full force. Now they looked incredibly pitiful and drained of all energy. Eva glanced at her friend sitting next to the window. Tom sat staring out at nothing in particular. Her heart ached. It never stopped to amaze her how many beautiful men she had met throughout her life. Age or time of place were no barriers to meeting wonderful people. Tom was one of those people, but this time it was too late.

The night attendant marched into the room and promptly switched off the television.

"Bedtime people," he announced. Neither Eva nor any of the other residents had ever objected, mainly because there was never anything interesting on in the first place. Tonight was different.

"But I was watching that," Eva protested. "Those are old friends of mine."

"On the Tonight Show? Wouldn't you just wish," he remarked cynically. "Your friends are here, lady."

Eva looked around at the empty staring faces, which were probably wondering what the commotion was about.

In the quietness of her room Eva sat on the edge of her bed. She had always been a fighter but going up against the regime in the home took more energy than she could muster. She knew she would probably end up like the others one day. The thought depressed her even more.

She looked up at her guitar on the wall. For most of her life it had been her only real friend until chronic fatigue syndrome forced her to stop playing seven years ago. For years she found it difficult to stay awake for more than four hours a day. When she was awake she hardly had the energy to hold a cup of coffee. Most of her friends turned their backs on her. To them she was old, lazy, an irritant. All she wanted was peace and quiet. With her approval her family placed her in an expensive old folks home where everyone was nice and respectable but few shared the same interests. When they finished plundering her bank account she had to be moved to the paradise she now resided. She could have brought a court action against them but she neither had the will nor the energy for it. They were still her children, and no matter how they behaved towards her, she still loved them.

Everything seemed nice and proper when she first moved in. The staff were attentive and they always made the time to talk. Activities such as light gymnastics, table tennis and ballroom dancing were all part of the daily schedule. Most importantly they had fun. Eva always had the energy to laugh.

But after a couple of months the more qualified staff went to work for another home that paid more. They were quickly replaced by people with a prison warden attitude. Non-communicative, rule regulators, who had absolutely no respect for the elderly. Nearly every other day she either felt humiliated or was humiliated.

Eva removed her guitar from the wall. During the last few weeks she found her strength slowly starting to return.

Eva began to play softly. At least she didn't have arthritis like some of the people in the home. Some hands so badly deformed it was impossible to hold a knife and fork, let alone play a guitar. If she had been struck with it her life would end. Eva strummed some chords with no particular tune in mind when an attendant entered the room.

"That will be enough of that." The attendant said sternly. You know we don't allow the playing of any musical instruments after nine." He took the guitar from her. "We don't want you upsetting the other guests." Without giving her a chance to defend her playing he took the guitar out of her hands and headed for the door.

"You can pick it up at the end of the week from the supervisor. You know the rules," he said, then left.

Eva sat with her head buried in her hands, sobbing.

That whole night she lay awake staring at the empty space usually occupied by her guitar. She knew the rules and accepted them when she moved in. The night attendant was just doing his job. A feeling of guilt began to engross her. A year earlier Eva had traded in her expensive acoustic guitar with metal strings for a Spanish guitar with nylon strings for a softer sound. She also discarded the metal finger picks she had used all her life and trained herself to pluck the strings gently. To dampen the sound even more she even took to playing the guitar under a blanket in the dead of night, but gave up for fear of being found out.

In the early morning she appeared at the attendant's door. The supervisor, watching an early morning game show frowned immediately when he saw her.

"I'm sorry I was playing the guitar. I'll put it back up on the wall."

"How many times have I told you. You just won't listen."

"Honestly, it won't happen again."

"This is the last time," he growled. "Next time we will confiscate it for good." He reached for the guitar and handed it to her. "Remember," he continued, "after nine no sound at all."

"I won't forget," she said, forcing a brief smile.

Eva stood at the end of her bed with tears in her eyes staring at her few possessions and photographs propped up on the cupboard. Her room seemed more cold and uninviting than ever.

"Whose life is it anyway," she whispered. She lay her guitar on the bed then went to the recreation room. Tom Welling sat in his usual armchair next to the window. He used to be warm and talkative and always showed interest in her music, before Alzheimer's took hold. With the passing of time his interest in her and everything else was gradually replaced by passive silence and mixed emotions. Sometimes he would sit in his chair for days, closed off in his own gray world where nothing entered or left, an awakened comatose state in a total void. Finally he greeted Eva as a stranger, unaware of having talked and laughed with her every day for the past four years.

Eva sat down next to him, took his hand and held it to her cheek. She kissed it gently then left. Around the room she whispered her good-byes in the ears of others to whom she felt close. Five minutes later she was back in her room buttoning up her heavy winter coat. For the last time Eva closed her door and headed towards the entrance.

The receptionist looked up as she came into view. "It's not that cold outside," She said cheerfully.

"I feel a little chilly," Eva replied. "I don't want to take the risk of catching a cold."

"If they were all that careful I'm sure we would have a lot less illness around here."

"What's for lunch today?"

The receptionist checked the menu chart. "Green beans, boiled potatoes, and roast chicken."

"Delicious." Eva replied as she headed out the main front door with a wide smile. "I wouldn't miss it for the world."

Chapter twelve

The morning after the Leno show Rick and Kronin, now accompanied by Chris and David flew back to the Superdome to see the last of the preparations for the concert. The assistant sound engineer stood behind the first of the four microphones lining the front of the stage.

"Check. Test. One two one two." The sound cracked sharply from of the speakers. In the middle of the Superdome floor, a hundred meters from the front of the stage, the chief sound engineer adjusted the lower and middle frequencies of the forty-eight channel mixer.

"Check. Test. One two, one two." The sound engineer gave him a thumbs up, then the assistant moved to the following microphone. "Check. Test, one two, one two. More monitors," he called.

A second sound engineer behind a smaller twenty-four channel mixer in the wings of the stage adjusted the volume on the band's floor monitors in front of the microphones.

"Test one two one two. Okay," the assistant said, and nodded in approval as the decor was hoisted into place behind him.

Rick, Kronin, and Chris pushing David walked slowly down the middle of the stadium watching all the work going on.

"Thirty thousand people will be here for you." Kronin said proudly." I suppose this sort of thing brings back lots of memories."

"It looks and feels like the old days," Rick said.

"I can imagine. But now it's time for younger blood to make their name and follow in your footsteps." Kronin walked deeper into the stadium. Rick bent down and whispered in David's ear. "Your man's full of shit." A smile lifted on one side of David's face. Rick began to imitate Kronin's walk. They continued after Kronin, all three of them smiling.

Chapter thirteen

Eva set her suitcase down in front of the counter at the bus station. The previous evening she hid her guitar and small suitcase behind the bushes next to the main gate. Without any of the residents or attendants noticing she walked away from the gate and headed towards the bus station two blocks up. It would be early evening before anyone missed her or noticed the note she left on the bed. By that time she would be very far away.

The male cashier peered at her from over the top of his reading glasses. His bald head shone from the lamp hanging directly above him. He looked as if he recognized her or suspected her from something. Eva suddenly felt her heart pound in her chest. He was probably searching with his foot under the counter for an alarm switch to notify the police. Running away was a mistake, she should never have done it. They would bring her back to the home where she would spend her days rotting away like the rest of the residents.

"May I help you?" The cashier asked as he removed his glasses and smiled politely. His features suddenly changed from being quite stern to that of sympathy and understanding.

"How long does it take to go to New Orleans by bus?"

He studied the timetable in front of him. "Let me see. We have a red eye going to New Orleans although you have to change busses in Tilton. Roughly fourteen hours."

Eva had planned on buying a return ticket. If things didn't work out she would always have some way of getting back. A vague excuse saying she didn't remember where she was for the past few days would be easily accepted at the home.

"A one-way ticket please."

The cashier looked surprised, as if he was not expecting her request. "Sure you don't want a round trip?"

"Never more sure in my life." She said resolutely. "Definitely one way." Eva was tired of excuses and uncertainty. She knew she would never go back to the home. Wild horses wouldn't drag her back. This was her decision and she was sticking to it. From now on she would spend her life the way she wanted and not the way others told her to. The cashier had confronted her with a decision of being totally independent and she went for it. Eva felt totally uplifted from the experience. She placed the money on the counter, and the cashier handed her the ticket.

"Thank you. Thank you very much." She said with a smile as she placed it in her purse and headed for the bus.

"You're welcome." The cashier called after her.

Without turning back she waved in acknowledgment, smiled, and with an air of pride and self-assurance went through the open doors towards the waiting coaches.

After many hours the bus finally slowed down, and turned into a small station. Eva sat at the back, asleep. One hand rested on the guitar next to her. The driver's rough voice grumbled over the intercom. "Change here for New Orleans." A lady sitting next to Eva shook her out of her slumber. She had slept the best part of the journey.

"If you're going to New Orleans you better get out here," she said quietly.

Eva's eyes opened wide, quickly taking in the surroundings around her. The station was small with only room enough for three or four busses at most. She checked her watch. It was at least an hour before dawn, and the sun had not yet appeared on the horizon. White-washed buildings glowed red-yellow and gold all at the same time. Everything looked serene and welcoming, a beautiful beginning to a new adventure. She turned to face the woman whose soft voice still echoed in her ear.

"Thank you very much for waking me up."

"Did you have a good sleep?"

"Yes, thank you." she replied in her soft and gentle voice. "I had a wonderful sleep." Eva gathered her few possessions and left the bus. There were about nine passengers in the bus, mostly black. She wanted terribly to say goodbye to everyone but decided against it. It would be wise to keep a low profile since her escape. In the compound she searched for the connecting bus to New Orleans.

The tip of the sun just appeared on the horizon as the bus left the station for New Orleans. This time she decided not to take a back seat since the noise of the engine drowned her thoughts. Instead she took a seat diagonally across from the driver. Eva removed her guitar from the case and began to tune it. The driver watched her in the rear view of the mirror. Eva began to play, harder than she ever dared back at the home. The driver switched off the small radio next to him and listened.

Chapter fourteen

The early morning dew on the forest floor was impressive. Droplets of water clung to every blade of grass, leaf and branch, as if trying to prolong a certain death before the sun evaporated its moisture. Harlan awoke when a beam settled on his face and warmed his whiskers. He smiled. This was softer and warmer than a woman's kiss. Mother Nature was kind. If only she could fry some bacon and eggs and put on a pot of coffee then everything would be hunky-dory. He lay for ten minutes longer, savoring the sweetness of it all, then threw back his weathered sleeping bag.

Going on eighty-five Harlan still moved with the agility of a man half his age. He kicked dirt over the smoldering campfire, rolled up the blanket and placed it in the saddlebag of his old and battered custom Harley. He mounted the bike and kick-started it with passionate aggression. Dirt shot out from the back wheel as he headed for the road.

Robbie had not made better progress than with his usual mode of transport, but it was more enjoyable than he could ever have imagined. No stewardess to serve your every want and need, but the pioneering feeling when he stepped into the truck cabin was profound. At seventy-three he felt like a young teenager who had run away from home and was enjoying every minute of it. The trip took two days, seven rigs, two automobiles, and three pick-up trucks to get him to Metairie, a small town just west of New Orleans.

The truck stopped at a crossing. This was where he would part company. Robbie opened the door and gently eased himself down from the elevated cabin. "Thanks for the lift," he shouted to the driver, then slammed the door shut. The truck turned off, lifting up a dust trail. Robbie began to walk. Ten minutes later on the quiet back road leading into the city a bus raced past, covering him in a billow of dust. He reached for his water bottle in his bag, took a large mouthful, then contentedly resumed his journey.

Chapter fifteen

The sun appeared on the horizon behind the stadium. Youths in sleeping bags began to stir outside the main gate and perimeter grounds. Many had arrived the day before in the hope of getting tickets on the black market. Since Kronin had rushed the concert they were unable to name a complete band line up when the first tickets went on sale. The only band who actually agreed to play for free was Black Wing, but they would never draw the crowd he needed to make this concert a success. Only two days before the box office closed the line-up was complete, an hour before he appeared on the Tonight Show. Kronin pulled the hat out of the bag and came up with a lineup that would draw the crowds. Finally the rush to buy tickets took off, but it left too little time for the Superdome organization to expand the event and give Kronin more seats.

Within hours the crowd had built up to thousands, all anxiously waiting for the gates to open. Along the roads leading to the stadium people set up makeshift stalls. T-shirts of all the bands playing at the gig were going at discount prices. New-age groupies pleated colored beads into hair for five dollars a go, others sold hand-made hats, red Indian-beaded belts, and hand-knitted woolen socks. Although the crowd was oddly mixed with many different types of music lovers, a strong element of hippy revival was dominant. Sheepskin coats, wrangler jeans with holes covered with multi-colored patchwork and long hair brought a sense of nostalgia.

Backstage, in the bowels of the Superdome, a cloud of cigarette smoke laced with the smell of cannabis flowed out of Black Wing's dressing room. Kronin opened the door. His gaze shot quickly around the room, taking account of the members of the band and the state they were in. No alcohol to be seen, only joints. As long as they did not combine the two they'd make it to the stage in one piece. The band had formed two years previous in Seattle and had received mixed success on the club circuit after the release of their first CD a year later. They also had a reputation for being troublesome. Usually such publicity kept them in the public eye and added to their persona, giving them an air of mystery and adventure. Unfortunately for them it worked in reverse. People these days just wanted good music and no hassle, so their pulling power and sales dived. They drew a fraction of the crowds a year previous. A gig like this would be enough to put them back in the picture, at least for another six months.

"You guys all set to go?" Kronin asked.

Rangoon, the lead singer, sat on the floor against the wall staring starry eyed at the neon light right above him. The fringe of his black and shaggy oily hair dangling in his eyes did not seem to bother him. "Yeah sure. We're ready."

"Great. Keep it up." Kronin left as quickly as he entered. Hopper, the lead guitarist, took a last quick puff from his joint then handed it to Rangoon.

"What an asshole. We're doing this for nothing while he gets a fat cut from the proceeds."

Rangoon shook his head. "Put it this way. Maybe he's putting it down to costs, and we all have costs. Don't worry, we'll be putting in for our costs." Rangoon smiled at the joint before taking a long drag on it. "This is the life." He said as he inhaled the smoke deeply, holding it in his lungs for nearly half a minute.

Kronin stood on the stage with Henry Mallow, his personal assistant, and watched the crowds coming in. "This is filling up quicker than I expected." Kronin said casually. "We estimated no more than 45,000, but I think we could have filled it to the 95,000 capacity."

One hour before the opening act, the seating and standing area contracted to the concert was full to the brim.

"We could have rented more space," Mallow said.

"True," Kronin replied. "But the cost of getting in extra staff at short notice would cut dearly into the budget. Too many last minute bookings."

Just more than a million dollars was supposed to cover expenses and administration costs at the end of the day. However, this figure could grow extensively if the takings allowed it. That was the trick to putting together a good benefit. Unfortunately it was not looking good right now. At such short notice any additional help would demand a double rate. Many worked freelance and knew when they had the contractor over a barrel. No way was Kronin going to let anyone maneuver him into such a situation. Television coverage in the US would probably generate a couple of million. International options on broadcast rights to Europe, Japan, and South America were perfect, although the outcome and success of the concert would make it feasible for a broadcast or not. Dvd sales of the concert would also help fill the coffers, but by how much?

Since Live Aid in 1985 charity concerts had become a trend. Every year thereafter there had been at least two or three. Last year no less than twelve worldwide. Saturation point had been reached and the public were not responding like they used to. But this time Kronin's expectations paid off and he was more than content of the expected income. However, the mood among the crowd made him nervous. The public had been standing in the Superdome for nearly two hours and had had enough. Restlessness began to set in. They had done countless waves and where starting to get agitated. Security broke up four fights while first aid registered two near fatal overdoses, and the official opening was still half an hour away. By then the crowd could be going wild, and they could cause some serious property damage. Unfortunately the terms of the contract meant he would have to pay for it out of his own pocket.

Kronin turned to his assistant Mallow standing next to him in the wings.

"That's it. Let's get the show going. We can't wait any longer. Get the old boys and the opening band up here and have them waiting in the wings until I give the word. After that everything goes according to plan."

Mallow was taken by surprise. This was the first large concert Kronin had let him help organize. He thought he could do it by just sticking to the script. Improvisation was not part of the rules, especially in his book.

"But there is still a half an hour to go before the official opening. Some of the bands are not even here yet." Mallow pleaded.

"Then those dope heads from Black Wing get to play a longer set. What more do they want. Look at all the free publicity. If we don't act quick we'll be getting the type of publicity we don't need."

Mallow looked bewildered. "I don't think the band can play an extra half hour."

Kronin closed his eyes and took a deep breath. He had hired Mallow as an assistant. He thought he would be doing him a favor by giving him hands-on experience on the workings of a large charity gig such as this one. It was a mistake, and mistakes he only made once. Next time he would leave him where he was best at. Behind a desk and pushing a pen.

"Don't worry, I know what I'm doing. Please do as I ask."

Kronin's tone was one Mallow never heard before. It was very calm, but at the same time very threatening. Mallow quickly disappeared. Kronin informed the stage manager of what he was going to do, who in turn relayed the details to the sound and light engineers.

A couple of spotlights lit up the center of the stage, then Kronin walked out and took hold of the microphone. The crowd cheered.

"Thank you." Kronin shouted. His voice boomed and echoed throughout the stadium. "Thank you very much for being here. Today is a very special night. A day the music industry gets to do something very special for its own. I just want to mention that although the concert has not yet begun, we have already raised half the funds needed for the retired musicians."

The crowd roared. Kronin turned to the wings and saw that Mallow had his aging rock stars lined up on cue.

"Now let me introduce to you the man who is responsible for you being here. Ladies and gentlemen, one of the greatest Rock legends of all time. Rick Macken." The crowd roar.

Kronin turned with outstretched arms towards Rick, who with a slight push from Mallow hobbled onto the stage. For the first time in more than two decades Rick stood before a paying audience. He stared in awe at the throng of youth, who instead of shouting and screaming as they always did, gave him a standing ovation.

Chris placed his hand on David's shoulder as he sat motionless gazing blankly at the spectacle from the corner of the stage. The crowd applauded solidly for at least five minutes.

Finally, when it died down, Rick took hold of the microphone. The sound of him clearing his parched throat boomed from the speakers and stilled the crowd to a whisper. Rick tried to say something but his jaw had locked. The crowd remained silent in expectance. The lump in his throat had strangled his vocal cords.

"I...I...." Rick turned quickly away from the mike to cough. The sound of phlegm being shifted in his larynx was picked up by the microphone and sent booming around the stadium. He composed himself and once again placed the microphone to his mouth.

"I just want to thank you all for being here, and the people who are watching this on TV all around the country." The stadium remained silent. He looked to Kronin, who nodded with uncertain reassurance. Staring into the crowd Rick realized he was old enough to be the grandfather or great grandfather of most of the kids in the stadium.

"I honestly don't think you really know who I am." The atmosphere in the air finally broke, and the crowd laughed and cheered.

"I'm the old bogeyman your mother used to warn you about." A roar of laughter went up in the stadium.

"And if you think I'm bad you should see me mates. Some of them would have you for dinner." Rick's cackled laugh boomed out from the Superdome speakers. He turned to see Kronin looking stiff faced and ready to pounce on the microphone, then turned back to the crowd.

"What I would really like to say is thank you for being here. I only wish I had the strength to play for you myself. Thank you all very much." Rick stepped back. Kronin smiled and nodded in assurance once again. The crowd gave Rick a second standing ovation as he hobbled back to Chris and David.

Like a seasoned rock star Kronin grabbed the mike. "Ladies and gentlemen, let the show begin."

Rick collapsed into the arms of Chris who patted him eagerly on the back. "You were great." He shouted in Rick's ear.

"I've never been so scared of a crowd in all my life." Rick groaned, wiping the sweat from his brow.

"But you've done thousands of gigs like this."

"Gigs where we played for our keep. Now they are coming to see the other bands. We do sweet fuck all and get to walk away with the day's takings. That's very scary stuff if you ask me."

"I wouldn't worry about it if I was you." Chris reassured him. "Let's go down to the bar and have a stiff drink." Chris wheeled David's wheelchair towards the artists bar.

"I thought you were against me drinking." Rick said.

"I am. It's me who needs the drink. You're on fruit juice until the night is over. If you've got to get up on that stage again you'll be as sober as a judge."

"Jesus Mary and Joseph," Rick moaned. "You'll be the death of me."

Chapter sixteen

Robbie had walked about four miles from Metairie and in the distance he could see the outline of the stadium. He reckoned it would take at least half an hour to get there, a fraction of that time if he tried to hitch, but at the moment he felt he could do with the walk. He stopped to take a drink of water to wash away the dust from his mouth. Behind him an automobile slowed down and gently pulled up next to him. He turned to the driver of a police car. The way he was eyeing him up Robbie felt he had committed the most terrible crime imaginable, or maybe they had found what they were looking for: the rich old rock star who had strangely disappeared.

"Where do you think you're going old man."

Robbie studied the officer and his gum-chewing partner. Probably graduated high school because of a football scholarship. No way his IQ could have earned him his diploma. After three days of being on the road, Robbie knew he looked like a tramp. Yet this tramp was sporting a pair of three hundred dollar designer jeans, made to measure Nikes and a Rolex.

"Just having a nice quiet walk into town, officer."

"We prefer people coming into our town on planes and automobiles. People who just walk everywhere are up to no good." His partner showed no interest in the proceedings. He just stared at the cattle grazing behind a fence on the other side of the road.

There were different ways to handle this; he could either act smart, dumb, or cut it down the middle. Being smart with this bozo could get him thrown in jail and expose his identity. This would lead the groupies he left in Los Angeles right to him.

Playing dumb would probably do the same. Then reporters from every corner of the earth would turn up demanding exclusive rights to any story he or anyone else had to sell. No doubt this Neanderthal staring blankly at him would have his fifteen minutes of fame.

"As far as I know there is no law against it," Robbie finally replied.

"That's true, yes sur-ree, but don't let us hear of you causin' any problems in town, ye hear?"

As the officers drove off a disturbing thought crept into Robbie's mind. People like that had actually made it to the presidency. He broke into a song at the top of his voice.

"Take a look at the Lawman
Beating up the wrong guy
Oh man! Wonder if he'll ever know
He's in the best selling show
Is there life on Mars?"

Chapter seventeen

The bus pulled into the New Orleans Greyhound stop on Loyola Avenue. Eva's joints ached and felt fused by the amount of time she had spent in the cramped seat. She pulled herself up wearily and with great effort stepped onto the isle. She tried painfully to straighten her back. An equally old African American man who had been sitting across from her took her hand and helped her upright.

"A thing about them old bones," he said cheerfully, "it don't matter whether you're black, white, yellow, or green. Them bones never seem to get any younger."

"The seats in these buses don't help much either." Eva replied. She stepped out into a cloud of diesel fumes blasted by another bus pulling away. She coughed and choked and tried unsuccessfully to fan away the black fumes with her hand. Her fellow traveling companion caught her by the elbow and guided her towards an enclosed bus shelter.

"Thank you very much. I thought I was going to die out there."

The white haired man led her gently to a bench, then got her some water from the cooler.

"You better rest up here. Get your breath back."

"I have to get moving soon otherwise I'll be too late. Do you know how I can get to the Superdome from here?"

The old man scratched his head and shook it disapprovingly. "I don't think they have any football today."

"There is a concert I've been meaning to get to."

"You're a little old for that sort of thing aren't you?"

"My bones may be old but you are as young as you feel."

"And looking at you I bet you're not feeling a day over fifty," he joked. Eva gave a little frown. "But," he continued, "from the spark in your eyes I'd say you were no more than 25."

Eva laughed. "How did you guess."

"I don't know, a natural I think."

"Is this what you do? Spend your day chatting up ladies you meet on journeys?"

"I would if I could but my wife would never approve," he replied with a warm smile.

For the first time in years Eva was embarrassed. Her face flushed to bright red. It was a pleasant feeling.

"Do you have a ticket for the concert?" He asked.

"I was planning on buying one when I got there."

"The tourist office is just around the corner. Maybe you can get a ticket beforehand; it might save you a long wait at the box office."

"Good idea." Eva said cheerfully. "I think I might just do that. Thank you very much for your help."

The air-conditioned tourist office was packed with folders and flyers advertising every conceivable attraction and entertainment in New Orleans. She went straight to a young male assistant who greeted her with a bright smile.

"I believe I can get a ticket to the Superdome from here? I want to go to a concert that's playing today. Could you also tell me how I can get there?"

The young male assistant seemed amused by the old woman standing in front of her. "You won't get in there, lady."

"I think I have a chance." Eva replied.

"It has already started and sold out."

"Well I can still try."

"Besides, they usually don't give reductions for old age pensioners at rock concerts," he said with a smile. Not a typical smile that showed how pleased he was to have helped her. "I think you're making a big mistake," he continued.

"The only mistake I've so far on this journey is talking to you," she said then whacked her hand down on the counter and glared at the assistant.

"Just show me the way, will you."

"If you insist." He said, surprised and embarrassed since he was now being watched by his colleagues.

"I do." Eva retorted. The young man suddenly straightened up and pointed down the street. "Follow this street for two blocks then take a right. You can't miss it."

"Thank you. Goodbye."

The air outside was hot and humid. Eva had played in New Orleans before. She had even played at the Superdome in 1976, a year after its completion. The days when folk singers came out of the smoky clubs and cellar bars and onto the big stage. In the sixties they never believed the big stage was for them. They were just a niche in a market dominated by mainstream popular music. They played to audiences of twenty-five to maybe fifty or sixty people. If you played to an audience of a hundred you had, by folk standards, hit the big time. Dylan changed that by bringing folk music to the forefront, writing memorable tunes with words that played on the intellect, and, most importantly, got people talking about what was being sung.

Outside a television repair shop she stopped just in time to see Rick on stage waving to the audience then walking off. The picture panned the stadium showing a full crowd. Why hadn't she bought a ticket last week when she learned about the concert? Everything had gone so fast she never had a chance to stop and think about it.

She stopped just long enough to see Kronin introduce the first band, Black Wing. She had never heard of them. Eva looked around to get her bearings and headed towards the Superdome.

She turned the corner at Poydras Street and was taken aback by the size of the crowds outside the main entrance. Thousands of people were gathered and continuously chanting to get in. The swell of the crowd surged back and forth. Police were in force but kept their distance. It would be impossible to get past any of this, although she knew of a possible option. She could try the artists entrance door: even after all these years she still remembered where it was. Another option was to get a room at a small motel in the neighborhood and watch the concert on television from there. She could try waiting for them when the concert was over, and if that failed she could come back tomorrow to try to find out where Rick and the others are staying. But by then they could be in New York or Los Angeles or even Europe. She decided to use the motel only as a last resort; she had to try and find them now.

Eva arrived at the artists entrance where a few groupies hovered around two towering security men who blocked the entrance as if expecting a stampede. Their oversized name badges pinned to their military styled uniforms informed her that one was called Roy and the other Dwight. Eva wormed through to the front. Roy laid an ape-like hand on her shoulder as she tried to go around him.

"Sorry lady, you can't go in there." She looked up at Roy whose head was closely shaven around the sides and back. The top was an inch thick, looked rather woolly, and dyed a deathly white. She smiled, just managing to hold back a laugh.

"But I'm an old friend of Rick. I've come a long way to see him."

"You have a pass?" Dwight, the smaller guard asked.

She could say she left it back at the hotel. Or one of the crew had taken hers by accident. She could be a band member's mother, or judging some of them on television, their grandmother. How about one of Rick's former wives? That would really put them off guard. She looked carefully at the two mounds of steroid flesh and knew she could only give one answer.

"No, I'm sorry. I don't have a pass."

He bent down towards her. "You don't have a pass you don't get in. Simple as that," Roy said with a tint of delight in his voice, and a smile that reminded her of the assistant at the tourist office.

"You don't understand. I came a long way to see him. I can't go back to the home. They would never take me back after walking out like I did."

Roy sighed deeply and stared over her head. The groupies standing next to their hand painted Volkswagen van were putting together the biggest joint he had ever seen.

"After the show maybe," Dwight replied, still not looking at her. "But you are not getting in here now. So move along." He pushed her gently aside. "Move along, you're blocking my view."

Out of nowhere the roar of an engine blasted their ears and a motorcycle's back wheel skidded to a halt right next to Roy and Dwight's black polished shoes.

"Take your hands off the lady," Harlan ordered. Roy quickly removed his hand as Eva turned. She was stunned by the sight of the ancient biker dressed like a cowhand and whose hair was very long and brilliant silver.

"Harlan?"

"Jesus, not another one," Dwight moaned.

"I don't have a pass," Eva said. "They won't let me in to see the boys."

"I don't have one either darlin'. Don't matter, jump on the back. We'll go and wait somewhere until after the concert. We've seen them all before anyway." Eva carefully mounted the back of the bike.

"Goddamn." Roy shouted at the top of his voice. "Did you ever see such a sight? And I thought the young kids were nuts."

Roy clapped Dwight on the back and they both bellowed with laughter. Harlan revved up and started to drive away.

"Don't get lost, granddad." Dwight shouted.

Suddenly, Harlan hit the brakes hard and spun the bike around. "I've had enough of these two jokers." He pulled back on the accelerator. "Hang on girl. Let's see what these two are really made of." Harlan switched on the main beam of his headlights, and pulled back on the throttle. The engine revved up. The groupies quickly got out of the way. Dwight and Roy stood firm.

"What are you doing?" Eva screamed. "We'll get killed,"

Harlan released the clutch and raced towards the door. Roy and Dwight jumped to each side and tried to reach out and grab them as they passed. Harlan kicked out with both feet, catching them between the legs. Roy and Dwight hit the concrete moaning. Harlan drove in through the open door and down the tunnel-like corridor. The thunder of the engine echoed off the walls in all directions.

"Yaaahooo," Eva screamed.

The sound of the band playing on the stage rumbling through the passage ways of the Superdome was drowned out by the thumping of the Harley engine.

"Let's see if we can find Rick," Harlan shouted to Eva, who clung desperately to him.

The maze of corridors seemed endless. Surprised personnel jumped out of the way as the bike roared towards them.

Outside the Superdome, Robbie walked up to the stage door and looked down at the two moaning guards. He stepped quietly over them and into the Superdome. The groupies had already disappeared when they saw their chance of a free entrance.

As Harlan and Eva rounded a bend they could hear the sound of a band much clearer. Suddenly the passage before them opened up to a ramp taking him up to the next level. The band had just finished their last number when Harlan and Eva reached the top of the ramp and rode inadvertently onto the stage. The crowd roared. The bike screeched to a stop in the center of the stage. Harlan and Eva looked at one another in utter surprise, then waved to the crowd. A cheer went up in the stadium. This changed to boos and hisses when a flurry of security guards ran to the front of the stage from the floor of the arena, while others appeared in the wings.

Harlan waved to the army of security guards and smiled. Eva raised her middle finger and the crowd roared once again. Harlan revved the engine, then drove full speed down a ramp on the opposite side, back into the maze of corridors.

Twenty meters ahead of them a door opened. Rick stepped out into their path. Harlan rammed his foot on the brake and at the same time pulled hard on the front brake. Both wheels locked. The bike screeched to a halt, stopping just in front of Rick.

"You old fool," Harlan shouted. "I could have killed you."

"Saw you on the monitors." Rick shouted. "There is a speed limit around here you know. Ought to have you arrested." They laughed and hugged one another.

"Great to see you, pal," Harlan said softly in his ear.

"Good to see you too," Rick said, trying to keep his emotions under control. "Who's the chick on the back?"

Eva, laughing and crying at the same time, stuck her head out.

"Eva?" Rick stepped back and gasped. "Jesus Harry H. Christ, well I'll be damned."

"Picked her up causing trouble outside," Harlan said.

Rick kissed her on the forehead and hugged her tightly.

"Come on in. I want you to meet some old friends." He pushed the door open to reveal Chris, while David sat in the wheelchair next to him staring blankly ahead.

"David's had a little setback," Rick said. "But he'll be all right once we get a place of our own. This calls for a celebration." Rick grabbed some plastic cups and quickly handed them out, then opened a can of beer that fizzed and sprayed its contents over all of them. Eva dived for cover behind Harlan while the others cheered in delight. After the cups were filled Rick raised his.

"To old friends and new beginnings."

"To old friends and new beginnings," they all repeated. Each raised their cups together and drank. Rick finished his in one quick gulp "Jesus I needed that. Who wants another?"

"Anything stronger?" Harlan asked.

Rick delved deep into his pockets and pulled out a bottle of whiskey.

Eva pushed the plastic cup towards Rick. "That's just what I need. My nerves have just been fried from that bike ride."

He filled it without hesitation. Rick shook his head as he studied Harlan and Eva. "How did you all get here? Have you two teamed up or what?"

Harlan raised his hands in defense. "No offense but we're not a couple."

"Harlan just got me through the front door." Eva said. "It took me fourteen hours in a hot sticky coach to get here, and the hardest part of all was trying to get in to see you. But the stage entrance made it all worthwhile."

Harlan held up his cup. "I'll drink to that."

Suddenly the door flew open and the two security guards, Roy and Dwight, came rushing in with three uniformed police officers.

"That's them," Roy said pointing to Harlan and Eva. Rick put his plastic cup to one side and took a step forward, putting himself between Eva and the security officers. "You lay a finger on any of these people and I'll have your guts for garters." Rick warned. "They're my guests." He proudly threw his arms over Harlan's and Eva's shoulders.

"My guts for what?" Roy said, sounding confused.

"Jesus, kids these days don't even learn the basics." Harlan moaned.

"But they don't have passes." Roy replied.

"Shove your passes." Rick retorted." Anyone who turns up outside over the age of sixty you just march them in here. Now piss off."

Roy and Dwight hesitated, not exactly sure what to do.

"Do any of you want to press charges?" The officer with notebook and pen in hand asked. Roy and Dwight remained silent.

"If you don't want to press charges just leave," Chris said, breaking the nervous silence. The officer with the notebook didn't hesitate. He immediately put his notebook back into his breast pocket and headed for the door. The rest followed. Rick raised the whiskey bottle in one hand and the beer can in the other.

"Let's have another toast." He shouted.

"Is this a private party or can anyone join in?" A deep voice with a British accent surprised them from behind. Robbie stood in the doorway.

"Robbie?" Eva said as if seeing a ghost. "My God. Where have you been all these years?"

"This place sure draws them in like flies," Rick said, as he shoved a plastic cup into Robbie's hand, and filled it with beer.

"Well you started it," Eva said, poking her index finger into Rick's chest.

"Did you meet any more outside?" Rick asked.

Robbie shook his head. "Just a couple of guys who had difficulty standing up, but apart from that everything looked pretty quiet."

"How on earth did you manage to put this together?" Eva asked Rick.

"I'd love to say I did, darlin' but I didn't. The whole show is being run by a big shot who I didn't know I existed until a few months ago. He asked me if I wanted to go along with it, so I agreed. He organizes the circus and I do the promotional side of the business," Rick said, straightening himself up and adjusting his coat. "Without me there was no way he could ever get this thing off the ground. Isn't that right Chris?'

"Yeah, Rick. Sure thing." Chris mumbled.

"Come on, I want to show you something." Rick guided them out into the corridor and down the passage.

"We've got this thing organized like you've never seen before. There are two rooms down here I want you to see. One is used to collect donations from people phoning in during the concert. The other we use to try and trace elderly musicians. Most are happy where they are but there's still quite a few who spend most of the year crawling from stage to stage just to survive from the little money they make. They could really do with a place like the one we're putting together."

"Have you seen it?" Eva asked. "Is it nice?"

"Well," Rick replied, sounding suddenly unsure. "From the artists impression it looked great."

"Oh," Eva replied.

"Artists impression," Harlan said. "Sounds promising."

Rick quickly moved on. "Anyway, it's not that easy to find them, so we got this thing going whereby anyone who can bring in a musician who published a work or has always worked as a musician receives a small gift. But they can also ring in themselves to register for the house. They are not all raving mad you know." Rick stopped outside a door. "Take a look."

The room was not much bigger than the changing room they had just come from. Three computers and operators with telephone headsets were taking calls, and all wearing badges with 'VOLUNTEER FOR MOUNT MERRIAN' printed in large letters, with their first names scribbled beneath. Paula, Archie, and Annie. They stopped to listen to Paula, talking to a caller.

"What is your name sir?" Paula asked in a long Southern brawl. "yes... and what was the name of the band you played with?" Her nimble fingers quickly raced over the keyboard, typing in the details. "Yes I've got that. Where can you be reached... Yes we'll get back to you. Thank you for ringing Mr. Cocker."

Eva gasped in surprise, "Did you hear who that was?" she cried.

"Couldn't be the same." Rick said. "Joe settled down in England. There is no way he could have survived the British weather after all these years. It was always bloody drizzerable."

Paula rapidly finished logging in the Cocker file and was already onto the next caller. "Yes...yes...how old are you, sir." Paula asked. "I'm sorry but thirty-five does not exactly qualify you for a senior citizens residence. Thank you for calling."

The group turned to listen in on Archie, sitting at the second terminal in the middle of the room.

"You sang with who? And you played where? I'm sorry but the home is only for retired professional musicians. I'm afraid playing once a month at the local community hall does not qualify you for the home. Thank you for calling."

The group turned back to Paula. "Yes, you can register here for the retired musicians home.... is he an acquaintance or... oh I see, and what did you say your name was? All right. Please give me your number so we may get back to you," Paula asked as she scribbled down the number. "Thank you for calling." She hung up.

"Hey you guys," Paula shouted. "We found Elvis." They all cheered.

"I'm sorry Miss I can't hear you," one of the volunteers said trying to listen to her caller over the noise of the cheers. "Did you say CJ?"

"CJ?" Rick shouts. "I don't believe it."

"CJ!" Chris moans. "I don't believe it either. Oh God."

Rick rushes over to the volunteer and grabs the telephone. "CJ, is that really you?" Rick screams. "I thought we lost you…. aaaahhhhhhh it's so good to hear your voice. I'd recognize you from the grave."

Kronin entered the room, and looked dismayed at the joviality around him. "What's going on?"

"Hold on a sec sweety." Rick continued on the phone. "I have to run but one of the people here will look after you and give you all the details. They'll arrange everything sweetheart. You don't have to worry about a thing. I bet all the boys will be looking forward to seeing you… Here he is, cheers darling," Rick said as he handed the phone back to the volunteer.

"Nothing's going on," Rick remarked. "That was CJ. You remember her don't you? I mean, you're not that young are you?"

Kronin frowned, and then quickly turned his attention to Archie.

"What's the count on the calls?"

"We have taken in about four hundred. At least five percent have a chance."

"Looks promising," he said as he immediately turns his attention to Rick. "I'd be grateful if you and the boys would join me on stage to listen to the concert."

"No problem. Let's go, *boys*." Rick said mockingly.

Kronin managed a short quick smile then herded them out of the makeshift office and down the corridor, through the endless passages and up the ramp used by roadies servicing the stage.

The second Rick saw the face of the singer playing to the crowd his heart skipped a beat. It was the face of a man he had known, loved, and respected, and who was shot dead in 1980 in New York City. It couldn't be the same person. John Lennon was three years older than he was. This double on the stage was half his age.

"Is that Julian?" Eva asked.

He finished his song to resounding cheers and shouts, then the lights dimmed and a single spotlight lit up and focused on him in the center of the stage. Julian put his guitar to one side and the crowd quietened to a whisper. He stepped up to the microphone.

"When I was young my family taught me not only to be aware of our own music, but to be aware of the music of others. They made me realize that musicians had different styles such as rock and roll, rhythm and blues, folk, heavy metal, punk, bebop, disco, rap, everything you could imagine. Each of those styles supported thousands of musicians. And over the years that has built up to many more thousands. Eventually you wonder what happens to them all when they stop making records and performing on stage. There seemed to be so many. Most find other work and live other lives. Some carry on right up to this day and still manage to stay on top, while others fall to the wayside and don't have the strength to get back on stage. They only had one talent and that was making music. But now they are too old or too broken to make a living at it. Some of these people live on the streets, in the gutter, and many live in retirement homes where other residents have no relevance to their past. They get isolated into a silence that is alien to them, without either a friend or fellow musician around to share the memories of making music or traveling the road. These are the people society threw away after they finished enjoying their music." Julian paused. The stadium was completely silent.

"You know why we are here," Julian shouted. "We are here to change that." The crowd roared.

"We are the ones who are going to give something back." The crowds roar even louder. "We are not going to let them rot on the streets or get thrown in jail, we are here to help, we are here to provide them with a new existence so they may enjoy the rest of their lives in dignity, free from humiliation and drudgery. We are here to honor those musicians and to raise enough money to give them a home they deserve. A monument to their work for your enjoyment."

"Didn't know that." Rick said to Chris as he listened to the speech in the wings. "I never did it for their enjoyment. I only did it for my own."

A stage assistant handed Julian a note. He read it quickly then grabbed the microphone once again. "This is incredible. Listen to this. Since we went on the air we have raised three and a half million dollars."

"Bloody hell," Rick said in total surprise.

The crowd cheered as thousands of multicolored balloons fell from the ceiling of the Superdome.

Kronin stuck his large cigar in his mouth and leaned towards Rick. "Looks like you won't ever have to worry about a thing for the rest of your days."

Without a word of warning a brilliant spotlight lit up Rick. Kronin, smiling as if he had just won the lottery, ushered Rick, Robbie, and the others out onto the center of the stage. The spotlight was blinding, making it impossible for them to see the crowd. In utter bewilderment they waved into the darkness before them. The intense feeling of warmth, laughter and cheers from the crowd gradually brought their confidence back. They took one another by the hand and spread out in a single line across the stage. To a tremendous roar of the crowd they raised their hands together.

Rick felt both humbled and ecstatic. After so many years in the gutter he never imagined something like this could ever happen. In all that time no one ever went out of their way to help him or those like him. Of course the Salvation Army and other charities were there to help, but that was their job. That was what they were there for. Rick was under no illusion the crowd really came to see their bands, their idols. But to hear them cheer and applaud made him for a moment think otherwise. Rick, Eva, Robbie, Chris, and Harlan bowed together.

Rick's eye caught David watching from the wings. Seeing him sitting caged in his body, he hoped he could feel the incredible feeling of pride of what was happening around him. Rick knew David would give anything to be up there with them but he knew nothing could change the fact he would be spending the rest of his days in a wheelchair.

The reception afterwards was quite unlike the parties Rick remembered from rock concerts in the past. Women in their best evening wear and men dressed in expensive suits seemed to be in abundance. But that was to be expected. This was no ordinary rock concert. This was a prestige event attracting the high-and-mighty and a host of celebrities from the film and pop world who expected to see their pictures to make the papers for their association with a charity gig. Robbie, Eva, Harlan, and Chris managed to park themselves in a corner of the reception lounge and did a great job in hiding from the throngs of reporters, VIPs', and anyone else who wanted to talk about the good old days. Rick would love to walk out and leave them to it but if he was going to stay with this dreary and boring lot he might as well make the most of it. He decided to take the plunge. More than that, he was planning to jump in at the deep end.

He filled a champagne glass with sparkling soda, lit up a fat cigar he got from Kronin, and for the next two hours told wild stories non-stop about his famous band and their escapades around the globe.

Chris watched him from a distance. Rick was like a seasoned general recounting his years on the battlefield, depicting scenes of world tours, girlfriends, wives, and unending escapades of wild nights with the world's celebrities. The suits lapped up every word. By the time he finished with his captivated audience of about thirty guests, most of the others along with Chris, had long gone to bed.

It was four in the morning when Rick arrived back at the hotel. The only thing that bothered him was the fact that he was alone. All the young groupies who had been hanging around backstage had been picked up by the younger band members. The days when he left a concert with a groupie under each arm was definitely a thing of the past, and that really pissed him off.

In the weeks that followed numerous retired musicians phoned the special help numbers advertised everywhere or turned up at the Superdome itself. Those who had a right to the new home were given rooms in various hotels or nursing homes around the city. Rick, Robbie, Harlan and Eva stayed at the Marriott hotel in downtown New Orleans. Putting them all together in one hotel would have created too many problems since many had particular needs regarding medicine, special diets, or some handicap.

In the beginning there were heated discussions between Rick, Kronin and Chris on whether or not to let classical musicians use the home. This was resolved by the fact that only two had phoned for inquiries, and were never heard of again. Most of the men and women who applied for the house came from the rock, pop, blues and jazz scene.

Harlan and Eva's famous stage entrance was another point of discussion. Ron and Dwight decided to press charges after all, while accusations of mismanagement were brought against the security company. Finally all charges were dropped and the whole matter was swept under the carpet. This did not stop the video footage taken by security cameras of their ride through the Superdome on the Harley Davidson going viral and reaching all corners of the globe. Within days Harlan and Eva became household names once again, bringing with it numerous requests to appear on television programs worldwide; on a Harley

Davidson of course. But that was never their goal. They had not only hung up their instruments; they had both decided long ago to shut themselves away from public view. Riding the bike onto the stage was an accident. All they wished for was peace and quiet, and to be left alone in the company of friends.

Rick kept tabs of the money they raised for the benefit. Three weeks after the concert they had raised just over six million dollars, and money still continued to pour into the account; eventually they ended up with seven and a half million dollars. Exactly how much was left after Kronin, the Superdome and the bands that played deducted their expenses was a well-kept secret.

David was taken to a special remedial center in another state, making it nearly impossible for Rick and Chris to visit. Although his therapy would still continue he would need to be looked after round the clock. Rick knew they would never have the facilities to care for him at Mount Merrian.

Nobody talked about Preston, not even Kronin. Aggressive and mentally unstable, Chris had said. What would they do with him? Probably shoot him up with so many drugs the only thing he could do without assistance was piss and fart. But life was not as easy as that. Preston had caused too much damage to go unnoticed. Kronin had mentioned something about the police but never elaborated. Right now he was probably sitting in the corner of some nut house banging his head against the wall. Rick suddenly felt very sorry for Preston.

It would be a three week wait before they could move into the home so Chris decided to go back to New York with Rick and spend that time putting his apartment on the market and resign from the hospital. Selling the apartment was easier then he thought. Within a week an agent sold it for twice the price he hoped for.

Resigning from his job was much more difficult. Since Rick had found fame once again everybody at the hospital was aware Chris was not only an orderly, but a long forgotten musician and actor. Chris paced the floor of his apartment looking nervous as Rick lay stretched out and relaxed on the sofa.

"I've decided to make an appointment with the director, and personally hand in my resignation." Chris said.

"You should plan this so it takes as little time and as little effort as possible," Rick said, while gesturing with his right hand, as if directing an orchestra. "Write a short note, walk in at the planned time, not a minute earlier, hand it to the director, then leave immediately. No problem."

Rick got up from the sofa, grabbed Chris from the rear by his shoulders and guided him into an armchair.

"Now sit down and write," he said as he pushed pen into his hand and laid a piece of paper down in front of him.

Rick began to pace the room, again gesturing with his hand.

"I think you should only write two small sentences," he said.

"Really? What should I write?"

"Fuck your crummy hospital. I'm off."

Chris shook his head. "I can't write that. They have always treated me fair and with respect. I have to give it something more then I'm off. I have to explain why I'm leaving."

"Have you gone senile or something? They know why you're leaving. It was in every newspaper and on every television channel across the country. There is no way they could have missed it."

Chris wrote another couple of lines, crossed it out, then ripped the page out and threw it on the floor. He buried his head in his hands with anguish.

"Maybe you should tell them you're off to a better life. Something like that. Sounds more philosophical."

"Cut the crap Rick. If you don't want to take this seriously go out for a walk somewhere and leave me to write this in peace."

"Great idea," he said, then grabbed his coat and headed for the door. "I was never any good at writing letters anyway. Expect me when you see me."

"Don't be too late," Chris said, sounding anguished. "We have to be at the hospital at ten sharp tomorrow morning." The front door slammed shut.

After walking a block exploring the neighborhood, Rick suddenly realized he was alone for the first time since he ended up in the hospital. He felt lifted by an air of independence and freedom, something he had not felt in quite a while. In Central Park he sat down on a lonely bench and took off his left shoe. He removed his bank card from under the inlay and quickly stuffed it into the inside pocket of his jacket. It had been a couple of months since he touched his bank account, and knew he had more than enough to get what he needed. Rick decided to visit some old haunts and surprise a few friends.

After withdrawing cash from an ATM he headed for the nearest liquor store. The attendant, and all the liquor, were behind a wall of one inch Plexiglas that lined the entire shop.

"Give me two bottles of the most expensive whiskey you've got." Without a word the attendant disappeared into the back store and came out carrying two bottles of Johnny Walker Blue.

"A gift or for personal use," the attendant asked.

"Both," Rick replied. This puzzled the attendant for a second, then he placed one of the bottles in an elegant box and wrapped it in fancy paper. The other he put into a plain brown paper bag.

"Is that all?"

"Give me a bottle of your best French wine." The attendant disappeared once again into the store and came back with a bottle. "Is three hundred expensive enough?"

"Magic. Wrap it up."

"Is it a gift or for personal use."

"You trying to be smart?"

"Just asking. It's service. It's what I do."

"It's a gift," Rick sighed.

"That's what I wanted to hear." The attendant wrapped the bottle. "Anything else?"

"That's it."

"That will be five hundred and fifty two dollars and twenty cents."

Minutes later he was in a taxi heading towards the harbor. How would they react when they saw him? Maybe they wouldn't even recognize him. His scraggly beard and long matted hair was replaced by modern grooming. The old army coat and tattered trousers were substituted for a neat suit and expensive overcoat.

The harbor was the same as ever with mounds of rubbish and building rubble littered everywhere. Rick scanned the grounds but saw no one. He made his way through the scattered litter towards their usual patch of ground. Barney, Harry and Stanley would all be sitting around the campfire or wander around the immediate area, scouring the semi-demolished buildings for firewood or anything else that would burn. However, they all never went off together, someone always stayed behind to watch for intruders. Now there was no one to be seen. He looked around in all directions and couldn't see a soul. This was a first. They were always around somewhere, but where? Did they all get arrested? Chased away by another gang? There was no way they could put up a fight, but where was the gang? Must have been the police.

Rick knelt next to the campfire ashes and ran his fingers through the embers. Still warm. The fire had been alight the night before. Rick placed the bottle of whiskey directly on the spot where Barney always sat. He then took out the second bottle and was about to place it on Harry's spot when he hesitated. Even stupidity had its boundaries. He put the bottle back into his coat pocket. Rick looked around once again. Still no one in sight. He had been looking forward to telling them about his latest exploits. Not that they would believe any of it, but at least they could get drunk, have a laugh and maybe a couple of songs. He turned and walked away from the makeshift camp.

"What's he doing now?" Harry asked in a faint croak.

Barney stuck his head out from behind a mound of rubbish. "He's walking away."

"Thank God for that. What's he doing here anyway?'

Stanley lay on his back, panting. He had spotted Rick coming towards the harbor while collecting wood and had run back to the camp as fast as he could to warn the others. In total panic they all ran a couple of hundred yards in the opposite direction to find a hiding place.

"I told you we never should have laughed at those stories he used to tell." Stanley said, with tears swelling up in his eyes. "He's going to be really angry."

"How was I to know they were goddamn true." Harry moaned.

"I knew," Stanley wheezed, "I knew he'd come back to get us for that." Stanley went into another fit of coughing which brought up a mouthful of green phlegm. He spit it out next to Harry.

"Wait a minute," Barney shouted. "He's heading back."

"Oh Christ. He's spotted us." Stanley said, now with tears running down his cheeks.

Rick strolled back to the campfire and took the second bottle of whiskey out of his jacket.

"He's taking something else out of his coat." Barney said in a near whisper.

"It's a gun." Stanly squealed like a little boy then buried his head in his hands. "He's come back to finish us off."

Barney shook his head. "I don't think so. He's putting it down on your spot next to the fire. It doesn't look like a gun from here."

"A bomb," Stanley cried. "It's a bomb."

Stanley had another fit of coughing.

"There was always something about him I couldn't put my finger on." Harry said. "That army coat he used to wear. Maybe he was one of those SAS people from the British army. A sort of commando; the ones who do all the dirty work."

Rick looked down at the second bottle he placed on Stanley's spot. The thought of keeping it for himself had suddenly seemed stupid. He had given his word to David in silence not to go on the binge again. It was time to clean up his act. Well, at least a little bit. Besides, the boys would enjoy it and probably appreciate it more. Since he had not been around in a while they didn't have the chance to get their hands on alcohol of this quality. He turned and walked away from the camp, unaware that every move he made was being carefully monitored.

Barney, Stanley and Harry looked on as he disappeared from view.

"What are we going to do now?" Barney asked. "If we go back to the camp the bombs might go off."

"But I want to sleep in my own spot tonight," Stanley said, as he started to cry again.

"We can always sneak up and see what he left. Maybe it's not a bomb" Harry said.

"I don't care what we do but I'm not going to do any running anymore." Stanley said.

When Rick had disappeared from view they climbed out of their hiding place and walked cautiously back to the camp. Barney squinted trying to make out the two objects Rick had left behind.

"They look like bottles. One of them is wrapped in fancy paper," he whispered.

"Molotov cocktails." Harry said.

"There's no burning rag sticking out of them, they're just sitting there."

"I never trusted him." Harry said bitterly.

Slowly, they get closer to the bottles.

"I bet it's poison. The type the doctors would never be able to trace." Harry picked up a large rock. "We better smash them before we get any closer."

Stanley also picked up a rock. "That's a good idea. If it's a bomb we'll be safe from here. If it's poison it will only kill a few fish." Stanley and Harry let the rocks fly.

Rick took a cab to the diner. Deep inside he hoped Jenny would be there, but he knew she wouldn't. She preferred the early morning shift and had probably left hours earlier.

Rick had always bragged about his exploits but she never believed him. Jenny could have missed all the publicity around him but he knew she was a Tonight Show fan and would never have missed the broadcast. Whenever she was in a good mood she would repeat some of Leno's jokes to the customers. He wanted to see her but at the same time he did not want to embarrass her. Rick had it all worked out. After signing his name on the bottle, he would leave the wine with one of the girls. Maybe after a few months he would call back to see how she was getting on, and talk about old times over a cup of coffee. Maybe they could even go to a concert together.

The cab stopped on the corner of 45th street. Smiler's diner was just around the corner. A sudden rush of panic set in. He got out of the cab and quickly checked for any loose threads or dirt from the harbor then combed his hair in a shop window. With the bottle firmly in both hands he headed nervously for the diner.

The sun had set an hour ago and the red neon lights above the diner flashed and flickered continuously. The familiar territory made him feel at ease. The sense of knowing he would recognize just about every face in the diner steadied his nerves. As usual, he stopped at the window like he always did, and peered in. The diner was quiet with only a few regulars sitting at their usual tables. He couldn't see anyone behind the counter. They were probably in the kitchen helping Jack put an order together. Rick brushed his hand over his hair then headed for the door.

As he opened the door Jenny suddenly appeared from the kitchen. She spotted him immediately, and a look of shock appeared on her face. "What are you doing here?" she yelled.

Rick lost his grip on the bottle and it crashed to the floor and exploded in all directions, covering his pants in wine and splinters of glass.

"You stupid bastard." Jenny screamed staring in horror at the chaos on the floor. "Look what you've done,"

Rick stared white faced at the pool of wine and broken glass at his feet. If only the ground would open up and suck him in.

"I told you before," she said with an air of definity. "You are not allowed to bring any booze in here."

Rick took one step back through the open door, then turned and ran.

"Jesus Christ." He heard her screaming in the background. "Just look at all this shit."

After two blocks he collapsed on a park bench, gasping and wheezing. The sight of the bottle smashing in all directions kept turning over in his mind. His hands shook from the shock of it all. But what struck him deeper was the fact Jenny was not surprised to see him at all. She never even looked at his new clothes and tidied appearance. He could not believe the anger in her beautiful brown eyes.

Murphy's law had taken over the entire day. Chris couldn't write the letter because of him. Barney, Stanley, and Harry who were always down at the harbor had disappeared. And Jenny had screamed him out of the diner. He had ruined everything. The day was a disaster. Nothing had gone right since he arrived in New York. His feeling of nostalgia for everything he left since joining up with Kronin had suddenly vanished. It was a mistake to come back because there was nothing to come back to. As soon as Chris got his act together and packed his belongings they would leave and never return.

It was after midnight when he finally made it back to the apartment. Chris was sitting in his favorite seat nodding in and out of sleep. The letter he spent hours putting together lay on the table in front of him in an envelope addressed to the hospital director. Rick gently took off his coat and quietly headed for the kitchen.

"Been drinking?" Chris asked in a tired voice. Rick stopped dead in his tracks. Chris was always a light sleeper.

"Haven't touched a drop."

"Must be some new after-shave then."

"Do you want anything from the kitchen?"

"I could do with a beer. Writing letters can be thirsty work."

"I thought you didn't keep any alcohol in the house."

"I went out and bought some just to celebrate our last evening in New York. You can have one if you want but I think you've had enough already."

"I told you I never touched a thing. I spilled some wine over my clothes but I swear not a drop went past my lips." A six-pack of Heineken sat on the kitchen table.

"Want a glass?" Rick shouted in a mocking English high class accent.

"Don't be silly, just give me the can."

Rick laughed and came out of the kitchen with two cans of beer. He placed the beer on the table in front of Chris.

"I thought maybe you'd visit your old friends?" Chris said.

"I did, but they weren't there."

Rick was about to sit down when Chris pointed to the armchair. "I think you'd better sit down there. You smell like a vineyard. I suppose you decided to douse yourself in wine to celebrate."

"It wasn't like that at all. I went out and bought a couple of bottles of whiskey for the boys but they weren't there. And that's the weird thing, they were always there. If they had to go somewhere one of them always stayed behind to keep an eye on everything so no one tried to pick their patch. There was signs of life because the fire was still warm. But now not a soul."

"Maybe they got picked up by the police." Chris said.

"For what? Being old and miserable? Anyway I left a little present so I hope they find it when they get back. After that I went to the old diner where I used to hang out. I bought a bottle of wine for one of the waitresses but it slipped out of my hand as I came in the door."

"You were bringing a lady a bottle of wine?"

"She's not a lady, she's just a waitress." Rick retorted, irritated. "Anyway there's no law against it,"

"True." Chris replied. "But you still manage to surprise me, that's all." Chris chuckled as he opened his can and held it out to toast Rick.

"Here's good-bye to New York." Chris said.

"Good-bye, New York. And good fucking riddance." Rick replied, and downed his beer.

Chapter eighteen

St. Ann's five story hospital looked painfully out of place next to the magnificent glass skyscrapers towering each side of it. Its whitewashed walls had long faded since they were last painted in the late eighties. Chris stood across the street from the building, staring at it with affection. Rick stood next to him.

"It looks so dreary." Rick grumbled.

"It saved your life."

"I bet I would have pulled through."

"No chance. Every bandage, pill, drop of medicine, care and medical expertise pulled you through. You would have lost that bet."

They crossed the road and entered the hospital. Chris nervously paced the floor of the very slow moving elevator as they made their way up to the administration office on the top floor. For the third time in so many minutes Chris straightened his tie.

"What's he like?"

"Who."

"The director."

"He's Ok," Chris replied casually. "Been here for about 10 years."

"So you're old mates."

"Hardly ever seen him. It's been years since I've been up here."

Mrs. Crew, the director's middle aged secretary, waved them into the office almost immediately. The room with its light tan carpet floor was sober and bright.

"Gentlemen, come in," said the director. "Take a seat. I've been expecting you."

He was a tall man with a meek face and wire framed glasses. He reminded Rick of an accounted he once had a long time ago.

Chris removed the envelope from his breast pocket and without saying a word handed it to the director.

He opened it without hesitation, read it, then put it to one side.

"Accepted." He said with a gentle smile, then stood up from behind his desk and shook Chris's hand.

Rick was startled. The director spent no less than three seconds reading the letter then accepted it without question. Something seemed very wrong.

"I can't thank you enough for everything you've done for this hospital. It has been a pleasure knowing you."

"You too, sir."

"Before you leave I would like you to go down and say good-bye to a number of the staff, including doctor Forest of course. He has always praised your work in the past."

Rick couldn't believe his ears. Chris was only the Goddamn orderly, and was being treated like the chief medical surgeon.

"Yes I will. Thank you very much," Chris replied.

The director then took hold of Rick's hand and shook it with vigor. "You have also helped put this hospital on the map and I would like to thank you for that. It was a pleasure having you."

"You're welcome, your Honor," Rick blurted out.

Rick did not utter another word until they were alone in the corridor waiting for the elevator.

"It's been a pleasure knowing you," Rick said in a poor imitation of the director. "What the fuck was that all about? You're only the orderly; you push people around, do the cleaning shit …."

"I'll tell you some other time."

"Tell me what some other time? No way, pal. I want to know right now. For a start what was in that letter. He read it in the blink of an eye."

"Well I didn't get to write that much last night."

"How much did you write?"

"Not a lot."

"How many words."

"Two."

"Two? That's what I told you. You stole my words.

"I didn't steal your words." Chris replied.

"What else could you write in two words." Rick asked.

"That was the easy bit. I just wrote *I resign*."

Rick looked at him dumbfounded. "You spent the whole evening putting two words together?"

"Do you think I needed to write more?"

"No, you're right. Two words were enough. You did a great job. I'm glad you took my advice," he said, patting Chris on the back and shaking his head in disillusionment. They stepped into the lift. Chris pressed the button for the second floor.

"But you still have not told me why he treated as if you owned the place."

"I do own it."

"What?" Rick shouted, an octave higher.

"Well..." Chris hesitated. "I don't really own it. But I did pay for it."

Rick was stunned. "What do you mean you *paid* for it? Other than that apartment you don't have a penny to your name."

"How do you know?"

"You left a bank statement lying about in the apartment and I just happened to notice it, that's all."

"We have all made a lot of money in our days and we all spent it. You spent it your way and I spent mine here. Every brick, every light fitting," Chris gestured to the surroundings, "every piece of equipment was paid for by me."

"Bloody hell," Rick moaned as the ground spun from under his feet. He grabbed the safety rail.

"Are you all right?" Chris asked, quickly grabbing him under the elbow for support.

"I don't know but thanks be to God we're in a hospital."

"There are only one or two people who know about this so don't say a word to anyone, ever."

"I won't mention it to a living soul. They wouldn't believe me anyway. Jesus Christ," Rick moaned. "Now I need a drink."

The elevator stopped on the second floor and opened to a rapture of applause and cheers from doctor Forest and the rest of the medical staff. Chris now felt his legs give way as they were hustled out of the lift and into the dining area. Rick stared in wonder at the hero's welcome they had organized for Chris. Balloons and decorations hung from the ceiling and the crowd sang "For he's a jolly good fellow...." They were guided towards two waiting chairs, while Doctor Forest climbed a table to address the crowd.

"I would like to be the first to admit I was one of those people who worked alongside Chris for many years and hardly ever got to know him. I would also like to say the popularity that surrounds him these days is not the reason why I'm standing here right now and giving this speech."

"But it helps," someone shouted from the crowd.

Forest laughed. "Think what you like," he replied.

"We do," someone else shouted from the crowd.

"And it's all true," another shouted. The crowd cheered and jeered.

"Anyway, to get back as to why we are here," Forest continued. "Chris has always been one of those figures who moved around the hospital doing his job to the utmost of his ability, and at the same time commanded respect and esteem from his colleagues. He achieved this because he worked for more than twenty years without complaint or criticism. In fact I can honestly say he did it so well his work went totally unnoticed by the rest of us in the hospital. In all those years there was never one complaint from any of the staff or patients regarding his work or manner. A test the rest of us can never hope to pass. But behind the man we knew who ran errands and cleaned floors was an accomplished musician, and a very popular one in his time I might add. An incredible fact he managed to keep hidden all this time. I would like to propose a toast to one of the most remarkable and distinguished people I have ever met in my life and I'm sorry to say we didn't have more time to get to know him." Forest lifted his glass high. "Here's to Chris."

"To Chris," the crowd cried out. They raised their plastic cups high to the ceiling.

Rick sniffed at the clear substance at the bottom of his cup and squirmed.

"I might also add that I am pleased to see an old patient of ours who, against all odds and the medicine I prescribed, is alive and kicking and looking in better shape than most of us. A toast to our old patient Mr. Rick Macken. May he and Chris live a long and healthy life in their new home."

"To be honest I'm not sure we'll ever get there with the piss water you lot are serving up here." Rick said, holding up a plastic cup. Everyone roared with laughter. Rick turned to Chris who was frowning and shaking his head.

"Don't be such a sourpuss. Come on, lighten up, have a laugh." He gave Chris an incredible whack on the back, which brought on another roar of laughter from the crowd.

An hour later they were on the street heading back to the apartment. Chris looked gloomy.

"Why do you always have to make stupid jokes like that? You really embarrassed me in there."

"You're getting old. Do you know that? There was a time when you could have a laugh like the rest of us but now you're turning into a grumpy old dog."

The next morning the furniture removal truck came for Chris's belongings. They stood on the sidewalk and watched it being loaded into the truck by a handful of sturdy men.

"I can't understand why you're putting it all into storage. Why don't you sell it. Get rid of it. You're not going to need it anymore."

"And what if it doesn't work out at the home?" Chris said. "What am I going to do then? I've had most of this stuff for the best part of my life. If I lose the home and I lose this I'll have nothing."

Rick took him by the shoulders and turned Chris to face him,

"You'll have me. I'll always be there. Just like you were for me."

"No chance. I want to enjoy the rest of my days. Not see it as a death sentence."

Rick roared with laughter. "Jesus, another miracle. You got your humor back."

Chris managed a wry smile for the sake of it. "Listen," Chris said, sounding nervous and hesitant. "I didn't want to bring it up but there is something I've been meaning to tell you."

"You can tell me anything you want as long as you can make me laugh."

"I'm afraid it's not a laughing matter."

Rick froze. "David?"

Chris shook his head. "I spoke to his therapist this morning. He's coming along great."

Rick clapped his hands. "They'll have him up and running around in no time," he said laughing. "It's amazing what they can do these days. Just take a look at me, a fucking medical miracle."

"It's Preston." Chris said.

Ricks' laughter vanished immediately. That was the reason why Chris had not brought it up earlier. Although Rick went on about Preston as if he never cared, it was quite the opposite. His affection for Preston was just as great as it was for David.

"What about Preston?"

"He's in a psychiatric hospital just out of town. I'm afraid he's not in the best condition and he's been asking for you."

"How do you know he's been asking for me?"

"When I contacted Kronin about of the home, he told me about Preston."

"What do you want me to do?"

"I thought maybe we could go out and see him before we get the plane."

"Let me think about it," Rick turned and walked away from Chris.

"If you don't want to go you don't have to," Chris shouted after him.

"I said let me think about it." Rick said without turning round. "I'll be back in half an hour." He disappeared around the block.

He thought about the Preston he knew from the sixties and tried to find something to connect him to the person he was today. There was nothing, no connection whatsoever. During his days on the street he had met other hobos with psychiatric problems. There was the kind who roamed streets and were the gentlest souls you could ever meet. There was also Preston's category. Bitter, stressed out, and occasionally violent. The world through his eyes was a hostile one. No enjoyment, no compassion, no friend to help him through the hard times, not that he'd accept it, but it remained nothing. Preston's world was a lonely hell hole, and he sat right in the middle of it.

Rick once looked at it as a sort of society shell shock with no cure. Shell shocked and traumatized soldiers were taken out of a war zone as quickly as possible and brought to a place of peace and quiet to recuperate. But with society shell shock the difficulty was removing them from the environment that caused the problem. The only way out was a psychiatric hospital and possible solitary confinement. This lacked any healing element. No flowers, trees or basic elements of nature to which a person could relate. Nothing except drugs to numb the nerves and induce sleep. Rick knew of the kind of hell Preston was in and the last thing he wanted was to look into his sunken, bloodshot eyes and see it, just like he did in Kronin's office.

Rick understood why Preston had been asking for him. He had recognized him as someone who could read his pain.

Half an hour later Rick returned to the apartment building. Chris was still in the same spot. "Ok. Let's go." Rick said.

Rick had never heard of the Ryder Psychiatric Clinic, but the moment he saw it he knew why. It was not a clinic for deadbeats and hobos. This was a thousand-dollar-a-night job. The large sprawling gray mansion with beautifully manicured lawns and hedges looked more like a five star hotel than a psychiatric clinic.

They entered the main door and headed straight for the receptionist, who had striking blond hair, large blue eyes, and a bust that made Rick's eyes squint while trying to get her into focus. Chris introduced himself. Rick just nodded, trying to keep his eyes off her chest.

"We've come to see our friend Preston Golding. There was an appointment arranged with Dr. Jabobs."

"Of course. If you would like to take a seat I'll call him," she said as she gestured to the waiting area across from the reception.

Rick sank into a luxurious armchair with a perfect view of the nurse across the hall, while Chris browsed through the rich supply of magazines that lay neatly stacked in small stands next to each of the four white leather armchairs. There was everything on psychiatry, mental care, art, fashion, and Time magazine. There was also a glossy about the clinic with star studded features about members of the staff. Dr. Jacobs featured heavily in their celebrity lineup. The article showed a full size picture of him standing before the front entrance to the clinic and an article that read like an obituary. Born in 1965, studied at Harvard, then spent two years at the Mount Sinai hospital before coming to the Ryder Clinic. He had three papers published in Psychology Today, and in various other scientific journals. Chris suddenly looked up to see Dr. Jacobs standing in front of him. "You've come to see Mr. Golding?"

"There was an appointment made through Mr. Kronin."

"Yes of course. Everything has been arranged. If you follow me I'll take you to see him."

With effort Rick pulled himself out of the deep comfortable armchair and followed Chris and Dr. Jacobs across the hall and up the flight of stairs to the first floor. He kept his eye on the receptionist for as long as he could. When he reached the balcony she looked up and gave him a warm smile. Rick's heart skipped a beat. He tagged on Chris's jacket and leaned in close.

"She fancies me," he whispered into Chris's ear.

"Grow up," Chris hissed. They went down a long corridor, then turned left to enter the back west wing of the building.

"How is he?" Rick asked.

"He's had a rough time," Doctor Jacobs said, sounding genuinely concerned, but he's slowly coming round. We have managed to lighten the stress he seems to have been under, I don't think you'll find him as aggressive as before. If he keeps up his medication he won't have many problems there. But there is another part of his illness I'm afraid we can't do anything about."

"What's that?" Chris asked.

"Although it is unusual to have it so late in life, he is suffering from early stages of Huntington's Chorea. This is a disease that affects body movements and slurs speech. As time passes there is also a progressive deterioration of mental functions. It can also cause alternating periods of excitement and depression. Like I said there is no cure but we can relieve some of the symptoms."

"Will it kill him?" Rick asked.

"Eventually."

"How long does he have?"

"Difficult to say. Ordinarily people who get Huntington's disease rarely get to reach this age. He must be one of the lucky ones."

"Doesn't sound lucky to me," Rick muttered.

Dr. Jabobs stopped outside a door with a small portal window at eye level. Rick looked through the glass to see Preston sitting on the edge of his bed staring at the wall in front of him.

Doesn't look so lucky either." Rick said in a barely audible tone.

Dr. Jacobs opened the door gently and entered the room. "Hello Preston. How are we doing today?"

Preston continued to stare at the wall.

"I've brought along some old friends to see you. You've been asking for them for quite a while and now they're here. Aren't you going to say hello?"

Preston did not move. Reluctantly Rick moved deeper into the room. He stood at the end of Preston's bed, staring at him in silence.

"I'll leave you alone."

"Is it safe?" Rick blurted out.

"Everything should be okay. If you need me there is always an orderly outside who can call me." Dr. Jacobs left, closing the door behind him.

The silence and the bareness of the room seemed unnatural to Rick. He slowly moved towards the bed and sat down next to

Preston. He stared at the same spot Preston seemed to be focused on, a blank wall painted light gray. There was no pattern on the wall, except for a few coffee stains, or was it dried blood? Rick tried momentarily to picture some recognizable shape or form in the markings. There was nothing. No rabbit's, bears, faces, not even Mickey Mouse. Without uttering a sound Preston gently rested his head on Rick's shoulder. After a few minutes he felt Preston's tears drip gently onto his trouser leg. Chris sat on the opposite side of Preston and tenderly placed his arm around his shoulder.

"I'm sorry for everything," Preston suddenly whispered.
Tears flowed down Rick's face. "It's all right old son," Rick whispered. "You don't have to worry about a thing. Everything is going to be just fine." Preston remained quiet after that. No one said another word. Rick and Preston just wept silently as Chris sat next to them with his head bowed.

An hour later, Rick blew out a deep breath of relief when the cab pulled away from the clinic. He laid back on the seat, and closed his eyes, utterly exhausted.

"To be honest it wasn't as I expected," Rick told Chris. "I expected to see Preston in a straight-jacket or in a padded cell."

"That's what Woody died of." Chris muttered, staring out the window of the cab.

" Woody?" Rick asked.

"Woody Guthrie." Chris replied. "He had always been Preston's hero back in the old days. He died in the late sixties of Huntington's Chorea. Strange to think Preston is going to die of the same illness."

Chapter nineteen

The air was hot and humid when Rick and Chris stepped off the plane in New Orleans, as if someone had left the central heating on full blast. The South had its great points but this was not one of them. Rick found it hard to understand people who preferred to live in a climate were you could roast to death just by walking down a street.

When they arrived at the hotel, Rick telephoned Harlan's room from the reception. No reply. He rang Eva and Robbie's rooms; no reply. Where was everyone? The receptionist confirmed they were still staying at the hotel but had no idea where they could be. They checked the hotel bar and lounge; nothing.

Exhausted after the long flight, Rick and Chris decided to call it a day. Together they took the lift up to their rooms on the eighth floor. Rick found a note that had been pushed under his door. GONE TO VIC'S KANGAROO CAFE. Chris found a similar note under his door.

Five minutes later they were both outside the hotel and climbing into a taxi.

"I thought you'd be curled up with your slippers and a book," Rick said, trying not to sound too interested.

"Not tonight," Chris said, peering out of the window as the taxi drove away.

"You never came before." Rick quipped.

"Well I need a break after a day like today." Chris replied.

"Oh." Rick muttered.

"What's so wrong about that?"

"Nothing. You usually stay in your room whenever anyone proposes to go to a bar. A bell always goes off in my head when someone starts doing things they normally don't do. And right now all my bells are ringing."

Chris turned to Rick. "Well why don't you use those bells to call a goddamn doctor." Chris replied, irritated.

Rick roared with laughter, then fell over to one side of the back seat of the taxi. "That's a good one," he screamed. "Second joke in twenty four hours. Things are looking up, me boys. Rick clasps his hands and rubs them together in a frenzy. "Things are definitely looking up."

Chris laughed and shook his head and settled back in the seat.

The taxi stopped right outside the bar on Tchoupitoulas Street, and as they stepped out of the cab Rick stared suspiciously at the bar and surrounding area.

"Hold on," Rick says, as he put his hand on Chris's shoulder to stop him entering the bar. "Doesn't look right to me."

"What's wrong?" Chris asked.

"The windows aren't smashed and there are no drunken old men blocking the sidewalk."

"Very funny," Chris mumbled. Rick chuckled and elbowed him in the ribs.

Vic's bar was not as packed as it usually was. There was no big crowd pulling artist tonight, only a handful of regulars. Eva, and Robbie were seated at a table in the center of the floor. To Rick's surprise Harlan was on stage with guitar in hand, and singing a ballad: the very one he wrote more than forty years ago, and made him famous overnight. It had sold more than three million copies, although few people in the bar recognized it.

When Harlan finished, the locals, used to something heavier, applauded lightly. Rick, Chris, Eva, and Robbie gave him a standing ovation along with cat whistles and shouts for more.

Harlan smiled and thanked them, then began to tune his guitar. "If I may I would like to do just one more song. This is one for my new-found friends and something I hope will see us through the rest of our lives."

"Which by the look of you lot will last about a month," a young man remarked loudly to his friends at the bar amid sniggers of laughter.

Harlan began to play the guitar.

"Hey Vic, I thought this was a Rock and Roll bar." The same man shouted for all to hear. "Since when are you caring for geriatrics?"

Vic, pulling a beer at the other end of the bar looked up. "Keep it down Lenny. We're all here to enjoy ourselves."

"I know Vic, but before you know it we won't be allowed in without a wheelchair." Lenny shouted back. His friends laughed even louder.

Harlan finished his song to the same applause and rousing reception, only this time Lenny and his friends booed. Rick ordered another round of beer and a club soda for Chris from the waitress when Harlan made it back to the table.

When the order arrived Rick toasted to Harlan's performance. "To Harlan, and a great performance."

"To Harlan," they all repeated, and hoisted their beers high.

"If that was a great performance then I'm a red eyed bug," Lenny said, sounding off from the bar. His friends around him laughed.

"Anyone want some nuts to go with the beer?" Rick asked them all.

"No thanks, Rick," Eva replied. "Plays hell with my digestion."

"Me neither," Chris said, shaking his head. "My dentures can't handle them." Robbie was willing.

At the bar Rick stood next to Lenny and his friends as he ordered the salted peanuts.

"I suppose if you can't get your nuts any more the only thing left is to buy them over the counter." Lenny joked, then turned back to his sniggering friends.

Rick tapped him on the shoulder. "Sorry? I'm a little hard of hearing, I didn't quite get that."

"I bet there's a lot you're not getting at your age pops." Lenny turned quickly again to his friends for more recognition of his instant wit, which was rewarded with another burst of laughter. Rick tapped him again gently on the shoulder; Lenny turned to him once again.

"I'm afraid I'm deaf in this ear." Rick told him pointing, to his left ear. "And I can't hear anything in the other. Could you repeat that?" Rick leaned in close to Lenny with his left ear.

"I'm sorry guys," Lenny said to his friends. "I just can't let something like this pass." He leaned in close to Rick's left ear.

"I said," Lenny shouted at the top of his voice. "I bet there's a lot you're not getting at…"

Rick flicked his head to the left and smashed it down on Lenny's nose. Lenny collapsed to his knees with both hands covering his nose, blood poured through his fingers.

"That's what they call a Liverpool kiss, sonny," Rick said, looking down at Lenny, "with a flip."

"You broke my nose." Lenny gargled through cupped hands trying to hold his nose in place. One of his friends, who was just as tall as Lenny and had more muscle grabbed Rick's jacket.

"Shouldn't have done that, old man."

As he pulled Rick towards him to line him up for a punch Rick grabbed his waiting bowl of nuts and smashed it over the side of his head. Lenny's friend hit the floor with a thud. Suddenly the other two made a dive at Rick and were about to land a punch when Harlan's guitar smashed down on their heads.

Rick and Harlan gave each other a high five. Seconds later the door of the bar flew open and the police stormed in.

The morning newspapers were full of pictures of Rick and Harlan being arrested at Vic's next to police mug shots. There were also photographs of Lenny and his friends bandaged up after their visit to the hospital.

It was three in the afternoon before Eva and Robbie came to collect them in a taxi from the jail. Charges of assault against Rick and Harlan were dropped. Outside, reporters questioned them about their night behind bars. Rick ignored them. The four of them were quickly herded into the taxi with help from the police.

"You okay?" Eva asked, as they sped away from the mass of microphones and the flashing of camera's. "Did they treat you all right?"

"Like royalty," Rick replied. "They realized a bunch of guys like us could never have started any trouble. We're too old and feeble to fight."

"Chris will be happy to hear that."

"I bet he will. Are we going back to the hotel?" Rick asked.

"We are." Eva replied.

"Great." Rick said, rubbing his hands gleefully together. I could do with a nice cold beer."

"Chris won't be happy to hear that." Eva said, sounding worried.

"Well that's his fuckin' problem." Rick replied. "Pardon my French sweetheart."

There was a small crowd of retired musicians who had joined the group during the last week waiting for them in the foyer. Chris was nowhere to be seen. The rest of the afternoon they spent in the lounge reading aloud newspaper articles about the fight. They cheered at reports about Rick and Chris and booed those about Lenny and his friends. As the beer flowed they went on to swap stories about illnesses and the cures they had received, or should have received from various doctors all around the world. They also shared stories about living in old folks homes and the problems they encountered. One thing was certain; this new home would never be anything like what they left behind. They would live their lives the way they wanted, and dare anyone to get in their way.

Monday morning at eight sharp a luxurious bus pulled up to the Marriott to take everyone to the airport. This was it: this was the day everybody had been waiting for. Their own home, their own friends, their own music, and their own life the way they wanted to live it. Rick was nervous. He sat on the toilet in his hotel room in a cold sweat with a look of fear on his face. He was shaking like a leaf. The only thing he knew was that he was not intending on going anywhere.

After celebrating their last night together in New Orleans, he had lain down fully clothed on the bed the whole night, pondering on the changes that were about to happen. Everybody looked to him; the central point of attention. If anything went wrong all fingers would point to him. Rick couldn't forget how his world fell apart so long ago and was terrified this whole project would go down the same road. Kronin was still regulating everything, but Rick felt like he was carrying the burden on his shoulders. He was the one they all turned to. None of the others had hardly seen Kronin. Because of him they were making the last and most important journey of their lives, and if he failed he would eventually die in shame; the only type of death he couldn't accept. What can go wrong will go wrong; and it always did for him. Wherever he went he was trouble. He had caused so much grief and pain through the years the thought of doing the same to these poor souls made him shudder. It had never bothered him before, but now it did. Maybe it was brought on by old age, he did not know, but for the first time in his life he was terrified.

When daylight broke and the effect of the alcohol had worn off, Rick sat contemplating on the toilet for at least a number of hours before everything became very clear. All the goals he set out to achieve were not for him but for David, Chris, Preston, and the rest. However, David was now being looked after in a first class rehabilitation center. Preston was in the most luxurious nuthouse in the country, while Chris and the rest had got what they wanted. Goal achieved, and now there was nothing left to do. For no more than a second he thought about going back to New York. Barney and the boys were probably somewhere still down at the harbor. As for the diner he could never show his face there again. The shock on Jenny's face when the bottle exploded was too much to bear. Apart from all that his worst enemy was the weather. He knew the doctors were right when they said he wouldn't last long on the streets of New York. First it would be a simple cold, then pneumonia, then lights out. Time to move to Sa Francisco where the mindset was cool and weather pretty much ok.

Suddenly there was banging on the hotel door. "Rick. Are you ready? We are all about to leave." Chris shouted. Unable to move or say a word Rick got off the toilet and walked nervously into the bedroom. Chris hammered once again on the door. "Rick are you all right?" Rick sat down on the edge of the bed, shut his eyes and put his hands over his ears, trying desperately to block out everything.

"No. I'm not fucking all right." He shouted. "Why don't you all just fucking leave me alone." Rick heard his door being opened by a porter. He got up quickly made a dash back to the bathroom.

"Rick?" Chris shouted in panic. Rick flicked the lock of the bathroom door a second before Chris entered the room. Rick sunk down on the toilet. Sweat poured down his forehead.

There was a knock on the bathroom door. "Rick, are you in there?"

"Can't a man have a shit in the privacy of his own toilet?" He shouted back.

"Come on. We have to go. Everybody's waiting."

"You go ahead. I'll catch up with you later."

"No chance. You've got to come now. We're not leaving without you."

Rick got up from the toilet and looked in the mirror. He was clean shaven and his hair was neat and tidy. Rick pulled on the wrinkles around is eyes, then poked his sunken cheeks. "Jesus lad, you really are fuckin' old," he muttered.

This was it. The last run of life. The last trot to the hole in the ground. "You stupid bastard," he muttered to himself then flicked the lock open. "Keep your hat on. I'm ready." The porter grabbed his bags next to the bed.

"Wait a sec." Rick said, stalling at the door of the toilet, then broke wind big time.

"Jesus Christ," Chris moaned.

"Have to sterilize the place before I leave Chris. You know me. I always like to keep things nice and tidy."

Chris waved his arms in all directions, trying to dispense the smell.

When they stepped out of the lift and into the foyer there was at least 30 people waiting. Suddenly a cheer went up and they began to applaud as Rick and Chris moved towards them.

"Right," Chris announced. "The flight leaves at ten-thirty. That gives us two hours to get out to the airport, check-in, and get everything together before takeoff. When we arrive there will be more coaches to pick us up and take us to Mount Merrian. Are there any questions?"

"I have one," Eva said. "Where's Rick?"

It was easy to give them all the slip. As soon as Chris began talking Rick tipped the porter with a twenty dollar bill, took his baggage, then headed for the back door. Outside, the air was cool and dry. The first thing he would do was get some cash. Credit cards left calling cards all over the place so he decided that one large withdrawal could keep him underground for at least a month. After that they probably wouldn't be interested anymore. The ATM took his card and asked for the code. Rick scratched his head. "What the hell was that number," he mumbled. He typed in four digits, and waited. Suddenly the screen flashed PIN CODE NOT CORRECT. He typed in another number. PIN CODE NOT CORRECT. "Jesus, don't do this to me. Oh my God, what the fuck was that number?" A flash came to him. "Yes, I remember." Rick quickly typed in another code. Within seconds another message flashed up on the screen. YOU HAVE TYPED THE WRONG CODE. YOUR CARD WILL BE SENT TO CENTRAL OFFICE. A NEW CARD WILL BE SENT TO YOU AS SOON AS POSSIBLE. Rick was stunned. He stared at the cash dispenser in total disbelief. "You bastard," he screamed. "Give me my fucking card."

He gave the only cash he had to the porter. Now, he did not only have no money, but he had lost the only means of obtaining it. In all the years he had the card he never forgot the number. And now he couldn't remember it to save his life. Feeling utterly defeated he picked up the two bags and headed down the street. What could go wrong did go wrong. The story of his life.

All the plans he made had just vanished with the credit card. It would take at least a week before he could get hold of a new one, but how would he get that together? He had no idea. The moon would have to turn green before he went knocking on her door. Maybe he could get it through one of the kids. He never saw them but there was no bad blood between them, at least he didn't think so. Suddenly he had the feeling he was being followed.

He turned to see the bus cruising next to him as he walked down the street. The door to the bus opened up.

Chris, Eva, Robbie, and Harlan stood on the door platform. "Where are you going? We were all looking for you." Chris shouted from the bus. "Come on, get on the bus."

"Come on Rick," Eva shouted. "If you don't get in we'll be late for the flight. What's going on?"

"I was short of cash, and the bastard just swallowed my card."

"You don't need any cash at the home. You won't ever have to pay for a thing. It's all been taken care of."

"Come on Rick, get in the bus," Harlan shouted. Then they all began to shout.

"Get in the bus Rick." Harlan shouted again.

"We can't go without you, everything will be all right." Eva said.

"What are you running away from Rick?" Robbie said. Suddenly, the bus shot past him, then stopped. Everybody jumped out and surrounded him in the middle of the sidewalk. Eva pushed her way through the crowd to face Rick.

"What's going on Rick." Eva asked.

Rick took a deep breath.

"I can't come. It's not the place for me."

"Of course it's the place for you. What the hell are you talking about," Eva replied.

"I didn't do it for me, I did it for David and all of you. I don't belong there."

"Stop talking bullshit," Harlan said. "Get in the bus and let's get the hell out of here."

"None of us want to miss the plane Rick," Eva said. "But we all will if you don't come."

"Don't be ridiculous," Rick replied. "If you go now you'll have plenty of time."

"You don't get it Rick," Eva replied. "We are not going without you. If you want to throw it all away then we will too. You made it all possible and we are not planning on anywhere going there without you."

Rick saw the desperate look on their faces. Right now he was only thinking about himself and he knew it. He had to make a decision. If he decided against going he knew they would be still standing here the next morning and not getting anywhere.

"All right, I'll come," Rick finally said. At least until he could figure out how to get a new credit card, he thought, then he would head for San Francisco. Harlan grabbed his bag while Eva and Chris ushered him into the bus.

Rick sat near the front of the bus next to the window, with Chris next to him. When the excitement settled down Chris began his usual read of the morning newspaper. As they got further away from the hotel Rick felt a hot flush run through his body. Sweat broke out on his forehead and down his back. His shirt was quickly becoming wet and clammy. He was burning up. This was too much. He couldn't go. The bus stopped at a traffic light and Rick stood up.

"What's up?"

"I have to get off the bus."

Chris stayed put, blocking Rick's exit. "If you forgot something don't worry." Chris said, still reading the paper and blocking Rick's exit. "Anything we may have left behind will be sent on by the hotel."

"It's not that. I just have to get off the bus." At that moment the bus pulled away and Rick fell back into his seat.

"Too late." Chris said, then tucked away the newspaper and reading glasses. "We're off. There's no turning back now."

Rick stared gloomily out the window. "Yeah, sure," he grumbled to himself.

Two hours later they were on a plane heading for Richmond. The flight was unusually quiet. Eva and Harlan seemed transfixed on the blue skies and a bed of creamy white clouds, while Rick slept during the entire flight, making up what he had missed the night before.

Rick awoke as the plane began its decent into Richmond airport. He stared out at the roving hills and the numerous shades of green that greeted them. So peaceful. Hundreds of fields as far as the eye could see with different-colored crops and freshly ploughed soil. Landowner's mansions had the appearance of dolls houses in the distance. Traffic on highways resembled dinky toys. A beautiful sight to look at but Rick only saw deception; in reality things were very much different.

As they circled the airport to line up with the runway. Chris removed his headphones and pointed out a large group of elderly men and women waving from one of the viewing points on the terminal building.

"Can you see that? Isn't that a sight." Chris said.

"I hope that welcome is not for us," Rick moaned. "There must be hundreds of them."

"Actually there are seventy-three," Chris replied. Rick stared at him with contempt. Chris was constantly a step ahead of the rest, and always knew what was going on.

Suddenly it dawned on him that not only the view was deceiving but the definition of deception was Chris himself.

"How do you know that Chris? How and where do you get all your information? I could have guessed you were in on this." Rick said, pulling himself upright in the stool. "You are the only one in the entire group who really knows what is going on, and only share the information whenever you feel like it. It is not as if you disappear every fifteen minutes to make a telephone call. You are always there, always in sight, always hovering around. You're like a fuckin' second shadow." Rick was pissed off.

"You know," he went on, "I don't think Kronin has really anything to do with this at all." The plane hit the runway and the engines roared. "You know what I also think?" Rick said, trying to shout above the thunder of the engines. "I think you're runnin' the whole fuckin' show! It's like that bleedin' hospital of yours. You were only the orderly. But the only hospital orderly in the world who owned the fuckin' building he was working in. For all I know you own Kronin and his whole bag of tricks. I bet before you go to bed at night you call him with some mobile yuppie thing and feed him all the instructions to follow the next day." The roar of the engines died down as they taxied towards the terminal building.

"Listen," Chris said. "I have tried to defend myself against your outbursts before but it usually inflames the argument. You slam doors shut and then silence for days after. Our friendship is worse than marriage, you know that? Divorce would be a beautiful way to get out of it, but we're married for life. You'll just have to be patient and with any luck you will kick the bucket long before me. And one more thing then let's leave it at that," Chris said calmly. "The only thing I never told you was that I contacted Kronin with the idea about the benefit concert. And the only reason I did that was because I didn't have the money or the organization to do it myself. Maybe David has, or Harlan, I've no idea but I don't think so. In any case, we badly needed the money to get us where we are going now. At least enough to get us what we need. Secondly, as a favor to me, Kronin has generally kept me informed about the progress of things, but as soon as we unpack out bags in Mount Merrian we are definitely on our own. I will not have any contact with him whatsoever." The plane came to a stop and everybody started to move out of their seats. "So whatever you are thinking get it out of your head right now." He unbuckled his seatbelt and reached for the overhead locker.

Chapter twenty

The airport lounge was full of reporters, photographers and old rockers Rick thought were either long dead or living in another country. Many names he couldn't recall straight off but they all knew him. The old musicians hugged and patted him on the back, telling him how great he was and how grateful they were. Adding pain to pride they tried to carry him to the waiting coaches outside the terminal. Some had not changed at all, only a few extra wrinkles and subtly receding hair-lines marking up the years. Others so unrecognizable he had no idea who they were until they introduced themselves. He was shocked at their physical change, probably brought on by drink, drugs and the hard life on the road, he thought. Memories of concerts, parties, drinking sessions and legal suites came flooding back. Rick never imagined he would be so overwhelmed by seeing everybody. Whether or not Chris was pulling the strings, it made him feel pretty good.
A blond woman aged about sixty grabbed hold of Rick, threw her arms around him and kissed him hard on the lips.

A large cheer went up outside the terminal. "Go get him CJ," someone shouted. Finally she pulled back from Rick who looked at her in a state of shock.

"CJ?" he screamed.

"Hello Ricky daaaaarling. Finally I've got you in my arms again."

"I'm so happy you made it." Rick shouted, and hugged her tightly. "They're all driving me crazy," he whispered in her ear. "At least you'll put some life into a few of these old buggers."

"Just like old times sweetheart, although I prefer my meat to be young and tender if you know what I mean." CJ said, and winked.

"You didn't say that when we first took a dive between the sheets." Rick said.

"I was only sixteen or seventeen at the time, and you were so famous, and looked so fabulous. Ooh I've got some lovely memories of those days."

"Shhhh. Will you keep your voice down? I could still get arrested for that."

"But I gave consent my lovely. In fact I opened the door." CJ replied.

"Doesn't matter. I could still get arrested and get my ass stuck in prison whether you opened the door or not." Rick said.

"Will they lock us up together?" CJ crooned.

"Get your hands off him CJ," someone shouted from the crowd. "Rick will never get to the house alive if you start." Everybody laughed.

"Daaarling," CJ shouted back. "I bet he's the only one among you who has still got a bit of life left in him," then grabbed Rick by the crotch. A cheer went up in the terminal. Rick removed her hand then guided her out of the terminal. "You haven't changed a bit in all these years."

"I am what I am darling. And I love it." CJ purred.

"And don't ever change that my lovely," Rick replied.

Outside the terminal building they were greeted by four coaches waiting to take them to Mount Merrian. Kronin stood on a small stage surrounded by various assistants, photographers and journalists. Rick and Chris were ushered towards the stage. Kronin tapped the microphone.

"Ladies and gentlemen, if I may have your attention for a second." Everybody quietened down to listen. "We have now reached a milestone. Today is the start of your new lives and we hope you will enjoy them not only in dignity but also in an environment where you will not want for anything."

The crowd cheered. The coach doors opened on cue.

"And now, if you would like to get on board we will bring you to your new life." Kronin announced, then stepped off the podium and gestured Rick and Chris to a waiting stretch limousine.

"Sorry pal." Rick said. "We can't let all these people down."

Kronin looked on in astonishment as Rick put his hand on Chris's shoulder and turned away to get on the coaches with the rest of the crowd.

Both coaches were nearly full. Rick sat quietly in the back stunned at the miracle of it all and wondering what it would be like sharing the same house with these new-found friends. If the atmosphere on the bus was anything to go by they were definitely in for a good time. The journey reminded Rick of school outings when he was a kid. Sixty kids aged about eight or nine singing every song that came into their heads.

Many had guitars, banjos, tambourines and mouth organs, and singing medleys of songs from the fifties, sixties, and early seventies. Rick recognized Steve Barlow, one of the session musicians who backed his band from time to time back in the sixties. By the look of it he was still wearing the same leader jacket he wore all those years ago. He still looked the cool, calm and collect musician as ever. He sat at the back of the coach quietly rolling a cigarette looking totally oblivious to all the commotion around him.

Directly across from him Jessie Colton and Stan Blake sat playing cards together. He could remember them as musicians who toured playing any type of music that brought in the money such as folk, rock, jazz, Irish traditional or whatever was the taste of the day. In fact they even played at one of his daughters weddings more than thirty years ago.

Others he knew had gone on to become legends in their own right, yet many here were those people who didn't write the songs, so they were paid per session, missing out on all the royalties earned from the recordings. Rick felt he had landed in Rock and Roll heaven.

Chris sat next to Rick with his eyes closed, totally oblivious to the party atmosphere. Was he asleep? Or just trying to avoid conversation. Rick leaned in close to see if he could spot Chris's eyes moving.

"I've been wanting to ask you a while now but never got around to it," Chris said without opening his eyes. Rick quickly reclined back into his stool.

"Go on, ask." Rick said.

"Whatever happened with you and the band?"

"I thought you'd ask that sooner or later. I've always managed to avoid answering that question. It's nobody's business, but I guess you have a right to know. There are so many rumors and gossip floating around maybe it's time I set the record straight. The truth is the band didn't split up in the normal sense of the word. They, along with the wife and kids, who were grown up already, simply left me. They had enough of my crazy antics on and off stage, scandals and law suits from pregnant girlfriends, not counting the millions blown on stupid whims and projects, there were so many the lawyers had a hard time keeping count." Rick took a deep breath, and rested his head on the seat headrest.

"I really fucked up," he continued. "I raided my wife's bank accounts during the divorce proceedings and sold off jointly held properties with the help of fake documents and newly hired lawyers who didn't know shit. When the missus found out she and the lawyers sued me for every penny I had. Since then I've never seen or heard anything from her, or the children, or any of the band. I never blamed her for the lawyers, and I've got no grudges to bear. I probably would have done the same myself.

The only connection I have, or had, was that credit card. The ex and the kids arranged a small monthly allowance that I could withdraw whenever I want. It's not a lot, about a thousand a month, but it got me food and drink and a place to sleep when I really needed it; that's if I didn't spend it all on drink."

How did you meet up with David?" Chris asked.

"We met up about five years ago. He lost all his savings when the stock market went belly up, then he lost his wife and kids in a plane crash. Two years later we met up in a Hare Krishna soup kitchen on the Lower East Side of New York. We've been together ever since." Rick paused and took a deep breath. "That's enough about me. What happened to your band?"

"Well I was always a loner," Chris begun hesitantly. "I never had a permanent band to call my own. Most of the people I played with were session musicians. I just never managed to create like you, and I never accumulated your wealth either. Maybe that was the best thing that could have happened to me. It would have ruined me as a human being, just like it ruined many of my friends." Chris threw a glance at Rick.

"What about the films?" Rick asked.

"Ok, there were some films but can you remember the names of any of them."

"Eh, not really, no." Rick replied.

"Exactly. Just like my music. Anyway, I got married, got divorced, got married again, then another divorce."

"I remember you demonstrating against Vietnam, nuclear energy, seal culling, whatever."

"True, but when I took to traveling to demonstrations people began accusing me of being a publicity parasite. Just to keep my name in the papers they said. As the years passed the only way I stayed active was visiting old friends in hospitals. After seeing just about every hospital in the state of New York I heard about an initiative to set up St. Ann's, a hospital dedicated to helping the less well-off and needy. When the state rejected the proposal for the third time due to lack of funds I decided to pay for it out of my own pocket. There were two conditions. Firstly, it should never be known that my money was used for the project, and secondly, I would be employed in the hospital itself. I paid for the hospital, got the job, and remained there ever since."

"It's different, I grant you that. I'm sorry I doubted you," Rick said.

"You're sorry you doubted me?" Chris replied. "I never thought you had a chance in hell in pulling this off. When you took off to see your friends in New York I never expected to see you again."

They both laughed as the busses slowed down and rolled to a halt before beautifully ornamented wrought-iron gates. People gasped and stared in awe at the sight of the mansion two hundred meters up the magnificent tree-lined driveway.

Rick could not believe his eyes. "Just what I thought," he said. "Our very own psychiatric clinic."

The Mount Merrian property was a twenty-acre site surrounded by trees and lush green fields and more beautiful than he remembered from the artists impression. The whitewashed late nineteenth-century mansion stood magnificently in the center of a very impressive estate. In its glory years it had been the biggest and best cotton plantation of the county, owned by the O'Malley clan, a family known for their relatively fair treatment of slaves and their generosity in helping the poor. When the last of the O'Malley clan died in the late fifties, large portions of the land were sold off to pay for the cost of setting up a foundation for the underprivileged. The house and surrounding grounds were retained as a head office. In later years the structure of the charity was changed to organizing collections and looking after the financial administration for larger charities, saving them millions on administration costs. With the O'Malley Foundation doing this work costs dropped to as little as ten percent, which meant the needy where getting a bigger share of the money supposedly collected for them in the first place.

Through the years the foundation grew into a multi-million dollar enterprise, and too large to remain in the O'Malley house. Finally they moved to a larger head office, and the estate was sold to the trust set up to control the account for the aging musicians.

The gates opened automatically, and the coaches entered the grounds followed by Kronin in his white limousine.

In the distance Rick could see the staff, nurses, assistants and kitchen help rushing out to greet the entourage. They quickly lined up in an orderly fashion as the coaches came to a halt before the grand white house.

The coach doors opened, and hordes of elderly men and women stepped out and stared in amazement at the building and the grounds. Many of these musicians had never achieved such fame or status as Rick or Robbie. Decades of touring with bands usually earned them just enough to get to the next town. No pension scheme, no official days off, no paid holidays, only a family waiting impatiently back home for the next check to arrive. To stand in front of a house like this was a dream, to actually live in it was unimaginable.

One old man sat down on the ground and wept.

"I don't believe it," the old man said as he buried his head in his hands. Another started hugging a tree, "I love you," he cried out. "I love you."

The house was indeed magnificent and beyond anything anyone could have imagined as an old folks home. It looked more like a governor's house or a millionaire's residence, with classically laid out grounds it had obviously been looked after with loving care. Behind the line of rich, green conifers that lined the driveway acres of neatly trimmed lawn, there were rose bushes and shrubs dotted throughout the grounds.

Kronin stepped out of his limousine and walked up to Rick. "This is one of the best retirement homes in the United States. And now it's all yours."

"Now I believe you," Rick said in a near whisper as his gaze swept over the front of the mansion.

Kronin gestured to a small group of people obviously waiting anxiously to shake his hand.

"These are a number of councilors from the local town who have come to welcome you to the home." Kronin said, as they all stepped up Rick. The first one to grab his hand was a tall suntanned man in his late forties wearing a dark blue tailored suit.

"We are delighted to welcome you to Mount Merrian. My name is Councilor Donavan," he said with an air of authority.

"Councilor Donavan," Kronin remarked, "is one of the people who holds control over your trust fund, along with Councilor Mannon and Councilor Labrinski." Kronin moved to one side as they reached over to shake Rick's hand.

"Very pleased to meet you." Councilor Mannon said. He was shorter then Donavan and overweight. "My dad had all your albums," he said in a jovial voice.

"And this is Councilor Labrinski." Kronin said, introducing a woman wearing a dark jacket with a red shawl all puffed up around her neck.

She shook his hand reluctantly.

"Very pleased to meet you. I'm sure you'll be very comfortable here. I know that Mr. O Malley, who died quite some time ago would have been delighted to have you here."

"Thank you your Ladyship. You're very kind." Rick replied as she quickly let his hand go. He turned away to gaze up at the house. "Now I'm here I finally believe it."

"You didn't think I was taking you for a ride, did you?" Kronin said.

"I can't imagine you did all this just to keep yourself busy." Rick said, and then turned casually away to look at the splendor of the grounds.

"I mean you did run up a lot of expenses with the concert and everything." He said with a cynical tone, followed by a self-congratulatory smile.

"You don't miss a beat, do you," Kronin remarked.

Rick turned to him and placed his hand on the shoulder and patted it gently. "It's the old guys like me that have to keep young blokes like you on your toes."

Rick's cynicism cut into Kronin. It had been nearly twenty years since anyone had spoken to him like that. Kronin turned abruptly away from Rick's hand. "Come on. I'll introduce you to the staff."

Kronin walked him towards the personnel who were lined up with military precision along the front of the house. Rick homed in on a woman marching towards them, with her arms open wide, and a beautiful warm smile. He had no idea who she was; but it was obvious she was the one running the show. Her graying dark blond hair was pinned up to perfection. In another change of clothes other than the three-piece matching suit she wore she could be anyone's sweet old grandmother. But right now she was the commander-in-chief. Rick judged her to be in her late fifties, and with a pearly pleasant smile that no doubt charmed everyone who met her.

"This is Mrs. Quinten," Kronin announced, "who will supervise the staff and the house. Mrs. Quinten has run some of the finest homes in the country."

Mrs. Quinten reached out to shake his hand.

"I'm very humbled to have been asked to take care of you and your friends," Mrs. Quinten said, "because I think it's wonderful what you did for them all. I'm so very proud to be here."

"Mrs. Quintens' father was also a musician," Kronin said aloud, as if announcing a national declaration. Rick's eyebrow rose with amused interest.

"Really," he muttered, trying to suppress his surprise. I'm afraid I can't remember any musician called Quinten. Did he work a lot?"

"Yes, he did," she said, obviously proud she could announce it to fellow musicians. "He was one of the best barbershop singers of his day."

"Barbershop?" Rick said in astonishment. He stared at her in disbelief. Of all the music styles he detested, barbershop had to be top of the list. A group of men sporting straw hats, dressed in the same ridiculous costumes, and singing in close harmony. He felt sick at the thought. Old-style jazz was another dislike, but barbershop definitely topped the bill.

"He used to perform all over the country," Mrs. Quinten continued. "He even sang at the White House and most of the Republican conventions."

"God bless America," Rick said, doing his best to force a smile.

"Unfortunately he died a number of years ago. But if he was alive today he would have loved to have joined you all here."

"And he would have been most welcome," Rick said, trying to sound as mournful as possible.

A short distance away Eva was standing next to Harlan. "I bet he was one of those boring old farty types," she whispered in his ear.

"You might have heard of him," Mrs. Quinten announced in a proud voice. "John James Quinten the third."

"Wrong Eva." Harlan muttered out the side of his mouth. "Hear that? John James Quinten the turd, a boring old shit." Eva buried her face in her hands trying to hide her laughter.

Everybody got into line behind Rick so they could also shake the hand of this wonderful woman who was prepared to look after them.

Except Harlan. For him, formalities were only for funerals, and then you'd still be pushing it. This sort of thing he could definitely do without. He picked up his saddlebag and headed into the house, unnoticed.

Rick, Kronin and Mrs. Quinten continued down the line with the rest of the introductions of the staff. They stopped before a young, well-dressed man, built like a professional body builder.

"This is Mr. Wesley." Mrs. Quinten announced as Wesley stepped forward.

"Mr. Wesley is responsible for security and heavy chores around the house, and he is also a trained medic." Wesley put his hand out to shake Rick's, but Rick did not respond. Kronin turned to find him gaping in wonder at five young women dressed in nurses uniforms. Kronin nodded a command to Wesley. Like a disciplined soldier he stepped back into line.

The nurses blushed and sniggered at the sight of Rick, staring at them, in a smiling trance. Their white uniforms were decorated with badges showing an outline of Merrian grounds placed neatly over the left breast. Rick couldn't help but trace the fine line of their white underwear under their uniforms. The nurses back at the hospital were not bad but these were babes from another planet.

"These five young ladies are trained for taking care of the elderly," Mrs. Quinten said.

"Well thanks be to Jesus for that," Rick blurted.

Kronin gently nudged Rick along to the next employee a large stocky man with apple red cheeks and a smile like a Cheshire cat.

'This is Zacharia, the cook." Mrs. Quinten said. "All the way from Moscow." Zacharia rushed past Kronin and Mrs.

Quinten and grabbed Rick's palm in both hands and shook it with incredible vigor.

"Go easy old son. That's not the neck of a chicken you've got there." Rick said. Zacharia bellowed with laughter.

"I'm sorry, mister Rick. You are funny just like my father. He was a Russian rock star. He died before our country was free. But you are a hero to him. He play your songs all the time."

Rick felt the blood draining out of his hand and joints fusing from the Russians powerful grip.

"Thank you very much pal, but if you don't let go very quickly I don't think I'll ever be able to play with myself again, let alone a guitar."

He immediately dropped Rick's hand. "I'm so sorry, very sorry. Please forgive me."

"No damage done." Rick said, while trying to shake some life back into his hand. "Great meeting you. You're just never going to see that hand again."

The cook was probably not the brightest person in the group but definitely one of the nicest. Here was an honest, down to earth, peace loving guy who would give you the world if he could. Rick knew he was going to enjoy his company.

"Thank you very much. Thank you." Zacharia said, nearly in tears. "I will never forget this meeting."

"Neither will I, son." Rick said, now massaging his hand, trying to rejuvenate the blood flow. "It was a pleasure."

CJ came up behind Zacharia and rubbed her hand up and down his neck.

"I love Russians," CJ crooned. "Some of the most wonderful men I've met were Russian."

Kronin ushered Rick along to the next in line, while the rest of the newcomers followed up behind, greeting the staff. Suddenly there was a shout coming from the back of the house and the sound of a splash.

"Oh my God," Mrs. Quinten screamed. "Someone has fallen into the pool!" She took off like a well-oiled tank, rushing past Rick and startled onlookers towards the back of the mansion. Kronin, Wesley, the staff and most of the newcomers followed quickly behind her.

Rick grabbed Chris by the cuff as they tried to keep up with the them. "Did she say pool?"

"Just the thing to continue David's therapy." Chris replied.

Rick never heard Chris's answer. He was struck by the five nurses running just in front of him. They all rounded the left west wing towards the back of the mansion. Rick passed a heavily bearded and scruffy old rocker removing his clothes along the way.

"Been waiting a month for a good bath. Now's as good a time as any."

They found Mrs. Quinten staring stupefied at Harlan, swimming with incredible ease around the large blue tiled swimming pool. Harlan flipped over onto his back and waved to the growing crowd of spectators.

"Temperature's great. Come on in." The bearded old rocker was the last to arrive. He went right up to the edge of the pool, dropped his pants and jumped in feet first. Rick, Robbie, and two other elderly men began to strip down to their underwear.

Chris stood in front of Rick, blocking his path to the pool. "What do you think you're doing Rick?"

"I'm doing what I should have done years ago. Enjoying my retirement." Rick pulled off his socks, leaving only his oversized underwear.

"You coming in?" he asked Chris.

"No I'm not."

"Then you'd better get out of my way quick because I'm coming through." After a few quickened strides Rick and Robbie jumped in with a splash.

Mrs. Quinten's clapped her hands and laughed.

"Isn't it wonderful to see people enjoying themselves so much?"

Kronin, standing next to Mrs. Quinten, calmly lit up a Havana cigar. "Looks like you've got your hands full."

Mrs. Quinten quickly composed herself. "Not at all. They're a fine bunch of men," she replied. "This is what I expected. Once they settle in and get to know the surroundings things will quieten down. Normal procedure."

They all splashed around in the pool for at least an hour before climbing out to lie in the grass and soak up the midday sun. Harlan pulled his well-worn leader cowboy hat over his eyes. Rick and Robbie lay flat out next to him.

"What do you think of it so far," Robbie asked Harlan.

"I think they must be mad to give this place to a bunch of guys like us."

"Speak for yourself," Robbie said as he turned over to sun his back.

Rick got to his feet and gathered up his clothes. "Better get checked in. I want to see the rest of this place."

"I don't think there is any checking in." Harlan replied from under his hat. "This is not a hotel."

"It's everything you want it to be mate." Rick cackled as he headed into the house while struggling to pull his tight fitting t-shirt over his head.

After inquiring at a small reception area just inside the main door, Rick was escorted up the grand stairs and down the corridor to his room by one of the nurses. The house was as immaculate on the inside as it was on the outside. Everything had been freshly painted in the original style. Cream white, soft pink and light blue dominated the color scheme. The carpet along the corridors was a deep royal red, flushed with sky blue and yellow throughout. It reminded Rick of the carpet in Kronin's office. Each of the rooms along the corridor had a number. The nurse who was guiding him to his room was just like the rest, beautiful. He couldn't take his eyes off the hypnotic contours of her body.

"Which room am I in," Rick asked.

"Room twenty-two," she replied with a smile. Rick felt his heart skip a beat. He was in love.

"Who am I sharing with?" Rick asked.

"You all have your own rooms, although in some cases there are doors adjoining the rooms next to you."

"You wouldn't happen to be in the next room would you?"

"I'm afraid not."

"What's your name?"

"Iris."

Rick leaned in close. "Did you know you have the most beautiful eyes."

"That's why my mother named me Iris," she said with a shy smile. "This will be your room." She stopped outside room twenty-two. Iris was about to open the door when Rick turned and put himself between her and the door, blocking the entrance.

Iris smiled, reached for the door knob under his arm and opened the door, placed her hands on his chest, pushed him gently backwards into the room, then delicately turned him around. Rick found himself staring at David in the wheelchair.

"David," he gasped. "Me old mate."

With great effort David raised his arm to shake Rick's hand. Rick quickly grabbed his hand and shook it eagerly. The right side of David's face lifted slightly in an effort to smile. Rick knelt down next to him, and David raised his right arm and pulled him towards him. They hugged each other closely.

"Jesus, David," Rick said, as moisture started to swell up in his eyes. He quickly wiped his eyes and took a step back. There were also tears in David's eyes.

"You're looking great. You'd hardly know there was a thing wrong with you." Rick said as he took David's hand with both hands. "You got a lot of movement back into that guitar arm of yours. Before you know it you'll be jumping around like the rest of us."

Iris rested her hand on Rick's shoulder. "We thought it would be better for your friend to have the room next to yours." An adjoining door to David's room opened and Chris appeared.

"You in there?" Rick asked.

"David's in this room next to you," Chris replied. "I'm across the hall. You should see the bath. You could fit three of us in there."

Rick climbed to his feet, and was again confronted by the shapely contours of Iris's figure.

"Three's a crowd." Rick said, and winked at Iris.

Rick's room was big and bright. Sparse, but well laid out and with a large walk-in wardrobe. Next to it was a beautiful bathroom, immaculately tiled and looking brand new. The room itself was painted white, with light gray paneling. A small radio sat on a small table next to the bed, and a flat screen TV attached to the wall the opposite side of the room.

"What do you think?" Chris asked.

"I've lived in better," Rick said. "Make a great summer home. But they don't know what they're letting themselves in for. They've gathered up the worst bunch of troublemakers you ever came across."

"Many of them are friends of yours." Chris replied.

"Don't blame me." Rick said. I'm not responsible for others. Anyway, what do you think of it here?"

Chris looked out of the window at the sprawling grounds in front of the house. "I don't think we did too badly," he said. "It's a beautiful house with acres of land to stretch your legs when you need to. I think we'll enjoy spending the rest of our days here."

"We need to drink to that." Rick said cheerfully as he grabbed David's wheelchair and headed out the door. "Let's see if we can find a cold beer."

"I'm afraid there is no beer on the premises." Iris announced.

Rick stopped dead in his tracks. "What?"

"There is no alcohol allowed in the house."

"Really?"

"House rules."

"You'll have to change that very quickly."

"Why?"

"There'll be a riot, that's why."

Rick looked down at David in the wheelchair. "Don't you agree David?" David grunted a reply.

"You hear that? He couldn't agree more." With surprising speed Rick wheeled David out of the room and down the corridor. Chris and Iris did their best to keep up.

Chapter twenty-one

A large congregation of men and women were gathered around Mrs. Quinten in the middle of the leisure room. Harry Banning, an old session-musician from Chicago stood in front of her. "It's not fair." He said, trying desperately to hold in his anger. "You have no right to treat us like children."

Harlan, standing in the entrance to the leisure room, adjusted the wet towel draped over his arm, then cut through the crowd in a beeline towards the center of the commotion.

"Mrs. Quinten, if you will pardon my interrupting." Harlan said, and smiled the smile he frequently used to swoon women half her age. She blushed. "It's not like these boys are alcoholics or anything like that, but there are very few enjoyments a man can carry into old age, if you follow my drift." Mrs. Quinten stared at Harlan, whose long loose hair now flowed over his shoulders.

Eva moved out of the crowd and stood next to Harlan. "In the other homes," she said quietly, "most of these folk have always been allowed a beer every now and then."

"And we don't intend to give up now," someone shouted from the back of the crowd. Everyone in the crowd mumbled and nodded in agreement.

"Ladies and Gentlemen," Mrs. Quinten said, gesturing everyone to calm down. "You are all such kind and wonderful people, and of course this is your home, but there are rules."

A tall elderly man with a goatee and cane got up out of a comfortable armchair in the corner of the room. "Excuse me, but may I say something?" He said in a strong Scottish accent, and approached Mrs. Quinten. Like in a bible scene, the crowd cleared a path as he gracefully made his way towards her.

An old man with a potbelly and a walking stick standing next to Harlan recognized the man with the red bow-tie.

"Hey, that's Charles Drewberry."

"The Scottish agent? What's he doing here?" Harlan asked.

"He was a musician before he became an agent." The old man replied. "Maybe that's how he got in here. He negotiated the biggest deals of the century before he took to the booze."

"I wonder if he's lost his touch," Harlan said. "And if he hasn't, our sweet Mrs. Quinten doesn't have a chance."

Dressed in a three-piece-pin-stripe suit Charles had a majestic sweeping mustache that would put a walrus to shame. With a pocket-watch in his waistcoat and the chain dangling elegantly from the pocket to the buttonhole, he carried himself with self-assured grandeur, acquired from more than forty years in the business of convincing people of his own judgment.

He marched up to her and stopped just close enough to make her feel uncomfortable and force her to look up to him. Surprisingly, instead of backing away, Mrs. Quinten held her stance.

Charles raised his cane with a distinctive sweeping gesture and addressed her as a King his servant.

"In this country you can get a drink almost everywhere. Airports, bus stations, bars, restaurants, and most of all... and where a lot of people prefer it... in the privacy of one's own home. This is now our home and you are telling all these men and women, who, for the most part legally came of age to drink liquor more than sixty years ago, are not allowed to drink in the privacy of their own home? You can't be serious."

"But there are rules."

"Yes, of course. Rules." Charles turned away from Mrs. Quinten and addressed the men and women staring at him wide-eyed. Many had heard about the great Charles Drewberry, his way with words, and his ability to slay the barons of the music industry who crossed him. But few had ever seen him in action. Now they had a ringside seat.

"Rules," Charles said in outspoken tone. "Are the basic elements that regulate a structured society and in turn keep the society structured." He paused for a second as if to test the tension.

"I suppose," Mrs. Quinten mumbled, sounding confused.

"Who made them?" He suddenly demanded, looking down at Mrs. Quinten as if he was just about to pass the death sentence.

She looked at him in total dismay. "Well..." Her words faded into thin air when she noticed all the elderly faces staring at her.

Mrs. Quinten tried to say something but nothing came out. Charles cracked the bottom of his cane sharply on the timber floor. Everyone, including Mrs. Quinten, jolted in the room.

"I said, and all the people in this room want to hear it. Who made them?"

Total silence filled the room.

Mrs. Quinten looked around at the expectant faces. "I did." She muttered.

"Well you know what to do with those rules don't you." Charles said.

"Pardon?"

"Change them." He said in a demanding voice.

"I'm afraid that's not possible."

"Do you have a father?"

"Yes, but he's passed on."

"Where did he live."

"At home. With me."

"Did he drink?"

"Yes, but not much."

"What do you mean by not much."

"Well I..."

"You had him on a quota?"

"It could get out of hand." She quickly said in defense.

Rick, who was standing in the door entrance behind David in the wheelchair, was surprised at Mrs. Quinten's sudden confession. Drewberry had broken through all her defenses. He had gone through the divisional wall of work and privacy and was now sitting in her living room, picking up all the information he needed. Charles suddenly smiled. "I think we could live with a quota," he announced to the room. Everybody except Mrs. Quinten nodded in agreement.

"I'm sure that most here need nothing more than a beer or two, or something of the equivalent on a daily basis. No excesses of course."

Anxious faces remained staring at her.

"I'll have to talk it over with the rest of the staff."

"I agree with you entirely. The quota will apply to drinking here in the lounge. Of course there will be no quota enforced in the privacy of their own rooms."

Quinten took a few steps towards the door when Charles tapped his cane gently on the floor. "We can wait." He announced. Mrs. Quinten stopped dead.

"Couldn't we do this tomorrow."

They all shook their heads.

"I'm so sorry, but at our stage in life *time* is of essence."

"I see."

"I'm sure you do," he said, and smiled.

"You realize it is not entirely up to me. I am only managing the house. There are other staff to think about."

"You said yourself you made the rules. I can't imagine you consulted the staff when you drew them up in the first place."

Mrs. Quinten turned and left the room in a quick march.

Rick went over to Drewberry with David and patted him on the back. "You haven't lost your touch, Charles. You were always one to negotiate a good contract."

"With any luck we should be drinking to that very shortly," Charles replied.

Minutes later Mrs. Quinten returned. She walked up to Charles and stopped just centimeters in front of him. Somehow it did not have the same effect.

"We agree," she said.

They all cheered. At the back of the room Jonathan, an old white-haired reggae musician, hit the button on his master blaster and the music filled the room. Jessie Colton and Stan Blake, who were sitting in the corner playing cards were joined by Jose Manzela who pulled up an extra chair and placed a bottle of tequila on the table. In other parts of the room cans of beer and bottles of liquor appeared out of pockets, from under cushions, and behind curtains.

"I propose a toast to Mrs. Quinten," Harlan announced, as he then held up his left arm which was still draped by the towel. He pulled it away to reveal two glasses of whiskey. Mrs. Quinten looked stunned. Charles took one of the glasses and bowed his head gracefully in acknowledgment.

"May she live as long as us in good health and prosperity, and to Charles Drewberry," Harlan continued raising his glass high.

"To Charles," they all shouted. "Cheers."

"Cheers me lads," Drewberry replied, bowed to the room and downed his whiskey in one go.

Chapter twenty-two

The dining room was the largest room in the building and by far the most stately. For more than a hundred years the room had entertained presidents, governors and celebrities who visited the region. it was also where the entire O'Malley clan from far and wide celebrated New Year's Eve. A tradition that came to an end when the only child, George O' Malley junior, left in 1944 on New Year's day to join the navy and was killed six months later fighting the Japanese in the Philippines. A tragedy that was the key for the family to devote themselves to charities.

In the early morning sixteen tables were laid spaciously throughout the room with eight chairs to each table. Along the wall an enormous breakfast buffet was laid out like in a four-star hotel. At the start of the table were cups, saucers, different sized plates and trays to carry everything. Then came the bacon and eggs, kept warm on hot-plates, cornflakes, muesli, fresh scones, croissants, sliced bread, butter, margarine, jam, and every other kind of breakfast topping imaginable, and at the end coffee, tea and orange juice. The old musicians lined up before three nurses who guided them to their choices and helped those unable to help themselves. Harlan, whose habit of rising at dawn never failed him, was the first in the dining room. He settled down to a sparse meal of muesli, yoghurt, and black coffee.

"Morning all," Rick announced an hour later in a cheerful voice as he pushed David into the dining room followed by Chris.

"You get a table," Rick said to Chris. David and me will put the breakfast together.

Chris went over to Harlan's table and removed a chair to make room for David's wheelchair.

Rick placed a large tray across David's arm-rests then proceeded to load it with everything he encountered along the way. By the time they reached the end of the breakfast line the tray was full to overflowing. David nervously held onto the tray with his good hand as they headed towards Chris.

"Why did you get so much," Chris asked. "We're not going to be able to eat all that."

"This is not for you. I've got to go back and get that. This is for myself and David."

"But David is on a special diet."

"I bet they're still giving him that so-called nutritious rubbish we got at the hospital. No way he's going to build up his strength on that sort of shit. What this man needs is real food." After unloading everything Rick went back to the table for Chris's breakfast. One scone, a croissant, margarine, and black coffee.

Rick cut up David's bacon and carefully fed it to him. David smiled faintly as he slowly chewed the bacon. It was when Rick soaked up the remaining liquid egg yolk with pieces of bread, and propped it into David's mouth that he really smiled.

"Not exactly the best British breakfast," Rick said. "I'll ask our Russian friend Zacharia to throw in some fried sausages and beans in tomato sauce the next time."

David smiled and nodded. The breakfast was good and hearty and second helpings were there for the taking.

Rick thought of Jenny, the waitress at Smiler's. He could imagine her standing next to the nurses, dishing up breakfast. For at least an hour Jenny would be as sweet as a lamb, and then her patience would crack. She'd have them sitting quietly in their seats while she waited their tables, and bark and yell at those who did not keep their hands to themselves. But right now she was nothing compared to the sight before his eyes. These nurses were younger, more beautiful, and would always be around whenever he needed them, day and night. Something he never could imagine with Jenny. Life had definitely taken a turn for the better.

A year ago it all seemed so different. He was in the gutter, living on booze, and never thought it would end any other way than that.

After breakfast Zacharia came around with canisters of tea and coffee, followed by a beautiful dark nurse handing out capsules to everyone in the room. She handed one to Chris.

"Your pills sir," she said.

"What is it." Chris asked, trying to read the minuscule writing on the side of the gray capsule.

"Just vitamins." She replied with a smile. "Vitamin A, which is good for the skin. Vitamin C, ascorbic acid which is for blood cell formation and bone and tissue growth, and vitamin E which is good for the nervous system."

"Sounds good to me," Chris said as he popped the capsule into his mouth, then washed it down with a glass of water. She stopped at Rick, and handed him a capsule.

"No thanks. The last time I took something like that the trip nearly wiped me off the face of the planet. Besides, my skin is beyond redemption, and I lost my nerves years ago in a fight with the wife's lawyers."

"Don't be silly," nurse said. "They're really good for you."

"Listen gorgeous," Rick said, putting his arm around her shoulder. "I have survived till now without them and I don't think they'll have any beneficial effects at this stage in life. If the others want to try them I have no objections. Is that all right with you?"

"But you also need them to keep up your strength."

"If you come up to my room tonight we'll see who needs the extra vitamins." Everyone in the room cheered at the remark, except Chris. The nurse giggled, then continued on her rounds.

"Hey superman," Harlan shouts at Rick. "What's on the agenda today?"

Rick stretched his arms and thumped his chest. "What do you say we do twenty laps in the pool followed by a quick jog around the garden."

"No problem, but at the end of the week you'll have about two people left alive in the building, and you won't be one of them." Harlan replied, as everyone in the room laughed and cheered.

After breakfast Chris wheeled David away for his daily physiotherapy. Rick headed towards the leisure room at the back of the house.

Eva sat in a corner playing her guitar and singing ballads to a group of people gathered around her. Chalky, one of the original members of Bear Tree, sat in the corner of the room doing a crossword puzzle. Fred and Bobbie, the other two members of the band, sat next to him reading a newspaper. Rick stared down at the puzzle. Chalky had three answers filled in and was working on the fourth. Rick tried to work out the encryption but quickly gave up. When he was on the street Rick tried to do crossword puzzles in old newspapers he found. The result was always zilch. He neither had the patience nor a head for it. It was one of those things you had to grow up with in an effort to make some headway. The puzzle Chalky was working on was one of the most difficult he had seen in years and carried a three thousand dollar prize.

"Looks difficult."

Chalky glanced up at Rick, smiled briefly, then returned to the puzzle.

"You won't get much out of Chalky," Fred said.

"What's wrong with him?" Rick asked.

"Nothing. He's always been like this. He never did say much." Fred replied. "Since we don't play anymore the only thing he's interested in is puzzles."

"Did he ever win anything?"

"He did once." Bobbie said. "Show him what you won Chalky."

Chalky chuckled toothlessly then pulled back his jacket to reveal a Mickey Mouse button pinned to the inside lining.

"Magic," Rick said in a near whisper.

"Yep, he's real proud of that. Not exactly first prize, but the jury got such a great kick out of the answers he sent in, they gave him the button and twenty bucks for the effort."

"Any of you play anymore?" Rick asked.

"As you can see we're all still together," Fred said, pointing to Bobbie in the armchair next to them reading a newspaper. "But we don't play anymore. Five years ago all our gear was stolen just before a gig. I didn't mind but Chalky took it bad. He accidentally left the van unlocked which meant the insurance people wouldn't cover the loss. He sort of cracked up. And you know how things are. We didn't want to replace him, so in the end we thought we were getting too old to be running around from gig to gig, then decided to draw our pensions and go for the easy life. Unfortunately that didn't turn out to be so easy after all. That's how we ended up here."

"It's good to see you guys anyway," Rick said, and then drifted further into the room. Many of the old-timers got up to shake Rick's hand, while others, too frail and weak, waved to him from the comfort of their armchairs. Rick stopped and chatted with most of them, remembering the songs they sang and the people they knew from way back when. They also brought him up to date on those who had passed away over the years. Rick was surprised to hear that so many were gone. Towering legends that not only died surrounded by their families, but also in automobile accidents, plane crashes, hospitals, gunfights, drugs, alcohol or secluded loneliness. Rick spent the entire afternoon and most of the evening drifting from one musician to the other, mostly listening.

That night he lay in his bed and stared up at the shadows on the ceiling, trying to remember the faces of lost friends.

Chapter twenty-three

Weeks passed into months as everybody settled into a life of daily routine and relaxation. There were no more conflicts with the motherly Mrs. Quinten, in fact she proved to be a real professional. The house was kept spotless and both the residents and the staff had rarely a complaint. Despite his bodyguard appearance Wesley turned out to be a useful man-about-the-house. He did most of the heavy chores and helped Mrs. Quinten with the running of the house.

Rick had never really taken notice of the drawbacks and sicknesses of old age until he saw it at such close range. Some people were still active and lively despite their age, yet saw the home as their last resting place. They had all but given up on life and subsequently had very little will to live. Their goals achieved or failed, now they waited for death itself, which resulted in some drawing themselves into a near permanent state of depression.

Relatively healthy residents who were slow on their feet received walkers. At first it showed a positive effect. They got more exercise but their dependency on the walkers grew so much their mobility and strength in general deteriorated quicker than ever. Eventually they got so dependent on the walkers they were unable to stand or walk without them.

Eight of the residents were in early or advanced stages of dementia, while a couple suffered from hallucinations. At least once a week Jimmy Drake, an old blues bass player, would arrive at the breakfast table looking tired and worn out. He complained of been kept awake the entire night by people coming to him to repair their spectacles.

At first, everybody thought that this might indeed be the case. Mrs. Quinten investigated, but none of the allegations turned out to be true. Even if it was true, it would have been impossible for him to carry out such repairs. Jimmy's hands were stiff and swollen from arthritis. His whole night of spectacle repair had been an illusion, yet so real to him he was getting physically exhausted from it.

After breakfast the reading room in the East wing became a favorite haunt, where the morning papers were split up and given to those interested in different sections. Drewberry spent most of his time scanning the financial pages. Chalky always got the funnies, and Eva waded through the obituaries.

Others went for long walks in the garden to help their digestion. Harlan took to the pool and began his daily session of fifty laps.

From early morning until late at night the pool tables in the leisure room were constantly in use. Chess and card tables were dotted around the room and in one corner there was a Nintendo game console, fitted with a pair of headphones so as not to disturb others. The adjoining fitness room had various exercise machines, a Wii sport, and weights for those active or able enough to lift them. Physiotherapy sessions were usually given by nurses in the early afternoon, either in the treatment room or private quarters.

After lunch those still interested in making music often gathered by the pool with some guitars for a relaxing jam session. Rick usually ended up jamming and dreaming up new songs with Jeff and Jonathan, old friends he had known from the early touring days in the sixties and seventies. They were also household names back then, but after so many years the gigs and the royalties dried up leaving them with nothing. Jonathan plucked on the strings, putting the last chords to his latest song.

"Hey Harlan, listen to this." Jonathan strummed the first chords on his guitar, and then sang:

"Your dreams enter my soul and I feel you.
To find someone to help you get through.."

Harlan recognized the song immediately. Jonathan had a hit with it decades ago. Two days ago he came up with another *new* song he called: After the Winter. Rick did not want to mention the fact it was another old classic, the very one that gave Jonathan recognition as a major songwriter.

"What do you think?" He asked Rick.

"Sounds great. Maybe you should release it. Make a few bucks."

"You bet," Jonathan replied, and continued to strum.

Jeff sat on a towel next to the pool with his legs crossed and concentrating heavily on finding the right cords.

"How's your song coming along Jeff?" Rick asked.

"Not bad. When it's finished I'll play it to you."

"You've been telling us that for months." Rick replied.

Jeff cursed then turned his attention back to his guitar. Since his nervous breakdown eight years ago, it was impossible for him to write a complete song. He spent four months working on the first twenty bars, after that it began to fall apart. When the frustration became unbearable he would start on a new song.

Rick got up to leave. "Got to go lads. Time for my physio," he announced.

Five minutes later he was wheeling himself through the corridor in David's wheelchair.

Halfway down the garden, Eva, wearing a long cotton dress from the sixties, and a necklace of beautiful turquoise beads strolled quietly with Robbie. Her hair was the same as it always had been, trimmed short and tidy, but it had changed over the years from jet black to a brilliant white. Fit and tanned, Robbie was dressed in neatly pressed beige cotton trousers and a short-sleeved shirt.

"Bet you didn't think you'd end up here," Eva said.

"It's quite nice actually. It's still better than living in a house with strangers."

"At least we lived to tell the tales. Not like some of our generation. We did bury a lot of friends didn't we." Eva said, shaking her head.

"Look at the life we have had. It's been fabulous. Even with all the shit in-between we still had a great life."

"I don't know," Eva replied. "Those shitty parts I didn't enjoy at all. I've been meaning to ask, and I hope you don't mind but why didn't you pay for all this? You have the money. I heard you gave millions to your own charity, so why not this?"

"Had the money," Robbie said, correcting her immediately. "You're right, it's true. But then the responsibility of all this would rest on my shoulders, and if that had been the case I could never have lived here. I'm retired, remember?" Eva smiled.

Along the way they encountered Chris, pacing back and forth and looking troubled.

"You all right, Chris?" Eva asked.

"There's nothing wrong with me," he answered irritably.

"Something up with David?" Robbie asked.

"He was coming along all right. But lately he hasn't been making much progress at all. I think his condition is getting worse and he'll get another stroke. I'm worried they'll send him back to the rehabilitation center."

"What does Rick think?" Eva asked.

"Don't talk to me about him," he said angrily.

"He hardly ever sees David these days. Claims he can hardly walk himself. Borrows his wheelchair when David's having his afternoon rest and wheels himself around like a cripple. He even gets physiotherapy three times a week. To keep the circulation going he says. He's getting it right now."

Rick lay naked on his back in his room. The door was locked. Nurse Iris was also naked, and sitting on top of him. Slowly she rhythmically moved her hips back and forth. He moaned. She leaned over and pulled his face into her large breasts. He moaned even more.

"How's the circulation Rick?"

"You just keep pumping and the circulation will hold it there for at least another half hour."

"Really?" Iris said and sat once again upright and increased the rhythmic action. "I've got other things to do today. Let's speed things up a bit." Rick cupped her breasts with both hands and moaned even louder.

"Please Lord. Don't take me right now."

"Are you Ok?" Iris asked, sounding worried.

"Yep, no problem. But if I die, I'll die a very happy man."

Iris laughed. "I think you'll survive."

"I hope so. There's no way I could get to do this in a box six feet under."

The leisure room was quiet and relaxed. Some of the men and women read newspapers or magazines, while others stared blankly out the windows. The radio was turned down low. In a deep armchair next to a window, lyricist Jack Hammer's head bobbed peacefully up and down as he fell in and out of his midday snooze. Directly across from him his old writing partner Burt Banner, who sat quietly reading a book. He was a small tanned man who as far as anyone could remember was always dressed in golfing slacks and white runners,.

Suddenly Jack woke up with a jolt. "What time you got," he shouted across to Burt.

In no great hurry Burt lowered his newspaper and squinted at the minuscule dial on his watch. "Going on four."

"Will someone turn up the radio?" Jack croaked. "Golden oldies is on."

Fred, sitting next to Chalky, leaned towards the radio and switched on the radio. The presenter bellowed throughout the room, which had now come back to life.

"Thank you for joining us for another hour of golden oldies. Today we are going to kick off the program with a famous golden oldie from nineteen sixty-four. Do you remember this?"

The rhythmic music of "The Last Dance" echoed throughout the room. They all rocked in their chairs.

"Hey Benny," Jack shouted, "it's one of yours."

Benny James stopped his pool game and bowed to Burt and Jack. "Thank you for the kind recognition gentlemen." Benny bowed once more then returned to his pool game. Wesley, who was helping ninety-three-year-old Karl Rivers to his chair did not recognize the tune.

"So that was a big hit in your day?" Wesley asked.

"Sure was, Wesley old pal," Benny said proudly. "Sold over three million."

Wesley's face lit up. "Must have made you a fortune."

"It paid the expenses." Benny replied.

Wesley whistled. "I wish I had expenses like that."

"Tell him about the others, Benny." Jack yelled.

Wesley was stunned. "Others?"

Benny tried to get back to his pool game but surrendered to all the old faces around him urging him on.

"Oh, it's nothing." Benny said, trying to shy it off, then turned to concentrate setting up another shot on the table.

Wesley eased Karl into his armchair and turned to Benny. "No come on, tell me. I'm really interested."

Jack climbed out of his chair and hobbled over to Wesley.

"Mr. Benny Robinson had fifteen hits. Sold millions worldwide."

"Come on you guys, give it up." Benny said, trying to line up another ball.

"What? Really? Wow." Wesley's said in surprise.

"That's a fact." Jack said. "Ain't that right, Benny. Seventeen million worldwide."

Benny gave up on the pool. "I know what you're up to," Benny said. "Stop winding the kid up. Yes, I sold a few million records. But nothing compared to you. The both of you sold at least three times that much."

Wesley looked on in shock. "Is that true?' He asked.

"It's true, all true," Jack replied, as modestly as possible.

"Then what are you doing here?" Wesley asked Benny.

"You were a tramp when we picked you up. You could own this place."

"It's all gone son, all gone."

"On what? Where?

Benny smiled a toothless smile. "On sex and drugs and rock and roll," he hollered proudly, and a cheer went up in the room.

"But what about the royalties? They still play that song a lot."

"I played the music. I didn't write the songs. The man who wrote that and the others is long dead, young man."

"Shit?" Wesley said. "What did he die of?"

Benny threw his arms up high and screamed. "OF SEX AND DRUGS AND ROCK AND ROLL!" Another loud cheer went up in the room.

Rick came in.

"How's the circulation, Rick?" Jack asked.

"Found the spot. Haven't done any physio in years. But once you get a good warm up the circulation just about works on its own."

"You dirty old rat," Jack said, as others in the room tried to hide their laughter. Rick smiled, then turned and headed out to the back garden.

The air outside was warm and humid and the sun shone in a clear blue sky. Rick stood on the verandah and surveyed the grounds before him. In the distance the gardeners trimmed back the shrubbery. Jeff and Jonathan were at the pool. plucking away on their guitars. Eva and Robbie were in the distance, walking around the grounds. Others sat either in wheelchairs or comfortable cushion-laden wicker chairs drinking ice tea or lemonade. To the left he could see something that looked like someone's shoe, sticking out from behind a large bush. Suddenly it disappeared. Then he noticed a shadow of a figure crouched down behind the same bush. It looked like Chris but he could not be sure. As he strolled over he saw David sitting in his wheelchair with Chris crouching down next to him.

"Chris? Are you all right?"

Chris crept out from behind the greenery. "No problem. I dropped something and I was just looking for it."

"Did you find it?"

"Ehm. I did yes. Thanks for asking."

"You're not trying to avoid me, are you?"

"Don't be stupid," Chris replied.

Rick squatted down in front of David in the wheelchair. "How's it going' mate?"

"He's all right," Chris replied. "But he doesn't seem to be improving as much as he was a month ago."

Chris was right. The last couple of months David did not seem to be making much progress. The doctors had done all they could. Because of this Rick had found it more and more difficult to express himself to David. Nothing could remove his feeling of guilt about leaving him alone with Barney, Stanley, and Harry. If he had been there when the first hemorrhage occurred David would probably not be in such a state. He had let down the only friend he ever really had, and that hurt more than anything. The David he had known as friend, musician, was gone. He found it extremely difficult to relate to the shell of him in the wheelchair in front of him. Even finding it more painful to look him in the eye.

David jerked his head towards Rick and stared at him blankly. A dribble of phlegm ran down his chin.

"He can say a few words though," Chris said, trying to be cheerful. "Can't you, David. Go on say something to Rick." David tried to say something but it was incomprehensible. He quickly gave up, then began to rock back and forth in the chair.

"I think he wants you to come closer," Chris said.

Rick hunched down in front of the wheelchair. David tried again. He only made grunting sounds.

"Are you sure he's all right? He's not having another attack or something like that is he?"

"No, he's all right. I've seen this before."

David rocked again. Rick was perplexed.

"R...R...R...Rick." David slurred with great effort.

"Christ, he said it. He said my name. Did you hear that? Yeah David, me old mate, it's me. You're going to be all right, pal. We'll look after you proper now. Anything you want mate."

David rocked once again in the chair.

"He wants to tell you something."

Rick leaned in closer. "What is it, David? Tell me."

"Ffffuuuck offfff!" David screamed. Rick fell back from the wheelchair and rolled on the ground roaring with laughter, slamming the grass with his hand. David rocked and reeled in the chair with laughter. Chris also roared with laughter, as he doubled over the wheelchair clamping his crotch with his hand.

"Please, I can't hold it." Chris cried. Rick fell over on his side, still laughing.

When Rick finally opened his eyes, moist from all the laughter, Mrs. Quinten stood next to him, looking at him rolling around in the grass.

"What is going on here?"

The sight of her was just too much. He roared out another bellow of laughter, and continuously slapped the ground screaming. Unexpectedly, she did not storm off, but remained staring at the three of them, waiting for an answer. Rick climbed to his feet and did his best to compose himself.

"Mrs. Quinten, you're a fine woman." He said, and rested his hand on her shoulder. She looked at it with contempt. He quickly removed it. "And David wants to tell you something."

"Oh, no," Chris moaned, then dropped to his knees behind the wheelchair, trying to conceal his laughter.

"Yes David, what is it you want to tell me?"

David, doubled over, quickly sat up straight, and shouted in Mrs. Quinten face. "Fuck off."

Rick roared with laughter and fell to the ground once again. David, his face lifting on one side from the laughter slipped out of the chair, and fell on top of Rick. Mrs. Quinten stared in disgust at the three old men going to pieces before her.

"I didn't think you could be so childish," she said, and stormed off.

Their laughter continued and could be heard all around the grounds.

Chapter twenty-four

The golden oldie show was still on the radio in the lounge.

"And let us go back to nineteen fifty-eight. A singer who achieved his seventh hit in that decade," the dj announced.

"Shut up, you old fart," Jack moaned. "We know that. Just play the goddamn music."

"And the name of the singer is..." The first note rang out of the speaker."

"Little Archie," Jack shouted.

"Little Archie," The dj repeated.

"Ten points for us." Jack said.

"And the song is..."

"Twist on Fire, dickhead."

"Twist on Fire," the presenter repeated.

Burt scanned the room. "Where is Archie? He used to do this number all the time. He'll want to hear this."

"He was here a minute ago. Somebody give Archie a shout."

"Hey Archie." Jack shouted.

Archie came out of the kitchen licking some cream off his fingers. "Where's happening brothers?"

"Listen." Jack turned up the volume once again.

"Hey, that's my song. I haven't heard it in years."

Archie shuffled and twisted to the music across the floor towards the piano. They cheered him on. Zacharia came out of the kitchen to watch. Archie flipped open the piano and started to sing in sync to the record. Everybody in the room started to clap to the music. Charles Drewberry remained comfortably in his usual armchair while tapping his cane on the floor to the beat.

Zacharia helped one of the old ladies out of her chair and started to jive with her.

Suddenly Mrs. Quinten entered the room. "Gentlemen," she yelled sharply. "Where on earth do you think you are?"

"At home," Little Archie shouted back. "You wouldn't expect me to do this anywhere else would you? I'd get arrested if I did."

They all laughed. Little Archie continued to play. Mrs. Quinten rushed over to the radio, switched it off then turned on Zacharia.

"You shouldn't be encouraging this sort of thing. It's bad enough as it is. If I catch you at this once more you are out." She stormed out of the room.

"Watch out, Zacharia, "Jack said. "She's starting to show her true colors."

"She doesn't scare me."

"Maybe not. But you're no good to us without a job," Jack replied.

Wesley was working on the administration in his small office at the back of the house when Mrs. Quinten stormed in and slammed the door. He had seen her in a bad mood before, but now she was really seething.

"Is everything ok?" Wesley asked.

"No. Everything is not ok."

It took her nearly a minute to compose herself, then she finally settled down into the chair across from Wesley. "These people are worse than a bunch of children, and they are getting out of hand. I want you to increase the doses in the vitamin capsules," She said in a quiet firm voice.

"Do you think that's wise?"

"They will get whatever is necessary. I do not intend to let them get out of control and start going crazy in the house, especially when our new guests arrive." She got up and left the room before Wesley could object.

Rick spent the rest of the day with David, pushing him all around the grounds and telling him about what happened when he found him with Barney, Harry and Fred, and the hospital. David seemed to comprehend it all, although he was quiet and withdrew into his shell when told about Preston, the trouble he had got into, and the clinic he was in. Later they took refuge from the sun under a giant oak at the back of the grounds. David lay slumped to one side of his chair snoring, while Rick lay flat out on the grass next to him in a deep sleep.

In the weeks that followed Rick had more contact with David and Chris. They would go for daily walks around the grounds, but he still borrowed David's wheelchair at least three times a week. The only big changes in the house were the proposed cuts Mrs. Quinten had ordered. She reduced the amount of gardeners from four to two, and cut back the hours of Zacharias' assistant cook. Visits to hospitals by the residents were made in automobiles belonging to the home rather than hiring taxis. The mood in the house mellowed even more. Fewer people took to walking in the garden, and the leisure and games rooms quietened down considerably. More and more people took to spending more time in their rooms.

The first death of one of the residents was Mike Durrow. One of the few musicians to make his name in jazz, and then an equally successful career in R&B. He died peacefully in his sleep. Three weeks later Roy Fuller died of a heart attack an hour after breakfast. Roy was one of the few people who remained active right up to the day of his death. Every morning before breakfast he jogged two laps around the grounds of the house. After evening meals he preferred to spend his time working out in the gym. Everybody in the house believed he would live to be a hundred. Roy was seventy-five.

The high point for just about everyone in the home was dinner. Zacharia was not a bad cook and for many residents his meals were the best they had had in years. For others they were a time to get around the table with old friends and joke about times gone by.

Zacharia wheeled in a large trolley. Rick clapped his hands and rubbed them enthusiastically at the sight of the large steaming pots heading towards him.

"What have we got today, Zacharia."

"Your favorite mister Rick, Hungarian goulash."

Rick's enthusiasm suddenly disappeared. "Christ, not again. That's the third time this week."

"Mrs. Quinten told me I have to keep the costs down mister Rick. Anyway I thought you liked my goulash."

"Zacharia, I like it so much it's the first thing I see every the morning when I go to the toilet."

Robbie leaned back in his stool and closed his eyes as if going into a deep trance. "How about a nice Madras curry," Robbie said. "With boiled rice, and Chapatti's."

The old rockers look at each other in despair and moaned.

"What I wouldn't give to have that right now," Harlan said. "The only problem is that all the sewage pipes would be blocked up for a month."

Jack Hammer smacked his lips, and his eyes glazed over.

"An Italian Lasagna about six inches thick," he said. "Covered in melting Gruyere cheese, with a bottle of Vin du Rhone to supplement the taste buds."

"Sorry, people," Zacharia said. "Hungarian goulash is all I have to offer."

Rick put his napkin to one side and got up from the table. "Anyone for a burger, French fries and a milkshake?"

"Thought you'd never ask," Benny James shouted. He searched through his pockets, pulled out some scraps of paper, and waved them in the air. "I've got three vouchers for a happy meal."

Burt and four others stood up. "Think they will give us a group discount?" Burt asked.

"Maybe," Rick replied. "We could always give it a try. They do it sometimes for the kids and besides, according to some people, and I'm not mentioning any names, we're no different."

"Let's go for it," Burt said.

Bobbie, who had been sitting quietly in the corner pulling on the long strands of his beard, got up and headed for his room. "I'm not in the mood. I'm off to bed." As he disappeared out the door, Big John, one of the oldest people in the home climbed steadily to his feet. "Me too," he mumbled. Bobbie took him by the arm and guided him out of the dining room. Big John who was once a six-feet-eight inch towering human being, was now withered and bent and looked like a walking fossil.

Rick looked up at a disappointed Zacharia. "Sorry son, I think you better do something about that menu."

Without uttering another word or showing his usual cheerfulness, Zacharia dished out the goulash to those who stayed.

Chapter twenty-five

The following day Eva sat in the corner of the recreation room playing her guitar and singing a ballad. The group gathered round her was much smaller than in previous months. Chalky sat as usual in the corner of the room doing his puzzle. The television was turned down, and those sitting around it did not seem to be watching it. With great effort Ray Barker, one of her most loyal followers, pulled himself out of his chair, tucked his hands into the pockets of his frayed dark brown cardigan, then headed for the door.

"I'm sorry Eva, but I'm off to bed," he groaned. I need to lie down before I fall down."

Eva looked on saddened. "Are you OK Ray," Eva asked.

"I'm fine sweetheart. Your music is as beautiful as ever but I need to rest these old bones a little more these days, that's all."

Ray was one who always cheered her on and sing along to her songs. Always the spark of life itself. Now he looked half the man he was when she first came to Mount Merrian.

"Me too," Fred replied, and got up out of his chair. "I'm beat."

Fred followed Ray out the door. Eva turned to the remaining few, all asleep. They always listened to her ballads. For the first time since she arrived the room was totally lifeless. It reminded her of her life in St. Brigit's. Disappointed, she put away her guitar and left.

Except for some laughter coming from Rick's bedroom the entire house was perfectly still that evening. Rick sat at his table with Robbie, Harlan, and Chris playing poker. Much to the disappointment of the others he was on a winning streak and showed another full house to prove it. He threw down his cards and pulled in his winnings.

"Mine, all mine."

Harlan looked at the dollar notes being pulled in towards Rick. "How do you do it, Rick?"

"Cunning and bluff. Something I learned to perfect with my last ex."

Robbie pulled some extra dollars from his wallet. "And I suppose now you're trying to regain all the money you lost in the divorce."

"What did she cost you anyway?"

"Sixty mil. The lawyers, ten. The lawsuits brought by my company directors trying to gain control of my companies, forty. The lawyers who tried to prevent that, three. I paid another two mil in bribes trying to prevent it all but that disappeared down a black hole."

"Just like our money," Chris said, looking gloomily at the pile of cash in front of Rick.

Suddenly they heard the sound of a crash from another room. They charged out into the corridor just in time to see Ray rush into Big John's room.

"Quick someone." Ray shouted. "Big John has collapsed." They rushed into the room as Ray pressed the emergency button next to the bed. Rick, Chris and Harlan did their best to try and lift Big John back onto the bed, but his length and weight made it impossible. Nurses Iris and Sadie rushed in with Wesley pushing a portable medical unit. Wesley grabbed Big John with little effort and lifted him onto the bed. Rick and the others stood outside the open door.

Iris listened for a heartbeat. "I'm getting an erratic heartbeat. I think we've got an SCA."

"Sadie, CPR quick." Wesley shouted. Sadie immediately began to give mouth to mouth resuscitation while Iris ripped open Big John's shirt.

"I wish they'd speak in plain English so I'd know what's happening." Rick said.

"CPR is cardiopulmonary resuscitation," Chris said. "I used to see this all the time in the hospital. They have to keep oxygenated blood flowing to the vital organs such as the heart and brain. An SCA is sudden cardiac arrest. Big John's just had a heart attack."

Wesley quickly set up the defibrillation unit and placed the pads on Big John's chest. He checked the readings then shouted "Stand clear." There was a thump and Big John's body jumped from the spasm.

Iris quickly replaced her stethoscope, searching for life.

"He's still fibrillating," she said.

"Another", Wesley shouted. Big John's body jumped again as the electrical shock tried to jolt his erratic heart rhythm back to a normal heart beat. Nurse Sadie listened again.

"Nothing. I'm not getting any heart beat at all."

"Stand back." Wesley said as he put down the pads, placed his hands on his chest and started pumping while nurse Sadie kept up the resuscitation. They kept this up for a good five minutes. Sadie listened for a heartbeat once again.

"Nothing. He's gone."

"Shit!" Shouted Wesley. He was out of breath and sweating profusely.

An hour later, Chris, Harlan, Rick and Robbie sat around the poker table. A half empty bottle of whiskey stood in the middle. All their glasses were filled and they held them high in a toast.

"Here's to Big John," Rick said. "It was a pleasure knowing him."

"To Big John," they all replied, then emptied their glasses in one.

"He was a great artist." Harlan said, staring into the small shot glass he held in his hand.

"How many hits did he have?" Rick asked.

"About two or three," Harlan replied.

"Great songs," Rick said

"Classics," Robbie said.

"How did they go," Rick asked.

"I honestly can't remember," Harlan replied.

Rick and Chris tried to hum one of his songs, without success. Their humming finally faded. Finally they sat in silence, staring blankly at the cards on the table in front of them.

Harlan broke the silence once again. "Haven't seen your buddy Kronin around for a while."

"He's had his pickings," Rick said. "I don't think we'll see him around again." He looked to Chris for confirmation.

"What do you think Chris?"

"I wouldn't know," Chris replied.

"I wonder who the new people will be," Robbie asked.

"Yeah, I heard about that. Maybe Mrs. Quinten will move in a barbershop singer," Harlan mocked.

"If she does I'm off. Who are these new people anyway?" Rick asked.

"I don't know," Robbie said. Usually we get the names of the people who are coming in advance, but this time nothing."

"Not to worry, we'll see." Rick said. "Hope they play lead guitar. I was thinking of putting another band together."

"Big John played great guitar. He was a great guy," Harlan muttered.

"He was the third this month," Rick replied.

"It's still better than dying on the street." Chris said.

Rick poured everybody another round. "Only we didn't seem to be dying so quick out there."

"People die a lot quicker than you think," Chris said. At the hospital I've seen thousands of people die."

Rick disappeared into the bathroom and pulled a six-pack from his half-full bath. "But this is not a hospital, and besides, me and David left the hospital through the front door."

Rick broke open the six-pack and placed the beer in front of him. "Okay, the hospital's an exception," Chris went on. "But there are more than eighty very old men and women living here under the same roof. For most of us death is just around the corner. This is not a kindergarten. Three deaths up 'till now I wouldn't think is above average."

Rick pointed his finger at Chris. "You won't be saying that when your turn comes."

Big John's body remained in the room the entire night. The following morning a long line of fellow musicians lined up to pay their respects. Finally, Rick and Chris watched Big John's body being placed on the stretcher and wheeled out of his room and down the corridor.

An hour later Fred, Bobbie and CJ entered Rick's room. Fred took a small empty bottle out of his pocket.

"I found this in Big John's locker. I think it had something to do with his death."

Rick took the bottle and sniffed its contents. "If that had something to do with his death you'd better get the nurses back up here right away. Its whiskey and we've been having more than our fair share of the stuff."

CJ took a small metal sweet box out of another pocket. "I also found this." She opened it up. They all stared at the capsules inside.

Chris took one out, put on his reading glasses, and tried to read the small writing on the capsule. "These are our vitamins."

"Big John never bothered to take them so he put them away," CJ said. "yesterday he was feeling a little weak so I told him to take the vitamins. I know he washed them down with the whiskey."

"Don't be stupid," Chris said shaking his head. "You can't overdose on vitamins. You said yourself he was feeling poorly, and we all have to go in the end. Big John's time was up."

Rick took one of the capsules out of the box and studied it carefully.

Chapter twenty-six

New residents to Mount Merrian always created an air of expectancy. Friends and fellow musicians who were supposedly long dead or never heard from in decades would suddenly be announced by Mrs. Quinten, long before their arrival. A rush of excitement would sweep through the home. Stories and gossip about them would be dragged up from the deep and hyped to a frenzy. This time however, Mrs. Quinten only announced the arrival of the new guest by posting a small notice on the board in the entrance hall just shortly before her expected arrival. The name was Mrs. Orland, and nothing more. This puzzled the entire house. No one had ever heard of a musician called Mrs. Orland, or even a Mr. Orland.

Rick browsed through yearbooks on American and British musicians in the library but found nothing relating to the name Orland. Maybe she was connected to another genre of music such as classical or jazz. A category difficult to check because they had only one reference book from each of those sectors, which only covered the most successful performers. As far as Rick was concerned she could have been playing the organ in a church. There was no way of knowing.

Mrs. Quinten had erected an air of silence, refusing to give any information on the mysterious Mrs. Orland, claiming invasion of privacy. A point that hadn't stopped her before, since she was always the first to receive files on the musicians' careers she was usually the one who supplied most of the information up front. Many times she relished being able to provide more information than any of the patrons in the home. This brought a sense of distaste to most, but fed the curiosity of those interested.

The day of Mrs. Orland's arrival the atmosphere was inquisitive and in some cases enthusiastic. Musicians who had rooms at the front of the house overlooking the drive organized extra seating and refreshments for others who wanted to view the new resident. Rick sat in Chris's room together with Robbie, Harlan and David.

At three o'clock sharp a taxi pulled up outside the mansion. The driver helped Mrs. Orland out of the cab. Rick judged her to be in her seventies. She was dressed in a fur coat and weighed down with expensive jewelry. With great effort the driver unloaded three large trunks from the cab. Mrs. Quinten, followed by nurse Iris and nurse Sadie, rushed out to meet her.

"Right on time, Mrs. Orland."

"Yes I am, aren't I. I just couldn't wait. What a beautiful building." She marveled at the grand structure before her. Rick and many of the residents who hung out of the windows to get a better look at the newcomer drew back as Mrs. Quinten scanned the building.

"It is so much like my dear father's home many years ago."

"Really, how nice," Quinten replied. "Well I'm sure you'll feel right at home here."

"Thank you very much. I'm sure I will."

Hiding behind a long drape Rick stared down at Mrs. Orland. He couldn't imagine her ever playing an instrument or singing in a band. Maybe it was her husband, but spouses only had the right to get in with their partner. If the partner was deceased, they were also refused entry. Different genres of music were not an issue any more, as long as it was not barbershop.

"I hope she's at the wrong place," Rick said to Harlan while ducking in and out of the window trying to avoid Mrs. Quinten's eagle eyes.

"Doesn't look like it," Harlan replied.

"If you will follow me," Mrs. Quinten said, as she rushed Mrs. Orland, flanked by the two nurses, towards the entrance and into the house. "I'll show you directly to your room." Quinten continued. "One of the nurses will be happy to help you unpack your things." They were half way into the lift in the lobby when Mrs. Orland noticed some of the residents sitting in the leisure room, listening to the radio.

"Oh. There are some of the other residents. Maybe I could go in and introduce myself."

"Could we possibly do that later. They are listening to one of their favorite programs. I wouldn't like to disturb them."

"What a pity," she said as Mrs. Quinten hurried her into the lift and up to a room in the little used east wing of the great house.

Jack and Burt huddled around the radio listening to the Golden Oldies program. The presenter introduced the next record.

"This one goes back to nineteen seventy-one. Do you know who this is?"

We hear a female voice sing "Tonight your mine…"

"Carol King." Jack and Burt shout, and throw their arms up in the air to give each other a high five.

"Whatever happened to Carol? Burt asked. Jack scratched his head.

"No idea. For all I know she could be upstairs with Rick.

"Don't think so, she was never his type."

Rick walked along the trees that lined the walkway down the center of the garden. The rest of the grounds were littered with a rich mixture of Conifers, Poplar, Birch, Cedar and Willow, giving everything a look of serenity and peacefulness.

Rick was looking for Steve. At this time of day he knew exactly where to find him. He pulled back a branch under a weeping willow at the back of the garden to find him smoking his favorite blend of tobacco laced with marijuana. He handed the enormous joint to Rick as he sat down next to him against the tree trunk.

"Thanks, Steve, I sure need it." Rick inhaled deeply.

"Have my own supply. Nephew sends it up from California." Rick slowly released the tobacco from the depth of his lungs. His eyes were closed. He relished the moment.

"Can I put in an order," he finally said.

"No problem."

"You know a little about drugs don't you."

"True. Before I got into music I was heading for a career as a chemist. And after I got into music I made the best brain busters in the business."

Rick took a few capsules out of his pocket and gave to Steve. "Think you could find out what's in these?"

Steve studied the capsules. "These are our vitamins," he said promptly.

"That's what it says on the outside. I'm not sure what's on the inside." Rick replied.

Steve opened the capsule and tasted a sample on the tip of his tongue.

"Seems okay to me, but what you really need is a lab test. My nephew might be able to help you out. He's got lots of equipment that beeps and farts and squeaks and can analyze everything down to the very last atom."

"If that's no problem then I'll leave them with you," Rick said as he dropped the rest of the capsules into Steve's hand, then leaned back against the tree trunk to enjoy the effects of the joint.

"I didn't know you were going to be a chemist."

"It's true, but I couldn't get away from the music and the women and the fun of it all."

"Those were the days," Rick said. "Back then everyone was an expert on drugs. We tried everything, didn't we? Kids these days don't know shit. We were doing speed and acid and plenty of these little stickies in between." Rick said, holding up and admiring the joint. "We used to enjoy our drugs. Most of us knew when to stop, or in any case use them in moderation. But you never gave up the joints."

"This?" Steve said as he held up the joint. "A few of shots of bourbon will buzz you a helluva lot more than this ever will, and that stuff is legal."

"Too true," Rick said, as he rested his head against the bark of the tree and closed his eyes. His thoughts went back to the hobos down at the harbor and he wondered if they were still there. He missed the drinking sessions and the insults. But that was about all. This was now home.

Gossip around Mrs. Orland ceased the next morning when she stood in the middle of the dining room and introduced herself to all the residents.

"My name is Mrs. Orland and I'm so happy to be here with you."

"And we are so happy to have you here with us," Eva replied with a broad smile. "But we have never heard of you in the music business. Did you sing or play an instrument?"

"Well, I can play a little piano," she said as everybody listened and nodded in agreement. "But I'm not a musician."

"Oh," Eva said with a smile. "Then your husband was a musician?"

"Well actually he was a garage owner in Illinois. I'm afraid he didn't play anything at all. After he died I went to live living with my daughter and son-in-law's family in Orange County. But that didn't work out. During the past year I have moved from one retirement home to another across three different states. I never really fitted into any of them. You see I'm still very active and try to keep up with everything that was going on in the world.

"We're pleased to hear that." Eva replied.

"Thank you." Mrs. Orland said.

Although she was not a musician everyone in the room seemed to relax and welcome her immediately.

"But," she continued, "after reading the advertisement in the newspaper about Mount Merrian I knew I had found exactly what I was looking for. It's expensive, but cashing in my husbands shares and bonds will be enough to finance my stay for the rest of my days.

"Advertisement?" Rick suddenly said.

"Yes," she replied. "I feel so lucky."

At that moment everyone went silent in the room. Eva got up then guided her over to the breakfast bar.

"Come, let me help you get some breakfast."

Rick stared at her in amazement. This was supposed to be a closed facility open for retired musicians only. Now, advertisements seemed to be floating around opening up the home to anyone who cared to apply. Which meant that Mrs. Orland was definitely not the last non-musician who would be coming to Mount Merrian. Why had they not been told? What was the reason behind it? Something very strange was going on, and he was going to find out what that was.

After a few days the commotion around Mrs. Orland settled down. She mixed in with the residents better than anyone had imagined. She even spent time pushing David in his wheelchair around the gardens, telling him all about her life as a dutiful housewife and about her children growing up. David seemed to listen intently, although no one really knew if he could follow it all.

After dinner Rick made his daily trip to Steve at the back of the garden to relax and have a few puffs of his joint. They sat discussing Mrs. Quinten and days gone by. Usually they ended up comparing ex-wives and difficulties between the IRS in the US and the good old fashioned British taxman. They also discussed Mrs. Orland and the possibilities of things to do. An hour later, Rick left Steve to smoke the rest of his joint and watch the sun set in the West.

When he entered the leisure room he was still smiling from the effects of the marijuana. But his smile disappeared as he viewed the sight. What used to be a hive of activity now resembled a morgue. Only a couple of old men reading, others dozing in their armchairs.

Time for short sharp jolt. He took a small paper bag out of his pocket blew it up then burst it. The loud bang went like a shock through all the room.

"Wake up everybody!" Rick shouted. "It's like a cemetery in here."

Drewberry, who was reading a newspaper, stared at Rick over the rim of his reading glasses. "Have you been taking something, me lad?" He asked, sounding like a school principle.

"Hardly touched it." Rick replied, then continued through the leisure room and into the kitchen.

"Where's me old mate Zacharia."

Zacharia was bent over the sink, scrubbing some pans. Sweat rained out of every pore in his body as he viciously attacked the charred bottom of a soup pan.

"Everything all right my son?" Rick asked.

"This is penalty of leaving pan on a low flame while listening to rockers talking about their past after main evening meal. This is punishment for such enjoyment. Rick, you come to help?"

"Don't be ridiculous. I'd have a heart attack doing that job. But I hate to see a man suffer. Give me that steel brush and pan and let me at it."

"No, I was only joking."

"Come on, give me the pan."

Rick tried to grab the pan out of Zacharias' hand. Zacharia held it in the air with one hand while he held Rick back with the other. They laughed and screamed at one another while Rick made mock attempts to retrieve the pan. Finally, after trying to dodge Rick in a cat-and-mouse chase around the oven in the center of the kitchen, Zacharia receded. He collapsed into a chair in the corner of the kitchen and handed Rick the steel brush and pan.

"It's yours," he said, totally out of breath.

Rick stood next to him half bent over panting, trying to catch his breath.

"Too late. You've finished me off. Just leave it there and I'll come back and do it tomorrow."

Zacharia rolled back with laughter and slapped Rick hard on the back. "You so funny, mister Rick. You really don't have to. It's my job and I don't mind doing it, especially when I know whom I'm doing it for. But let me get something for your thirst after all this running around." Zacharia opened the gigantic fridge in the corner of the kitchen and took out two beers, and handed one to Rick.

"To the Bolsheviks," Rick toasted.

"Yes, to the Bolsheviks," Zacharia shouted. "The bastards." The bottles chinked as they laughingly toasted a salute. After downing half the bottle Rick looked up towards the ceiling and belched loudly. Zacharia laughed heartedly.

"God", Rick says, through a second belch. "I needed that. Listen I wanted to ask you if you know anything about the new arrival, Mrs. Orland. She's a nice old soul but she's not a musician. I've heard that there are advertisements floating around, inviting all sorts of people to come and live in Mount Merrian. What's Quinten really up to? Do you know what's going on?"

"The morning Mrs. Orland arrived," Zacharia replied. "Mrs. Quinten told us that the new people pay a lot of money to get in here. She talked about turning this into one of the most elite retirement homes in the country. Not mention anything about musicians. That is all I know."

"Ok. Thanks mate," Rick said, patting him on his massive shoulder. "You know Orland might be the first non-musician to reside in Mount Merrian, but she is not going to be the last. Why does Quinten want to turn this into an elite retirement home? Are there no more rockers out there in need of a home? Are they all dead?

"I really don't know mister Rick."

"We're going down a one way street here, sunshine. In a couple of years there'll only be a few of us left. Mount Merrian as a home for retired musicians could eventually disappear. We have to do something about this, Zacharia. Could you try and find out some more for me?"

"Yes, mister Rick, of course I will." They finished off another beer, then Rick went cruising for Iris. He felt badly in need of a massage.

Chapter twenty-seven

The wait for new arrivals did not take long. A week after Mrs. Orland arrived, a limousine pulled up to the front of the house. The only difference between these new arrivals and Mrs. Orland was that no announcement had been posted on the notice board informing anyone of their arrival. Only Wesley and one of the nurses were aware of the newcomers. Zacharia and the rest of the staff were kept in the dark.

Mrs. Quinten, Wesley and a nurse rushed out to greet them as the driver pulled up to the main entrance. With help from Wesley and the driver, the two elderly newcomers stepped briskly out of the limo and into the late afternoon sun before the great mansion.

"Mr. Underwood, Mrs. Edwards, welcome to Mount Merrian." she announced. "I'm Mrs. Quinten, director of the home. I spoke to you on the phone."

Mr. Underwood gave her a skeptical look, scanning her and the others from head to foot. "Thank you Mrs. Quinten, nice of you to welcome us. That's exactly the way I like it, punctuality and neatness." He said sternly. Mr. Underwood was tall and carried a walking stick, which he seemed to use to assert authority rather than any disability. He had a shock of white hair and his face was set in a permanent state of harshness.

Mrs. Edwards stared up at him in awe, then turned to Mrs. Quinten. "Mr. Underwood spent years in the army. I've never met anyone so neat and organized in all my life. It's a joy."

He gazed down at Mrs. Edwards as if she had just announced her own death sentence.

"I couldn't agree with you more, Mrs. Edwards," Mrs. Quinten said. "That's exactly how I like to run things." She gestured towards the entrance.

"If you will follow me."

"The last place didn't," Mr. Underwood grumbled as he remained put, carefully watching the driver unload their luggage. "You should have seen their faces when we told them we were leaving."

"Yes," Mrs. Edwards replied. "And they were speechless when we told them we were coming here."

David sat in a chair in Chris's room looking out of an open window and could hear everything that was being said outside. Behind him Chris lay sleeping. It disturbed him immensely.

"This is a definite improvement on where we were staying," Mrs. Edwards remarked.

Mr. Underwood studied the house and the surrounding grounds with a critical eye. "I should say so for the price we are paying," he snapped.

"I'm sure you have fine people staying here." Mrs. Edwards said.

David had heard enough. He started to rock back and forth in the chair. Chris stirred from his slumber.

"What's up, David?"

David tried to shout but the words were unintelligible. Chris quickly sat upright in his bed.

"I hope you're not cracking up on me pal."

"Oo..oouuuttt...sssiiiide." David shouted in a slurred voice.

"What on earth is that?" Mrs. Edwards asked.

Mr. Underwood and Mrs. Edwards looked around, searching for the puzzling sound. She put her hand to her ear, trying to discern the nature of the sound.

Mrs. Quinten tried to hide her panic. "Nothing. Nothing at all." She said, as she tried to usher them into the mansion. "Please, follow me."

In the hall they met Rick, wheeling himself in David's wheelchair, heading for the leisure room. He had just completed one of his intense massage sessions and felt dynamic and invigorated.

"Hello folks, great to see you. Whatever you do don't miss the massage sessions. Gets the old blood going in places you never dreamt possible. Highly recommendable."

Rick winked at Mrs. Edwards as he rolled by.

"What a strange man." Mrs. Edwards said with a polite smile.

Mr. Underwood scratched his head with the silver plated handle of his walking stick. "I do believe I recognize him from somewhere, but I just can't place it."

Mrs. Quinten did her best to herd them quickly into the lift.

"I'll show you to your rooms."

Jack quickly hobbled over to Rick as he wheeled into the leisure room. "Hey Rick. Steve has been looking for you. He's in the garden."

Rick gingerly stepped out of the wheelchair. "Do me a favor, Jack?"

"Sure."

He wheeled the wheelchair around to the back of Jack and pulled him into it. "Wheel this back up to David. He's up in Chris's room. I won't need it anymore today."

Rick found Steve sitting under his usual Willow tree smoking an impressive joint, and sat down next to him.

"Here. Try this." Steve said as he handed the joint to Rick. "I got the results back from my nephew. Those capsules did contain vitamins."

"Ok," Rick replied, dragging hard on the incredible joint. "Then everything's all right."

"Not really, he also came across benzodiazepines, a mild sedative. Not enough to have much of an effect on a normal person but when you get to our age it would definitely slow you down a bit."

Rick was not surprised. In fact he sort of half expected it. He inhaled deeply and blew a couple of smoke rings towards the branches above him. "No wonder we're all turning into a bunch of old folk. The house is like a zombie hotel," he said, as he handed the joint back to Steve.

"We have to do something about it," Steve said. "But it's not easy. The amount of sedative found in the capsule was minute. If we started a court action against Mrs. Quinten we'd have a fight on our hands that could take years of legal battling. By the time it's over half of us will be pushing up daisies. We've got to do something while we're still able to do it, but I don't know what."

Rick blew out another perfectly formed smoke ring, then a wide grin covered his face. "I know just the thing."

One week later, in the deep of the night, Harlan, Steve, Rick and Chris sat around the poker table in Rick's room.

"I'm nervous about this." Chris said. "I've never done anything like this before. What if they find out?"

"So what," Rick said, shrugging his shoulders. "They have been doping us for the last six months. They're up to their ears in shit. If anyone is going to get into trouble it's not going to be us."

Robbie entered the room with two large canisters of capsules from the infirmary. "Got them," he said as he placed the canisters on the table.

"No one saw you?" Chris asked nervously.

"Nope." Robbie replied with calm assurance and opened up the canisters of vitamin capsules and placed them on the table.

"Okay. Steve, let's have your lot." Rick said.

Steve lifted a plastic shopping bag onto the table and took out two smaller plastic containers. He opened the containers carefully to reveal a light gray powder.

"Robbie, Chris, and Harlan, you start emptying out the vitamin shit," Rick ordered. "Steve and me will do the refill."

Robbie, Chris and Harlan popped open the vitamin capsules and emptied the contents into small soup bowls in front of them, then put the two empty halves of the capsules into separate bowls. Rick and Steve in turn took the empty shells and ran them through the containers with the gray powder, filling the capsules to the brim. Within ten minutes they had the emptying and refilling of the capsules going like a regular assembly line.

It was after five in the morning before all the capsules were refilled. They were exhausted. Rick studied the mound of refilled capsules.

"Just one question about this new substance, Steve," Chris asked. "What does it do?"

Steve took one of the capsules in his hand. "These are the ultimate vitamin pills. Not only do you receive all the vitamins you need, but they also give you a little boost to help you get through the day."

"Is it dangerous?."

"You can take up to six of these a day without any real problems. The only side effect you can get is a hard-on from here to Tokyo."

Rick popped one into his mouth. "Just what I need." Harlan, Steve and Robbie also swallowed a capsule.

Chris hesitantly put one into his mouth. "Are you sure these are safe?"

"No shit. Most of this stuff can be picked up at any good health food store."

Rick handed the containers to Robbie. "Better get these back before we're found out."

It was six in the morning before they all finally managed to get some sleep.

In the early afternoon, Rick and the others awoke from the sound of a woman screaming in the corridor. Outside, Ray was chasing after a nurse. In the distance he could hear a radio playing rock music at full volume. Chris, Harlan, and Steve joined him in the corridor.

"Sounds like it's coming from the leisure room," Rick said.

In the leisure room Jonathan danced around with his master blaster on his shoulder. Burt and a group of old men danced to the music with some nurses.

"That's more like it," Rick yelled. "This is definitely my idea of a retirement home." He turned to Harlan and Steve. "Hey guys. What do you say we go out on the town tomorrow night. Have ourselves a bit of fun. After all we haven't really met the locals yet?"

Harlan nodded. "We haven't been out since we got here. It's about time we checked out the local bar."

"Maybe even go to a disco." Rick said grinning and rubbing his hands in glee.

The dining room was packed that evening, and for the first time in months everyone had a real appetite. At last, Zacharia wheeled his large dinner tray out from the kitchen and into the center of the room.

"What type of goulash are you going to try on us today Zack?" Rick called out.

"No goulash today, Mr. Rick."

"What? Don't tell me you've run out of countries. We've already had Hungarian, Rumanian, Russian, and Yugoslavian. We've gone through just about the whole Eastern bloc."

"Sorry. No, Mr. Rick, tonight we have something completely different. Tonight we have spare ribs." Zacharia lifted the lid off the tray to reveal the steaming ribs. A cheer went up in the room.

"Hey Zack, me old son," Rick said. "If we get the spare ribs, who gets the real ones? I bet you smuggle them up to that new couple who arrived recently."

Zacharia was confused. "I'm sorry Mr. Rick, but these are the only ribs I got from the butchers. If you want I'll go back in the morning to try and get the rest."

"It's all right lad. The spares will do just fine."

Zacharia dished up the ribs onto Rick's plate, followed by French fries and salad.

"Why don't the newcomers eat down here with the rest of us?" Rick asked Zacharia.

"I do not know mister Rick. Maybe they prefer to be alone." Zacharia said, then disappeared into the kitchen.

"I wonder what capsules they are on?" Rick whispered to Chris.

After dinner Rick wandered aimlessly around the house, taking in the changes that had occurred since that very morning. Steve as usual headed for the Willow at the back of the garden. Eva played to a full and enthusiastic crowd in a packed fitness room. Life was indeed looking up. If only he could find nurse Iris for a quick massage, that would make his day complete.

Chapter twenty-eight

The following morning the postman turned off the main road and onto the driveway of Mount Merrian for his daily delivery. Old Joe Riley had been looking forward to this for the past three weeks. This was the day. Since dawn he had been on the look-out with his binoculars from his room on the first floor at the front of the house. Fellow residents had brought him breakfast so he would not miss anything. Finally the postal truck came into view and he jumped to his feet. "He's here," Joe shouted at the top of his voice. "He's here."

His shouts echoed throughout the entire house. He hobbled quickly out the door and down the corridor as fast as his old bowed legs could carry him.

"Out of the way," Joe shouted at a nurse helping a resident into a wheelchair, "coming through, coming through." he repeated as hard as he could, then went down the stairs and dashed past Mrs. Quinten emerging from her office with nurse Sadie.

"What on earth is the matter with that man?"

"I believe the post has arrived." Sadie replied.

"What could be so important about that?"

"Last Friday of the month. Joe receives his monthly magazine."

Outside, Joe grabbed his post, thanked the mailman as much as humanly possible, then ran quickly back to the house and into the leisure room. He sat down into a comfortable armchair and began to unwrap the magazine. Many of the people in the room, including CJ, Steve, Chalky and Fred, gathered round him. Joe had been talking about it for months, but this time she promised him she would be in there.

Joe opened up the centerfold. "There she is," Joe said with pride.

"Good God," Fred said. "They don't make them like they used to. Not bad at all."

"Is that really her?" Steve asked.

"Yes, sir. That's her. That's my granddaughter Tracy."

"She's got your eyes." Fred said.

"You think so?"

"Sure happy she hasn't got the rest," Steve joked.

"My my," CJ says, "reminds me of all those parties after the gigs, except everything was au natural back then." CJ grabs her breasts with both hands. "Mind you, so are mine although not exactly in the same place anymore."

Mrs. Quinten entered the leisure room.

"Here comes Mrs. Quinten," Fred whispered. "Quick Joe, show her the photo."

Joe shook his head. "Nah, it'll only make her jealous."

""I heard that gentlemen." She said, heading towards Fred. "Jealous? What would I be jealous of, gentlemen?"

"Of his granddaughter. Tracy got her photo published in a magazine," Fred replied.

"Really. How wonderful. You must be very proud."

"You bet I am." Joe replied.

"Go on, show her Joe," Steve said, nudging him in the back.

The men moved aside to let Mrs. Quinten through. Joe turned the Playboy centerfold to her and held it up high for her to see. Tracy lay naked on a bed of silk sheets.

"Isn't she something?"

Mrs. Quinten looked on in shock.

"Make your eyes water," Steve said.

She muttered something unintelligible, turned abruptly on her toes, and stormed out of the room.

"Some people don't appreciate beauty when they see it." Steve said.

"I bet she wished she had a body like that." Fred said.

"That's right darling, she just jealous." CJ replied.

For the first time in months Harlan trimmed his beard and took the time to neatly braid his long silver hair. Rick changed into his best clothes, and after a clean shave doused his face with Old Spice. Going out was a celebration and he was determined to do it properly. Rick, Robbie, Eva and Steve gathered in the entrance hall. Much to their surprise, Drewberry also turned up.

"I didn't think you were into the night life, Charles?" Rick said.

"I've had my days," he replied, "but I'm not dead yet. Perhaps you could look on me as a sort of chaperone. Someone to bail you out when you get locked up by the local sheriff."

Finally, Chris arrived, pushing David in his wheelchair.

Rick was more than surprised. "You're bringing David?"

"I didn't want to leave him here on his own." Chris replied.

He looked at David in the wheelchair

"You really want to come along David me old son, don't you." A smile came to one side of David's face.

"Leeettts ggoo." David mumbled.

"Oh what the hell. We used to go everywhere together, anyway, so why not now. You're the lucky bugger David," Rick said. "You've got the wheels. We have to leg it."

"Touuggh shiiit." David replied laughing.

No one in the house noticed them walking down the driveway and out the gate. Rick felt uplifted, and in a strange way free. The house had no rules about leaving the grounds, everybody was free to come and go as they pleased, as long as someone in the house knew where they were going and what time they would return.

"Where are we off to, Rick?" Chris asked.

"Anywhere that will have us."

"Say anything to Mrs. Quinten?"

"We don't have to tell no one nothing Chris. It's our bloody house, right?" Rick retorted.

"Then how do we get in later?" Chris asked.

Rick held up a bunch of keys. "A little present from Iris," he said, rattling them in their faces.

"Nice one." Steve replied.

The walk into town was filled with jokes and the usual reminiscing.

"You never got to make world tours like I did?" Rick said to Harlan. "Why not?"

"I never got into the trouble like you either." Harlan replied. "I bet you got kids on every continent on this planet."

"A man's got to keep the gene pool going. I'd hate to be the last of my line."

"Your ex's wouldn't agree with you there." Harlan said.

"You got kids Robbie?" Rick asked.

"A couple that I know of. You can never tell in our line of business. The ones you think are yours are usually from someone else, and the ones you think are not yours, are. You just can't win. What about you, Charles?"

Charles looked at him sternly and shook his head. "I'm afraid my view of the female sex has always been tainted."

"By what?" Rick asked.

"Young men." Charles replied, and smiled devilishly.

"Aha," Rick replied, and laughed.

"Shouldn't we check in at the sheriff's office first?" Harlan said. "Let them know that the famous geriatric gang is in town."

"Very funny," Rick remarked.

The town square was old-fashioned and quiet. As they walked across the green, David's gaze was fixed on the large white church that dominated the town center.

"Don't worry lad." You won't be going in there for a while yet," Rick told him.

David smiled. They jostled down the sidewalk and stopped outside Hanley's, a bar on the corner of Main and River Street. Outside it looked run down and badly in need of a paint job. Steve peered in through the window.

"They've got pool tables," he said.

Rick shook his head. "Looks a bit dead to me."

Harlan headed for the door. "We can always have a look," he said as he opened the door. He went in, and the rest followed. Two middle-aged men sitting at the bar stared as they came through the door, followed by Chris and David in the wheelchair. Two younger men standing at the pool table stopped playing to study the assortment of old folk entering the bar. The atmosphere in the bar was one of curiosity and unfriendliness. This was probably their local watering hole since time immemorial, and now they had intruders.

Without hesitation Harlan, still followed by the rest, walked through the bar, around the pool table and back out the front door.

"Like a cemetery," Steve said when they finally got out onto the street. "Anywhere else?'

They carried on down Main Street surveying the shops and small restaurants. Rick and Harlan stopped to study the menus stuck to the inside of the windows.

"Would you look at these prices," Harlan said. "They ain't what they used to be. I can't understand how people can afford to eat out these days."

They carried on down the street and stopped outside a music shop.

"Look at the price of those instruments." Harlan said. "In my day you could pick up a good guitar for a couple of bucks. Now you can't eat or play a song without having to part with a fortune."

Further down the street they came to another bar. The sign on the window read, "The Royal Bar".

Rick studied the sign. "Sounds like a tie and tails job to me."

"An excellent choice, Rick," Drewberry said as he primed his bow tie, getting ready to enter.

"I don't think so, Charles," Rick replied. "Definitely not for us. What do you think David?"

In a jerking effect David shook his head. "Aaah loooad off shhhit" he shouted.

"That's me boy. David knows his bars. Sorry Charles, you've been overruled."

They continued down Main Street and came to a halt outside a Hard Rock Cafe. The music was blasting inside.

"This sounds more like it," Rick said. He tried to peer in through the window, cupping his hands around his eyes to block the shade. "Hardly a soul in there. What do you think?"

Drewberry hesitated. "Wouldn't you prefer to go somewhere quieter?"

"Don't be silly," Steve replied. "It's only Rock and Roll."

"And I like it," Rick said, cutting in.

The look on the barman's face when they entered was one of both shock and surprise. They took a table next to the window and studied the surroundings. Posters and photographs of modern-day musicians where everywhere. Old electric and acoustic guitars hung from the ceiling and in one corner a complete set of drums. At the opposite end, behind the bar, hundreds of CD's were stocked up next to an impressive sound system, where a DJ regulated the music. The only other people in the bar were three young women sitting at a table and a couple of young men further up in the bar who seemed to be experimenting with their first beers. The bemused barman arrived at their table.

"You sure you're in the right place?" The barman asked. "Our music might be a little too loud for you guys."

"Don't get smart," Rick shouted above the music. "Us guys know exactly what we want. Just turn up the bass, and bring on the booze." He clapped his hands together and rubbed them diligently. "What are we drinking gentlemen?"

Drewberry dawned his reading glasses and studied the menu on the wall. "This will be my round and I think it's time we gave ourselves a treat. Barman, may I have five glasses of best Brandy there is, one beer and one soda."

Within minutes the barman returned with a full tray. Charles paid immediately and gave him a generous tip. Rick lifted up his glass to propose a toast.

"To Charles, our chaperone. May his wallet be bottomless and may he live long and healthy to a fabulous old age."

"To Charles," they all cheered. Rick and Harlan downed their drinks in one go.

"Thank you, gentlemen," Charles said. "But I think nights like these with you gentlemen will shorten my life span considerably."

"Don't tell me you can't handle it," Rick said.

"Well up to a few days ago I thought I couldn't." Charles said. "But recently I'm feeling on top form again. In fact I never felt better. It must be something in the food."

Harlan, Rick, Chris and Robbie looked at one another. Other than those who were in on the vitamin switch, no one knew anything about it. Had Charles guessed? Did he know something? As far as Rick was concerned, nobody had told Charles anything. Not that he couldn't be trusted, but they had all agreed to keep it to themselves. By the look on everyone's faces he knew they were not going to change that.

"I've got to do something about this music," Harlan said, shaking his head in disgust, and got up to head for the bar. None of them recognized what was playing, nor did they particularly like it. It sounded like a mixture between techno pop and house.

Harlan looked at the substantial music collection behind the bar.

"I don't think we have anything to suit your taste, pop's," the DJ said. "I'm afraid I've got no Frank Sinatra or Glenn Miller in stock."

Harlan ignored the remark and squinted at the CD's over the counter. "Can't read them from here. Mind if I come around?"

"Help yourself, pop's." Behind the counter hundreds of CD's were laid out in alphabetical order in neat racks nearly two meters high. He scanned the CD's, found the one he wanted, and took it out of the rack.

"Mind if I play a couple of tracks from this."

"Sure why not. Let me put it on for you. This equipment is pretty complicated."

The DJ reached for the CD, Harlan pulled away. "I can manage." Harlan said. He pressed a button on the CD player and the loading tray shot open. He put the CD in, pressed the same button, then the compartment disappeared into the machine. Harlan then pressed a button for track four, set the memory, track seven, set memory, track eleven, set memory. "That should be enough for the next thirty minutes." The DJ looked on in amazement.

Harlan then turned to the elaborate equalizer and scanned the eighteen faders. "This is all wrong. The middle and high frequencies are turned up so much you're practically distorting the music. You've got to bring them back somewhat so you can hear the authentic sound. A good studio engineer knows his job when he's cutting the track. If he heard what you were doing to his work he'd have you jailed. What you should do with a good equalizer like this is give the music a boost to suit the surroundings you're playing in."

Harlan fiddled around with the low and high frequencies, changing the faders with utter assurance. "I think that should be about right," he said as he pressed the start button. The sound of "When the lady smiles," from Golden Earring blasted from the speakers.

Rick jumped out of his chair and started to dance sexily towards the girls.

"When a lady smiles", Rick sang to the accompaniment of the music.
"You know it drives me wild
Her lips are warm and resourceful
When her fingertips,
Go drawing circles in the night
Then the mood is soft and sensual, hu-u"

Harlan picked up one of the guitars on the small stage and plugged it into an amplifier. Robbie got up and took a place behind the drums.
"And I love it," Rick continues to sing.
"yeah I love it
It's the answer to all my dreams
Every time it feels like the earth is shakin'
It doesn't matter, a glass is fallin',
I hear it shatter,
Maybe it's raining, faster and faster, shadow dancin'
Together oh I, I'm a bettin' on the game of love
Oh oh oh I, I'm bettin' that love is gonna come out
When the walls no longer shout, back at me
And I'm feelin' proud...."

Everybody, except Drewberry and Chris, got up to dance around the table. David rocked back and forth to the beat of the music in his wheelchair. The three young men looked on and clapped, while the girls left their seats to dance with them. When the song finished, Harlan put down the guitar and went back to their table with Robbie. Rick stalled at the girls table when they sat down.

"My names Holly," the girl said. "You and your friends seem to move all right for a bunch of old blokes."

"We're not old," Rick said. "Me and me mates are not a day over thirty. It's our hard living, playing in bands and being on the road that adds a little wear and tear to these incredible bodies."

"Hey Adonis," Harlan shouted at Rick when the music finished. "It's your round."

Rick bought a round for everyone in the bar. The young boys joined in the fun by trying to out-dance and out-drink Rick, but it proved impossible.

After an hour the boys left the bar drunk, with hardly any energy to stand up. Harlan and Charles took turns in selecting the music, which was mostly rock from the seventies. The girls, in their early twenties, were students at the local college. They kept up the pace and spent most of their time on the dance floor. The only problem that arose was an argument with Charles who refused to let the girls buy any of the drinks.

"He's old fashioned," Rick said. There is nothing more worse in the world than that."

Suddenly the dj played "Satisfaction" by the Rolling Stones. The girls and Rick wheeled David out onto the middle of the floor and began to roll and swing the chair to the rhythm of the music. David waved his good arm to the beat, then one of the girls grabbed his arm and began to rock and roll. David's wheelchair swayed back and forth as she held on to his arm.

They finally left the bar at closing time and carried on singing and laughing as they walked down Main Street. Rick and Steve had a girl under each arm. Drewberry weaved across the sidewalk, yet still managed to hold himself up with an air of authority. Chris pushed David, who was fast asleep and slumped over in his wheelchair.

In the distance the town hall clock struck one when they arrived back at the locked gate of Mount Merrian. Rick dug deep into his pocket and searched for the keys. Then he tried another pocket. Panic set in.

"They're not here." He said as he frantically tried other pockets. "Shit. I've lost the Goddamn keys."

"I knew something like this would happen," Chris said, shaking his head in disgust. "We should never have done this. We should have stayed in the house. What are we going to do now?"

Robbie studied the two meter high stone wall. "There's no way any of us can climb over that."

"Maybe it's not locked." Rick said, and tried the handle on the gate. The gates rattled but did not open. They were definitely locked. From inside the grounds a large Doberman ran towards them, barking.

"What the Fu..? Steve said, scratching his head. "A guard dog." He took a step backwards.

The dog skidded to a halt, bared its teeth and barked viciously. They all took a step backwards.

"I don't know about you," Holly said. "But right now I'm delighted that gate is locked."

"Is it to keep us out or him in," Harlan said.

Rick scratched his head. "I didn't know we had a guard dog."

"They got him after the new people moved into the house." Robbie said. "Must be trying to up-market the place."

Rick got down on his knees and faced the barking dog. The dog snarled and barked savagely. Rick barked back.

"I don't think he likes you," Harlan said.

"You've got to show him who's boss," Rick said, then barked once again.

"He doesn't think you're the boss." Harlan said. "He thinks you're dinner."

"Well then I'll try to convince him I taste like shit," Rick replied, and barked back at the Doberman.

Steve began to search his pockets. "I know just the thing for this guy."

"It's a girl," Rick said, still confronting the Doberman.

"Typical isn't it." Drewberry moaned in his drunken state. "They use a female to protect a bunch of old folk like us."

"Don't be such a sexist," Rick said. "She's doing a great job." Then he howled like a wolf. The dog howled back.

"I think we've got a thing going here," Rick said.

Steve found what he was looking for. He took the butt of a used joint out of his pocket, flipped his zippo and lit up. Steve got down on his knees next to Rick, and blew the smoke towards the dog. The Doberman shook its head a couple of times, but held its ground. Steve blew more smoke. Rick took the joint and blew some smoke rings.

"She seems to be enjoying this," Rick said, as the dog calmed down.

Finally, the dog backed off and walked away in a drugged state, weaving towards the house on all fours.

"She'll wake up with a smile." Steve said.

Rick put his arm around Holly. "Won't we all."

"Great," Robbie said. "But it is not going to help us get the gate open,"

"I know just the thing," Rick remarked, as he took a small penknife out of his pocket and opened it out. "Have faith old son."

"Pick the lock with that?" Harlan said, more than surprised. "It'll never work."

"You're right, it won't." Using the knife Rick tried unsuccessfully to pry the pin out of the gate hinges. "If some of you grab the gates and lift them enough to take the weight off I should have these out in no time. A little trick I learned from my dad, when my mum used to lock him out after being on the piss." Within seconds the first pin fell to the ground. Rick proceeded with the rest. When the last pin was pried out, they let go of the gate which crashed with a clatter and a bang to the ground.

"Ssshhh, you'll wake up the entire house," Chris whispered.

"That'll teach 'em to lock us out," Rick replied.

The following morning the dining room was humming with activity. All tables were full. Even Mrs. Edwards and Mr. Underwood sat at a table in a quiet corner. Zacharia was kept busy with ongoing orders of fried bacon and eggs, while his assistants dashed back and forth from the dining room to the kitchen trying to keep the buffet tables stocked. Hardly anyone noticed one of the girls walking down the long driveway, stepping over the gate and heading back to town.

Suddenly Mrs. Quinten stormed into the room.

"Who is responsible!" she screamed. "I want to know this minute. Who is responsible?"

Mrs. Edwards looked up. "Sorry?"

"I'm sorry Mrs. Edwards, I don't mean you. We have had a slight problem with our gate and we seem to have lost the guard dog." She scanned the room. "It's that Rick person. I know he is behind it all. I just know it. Where is he?"

There was no sign of Rick or any of the others in the dining room. As quickly as she had entered she stormed back out. Without knocking she entered Rick's room. Rick rolled over, opened one eye to see Quinten looking down at him. Holly lay asleep next to him.

"What have you done to our gate?" she shouted. "I know it was you. You're a trouble-maker. I knew it from the moment I saw you."

Rick closed his red shot eye and turned over. "Close the door when you leave," he moaned, then pulled the blankets over his head, revealing the dog lying at the other end of the bed, next to his feet.

"Brinier!" she screamed. The dog looked up. Quinten raised her arms and gritted her teeth.

"Oh, that's her name," Rick muttered from under the blanket.

"That's it. Things are going to change around here." She stormed back out of the room and slammed the door hard.

"Stupid cow," Rick groaned from under the blankets.

"What?" said Holly.

"Not you darling." Rick said as he wrapped his arm around her and pulled her closer. "Come closer," he whispered. "I need a little physio."

That afternoon, a meeting was called by Mrs. Quinten in the leisure room. All the residents, including Rick, were present. Eva sat in the corner of the room, quietly strumming her guitar, while Chalky continued to work on his puzzles.

Finally Mrs. Quinten entered, with Wesley hot on her heals. She took her place at the top of the room, directly under the enormous portrait of George O' Malley.

"Ladies and gentlemen. Most of you seem to think that this is a holiday camp. Well I can assure you it isn't. This is a place for peace and quiet, and that's the way it is going to be from now on." Mrs. Quinten gave a sign to Wesley, who unplugged the radio then carried it out of the leisure room.

"Because of the recent situation alcohol is now banned inside Mount Merrion." Mrs. Quinten announced. "If you want to drink you'll have to do it off the premises. If you wish to smoke you can carry on the example of our good friend and fellow resident Mr. Steve Barlow and smoke on the grounds and not in the house." Steve smiled at the unexpected compliment then stood up and bowed to the crowd.

"Residents are of course free to come and go as they please," Quinten said, continuing her speech. "But because of security reasons you will be asked to remain on the premises after evening dinner. At nine O' clock the main gate will be closed and locked, and no one, I repeat no one will be allowed in or out. For cleaning purposes the leisure and the fitness room will be closed to everyone after ten in the evening. And one last thing, I will have no more pornography in this building. I don't care if it is a relative; I think it's disgusting and I will not tolerate it. This is a respectable home and I'm going to keep it that way."

As soon as Mrs. Quinten left there was a rumble of chatter all around the room. A quiver ran down Eva's spine. Suddenly she felt she was back where she started; in a home governed by rules and regulations just to keep everybody in their place.

Charles Drewberry tapped Steve on the shoulder with his silver-topped cane. "Well Steve, I see you have got what you might call government approval for your little inhalation sessions at the back of the garden."

"You're welcome to join me anytime, Charles."

"No thank you, Steve. I prefer my little delights in a more fluid form. Preferably malt and at least twelve years old."

Everyone was taken aback. Everyone except Rick. He knew it was going to come to this sometime. There was no need to panic, nothing to get worried about. Except, how was he going to get round it all. He would have to come up with something, but what?

That evening, just after dinner, Rick, Steve, Chris, David, and Harlan headed out to the garden, down the path and towards the willow.

Outside it was hot and humid. Steve sat in his usual position against the trunk while Rick lay flat out next to him, staring at the hanging branches. Steve lit up a joint, took a few puffs then handed it on to Rick, who inhaled deeply. His eyes went wide and his face flushed a deep red. After ten seconds he finally exhaled.

"This is dynamite." Rick said with some effort. He stared at the joint he was holding.

"You like it?" Steve asked.

"You could make a fortune out of this."

"No sir. This is for private use."

Rick was about to hand it on to Chris when he stopped at the sight of Chris's frown. Rick knew he would never take it, but at that moment it seemed like a great idea. It would definitely help him break the news of his plan.

"You should try this," Rick said, offering the joint to Chris. "Take some of the edge off."

Chris shook his head. "No thanks. I've had my share over the years. I don't need it."

"You don't mind if we smoke, do you?"

"Not at all."

"Are you sure? Because every time we do you pull a face like you're sucking a lemon."

"I told you I don't mind." Chris said, his mood turning quickly sour. "Do you want me to stay? If you don't I'll go." Chris said as he was about to get up. Rick reached for his jacket and held him down.

"No, don't go. Really you're great fun. Just stay. I won't start again. We need to talk about what's going on."

Chris settled down. "What's there to talk about? There's nothing we can do..." Chris stopped and stared intensely at Rick. "You're up to something."

Rick could almost feel Chris's intense deep set eyes probing his mind. "Me?"

"You're up to something," Chris said again. "I know you are."

"I admit I may have messed up now and again," Rick said.

"You can say that again." Chris mumbled.

"But I only want us to have a good time here. After all, it is our home. What if we did something to cheer the place up a little?"

"You already tried to do that with your little pills and look where that got us."

"Nothing like that. I was thinking of something really genuine. What do you say we organize a little party for the entire house. We could even invite some people from the town." Rick said.

"Such as?"

"I don't know. Maybe some of the kids down at the bar."

"Yeah sure. Quinten would love that." Chris said.

"Then what if we invited some of the people from the town council."

Steve nodded. "That sounds interesting."

"What would we be celebrating?" Harlan asked.

"We don't have to celebrate something to have a party." Chris gave Rick a curious look. "What are you up to?"

"Nothing."

"Don't give me that."

"No really." Rick said, raising his hands in defense. "I just thought it would be a nice thing to do. After Quinten taking our privileges away like that I think we could all do with a little morale booster."

"Who are you going to ask from the council?" Harlan asked.

"I don't know. I was thinking maybe... councilor Donavan, Labrinski, Mannon, and a few of the others."

Chris gave an unexpected grin. "You clever old son of a bitch."

"What's going on?" Steve asked, then passed the joint to Rick. "What's so special about these people?"

Rick took a deep puff of the joint and held his breath.

"Those are the councilors who hold our purse strings." Chris answered.

Rick slowly blew out the smoke.

"What purse," Steve said. "I don't get it."

"The money from the benefit was put into a trust," Chris replied. "A number of people hold complete control over that trust and the management of the house, and Rick just named them all."

The joint began to take its effect on Rick. He closed his eyes and smiled.

For the first time ever, Rick was early for breakfast. He was surprised to see so many people, fifteen at least, at seven in the morning. Rick scanned the room. If they had not been there he would have waited. But they were, and sitting at their usual table next to the window.

He grabbed his tray with bacon, eggs, white bread, two slices of toast, butter, coffee, a glass of orange juice, and headed for his goal.

"Mind if I sit here?" Rick asked. Mr. Underwood and Mrs. Edwards were stunned when they looked up from their morning papers to find Rick standing at their table with a broad smile. They stared at each other in disbelief.

"Eh.. er..yes, take a seat," Underwood finally mumbled.

"Great," Rick said, as he eagerly set the contents of his tray on the table. "None of the others are down yet and I don't like sitting on my own."

"Of course," Mr. Underwood muttered, trying to ignore Rick and continue reading his newspaper.

"Anyway," Rick continued, "I've been wanting to ask you something."

"Us?" Mrs. Edwards squawked, as if the word got caught in her throat.

"I knew immediately when you came to Mount Merrian that your upbringing was better than most of the riff raff here so I thought I'd get your opinion on a little reception I wanted to organize."

"A reception? I do enjoy those occasions" Mrs. Edwards said. "Are we allowed to come?"

"Ssshhhh," Rick hissed. "I don't want everyone to hear. I haven't got everything arranged yet. It's still secret."

Mr. Underwood peered from over the edge of the newspaper. "Sounds fishy to me," he moaned, then went back to his reading.

"You don't have to worry about a thing," Rick said. "We have limited the guest list to the very elite. Nothing but the best."

Mr. Underwood sighed deeply, then lowered the newspaper once again.

"I hate to imagine what your idea of elite is," he said.

Rick leaned towards them across the table. "I was thinking of the mayor and a number of his colleagues," he whispered.

Mrs. Edwards looked up in surprise. "Really. That does sound exciting."

Rick knew that this would work on her. When she was married to Mr. Edwards she told everyone that she had always hoped for a life of gaiety and splendor, meeting government officials and being asked to charity functions all over the country. But life with Mr. Edwards had not turned out like that. She had never met any celebrities or had gone to grand galas. A year after her husband died she met Mr. Underwood. She had said her life would change for the better, and now it seemed to be looking that way.

Underwood nodded, put away the newspaper, then straightened his tie. Rick knew he had pushed the right button. "Well, that does sound interesting. I've never met the mayor."

"Our only problem is convincing Mrs. Quinten. I think if I put it to her she might have her doubts. We need someone with stature, someone Mrs. Quinten would listen to. A man like yourself is respected in this house, especially by the management."

"So you want me to be your spokesman," Underwood said.

Rick smiled, then reached over and placed his hand on Underwood's shoulder. "You do have something we are lacking."

Rick wanted to go further into that statement, but bit his tongue to prevent himself from doing so. "Of course there is no money in it," he said quietly, "but you would have the honor of representing all of us in the house."

Underwood straightened up and checked his tie. "I must say I'm honored. I'd be happy to oblige."

"Oh my goodness," Mrs. Edwards said, looking gleeful. "This is wonderful."

"If you are willing to do something like this," Rick continued, "maybe you could actually go on to represent the residents on a greater proportion. A spokesman for all their concerns. I'm sure Mrs. Quinten would have no problem with that. In fact, with the skills you have gained from years in the military you could probably even help her run the house. The possibilities are endless."

Harlan, Robbie, and Chris pushing David, finally arrived in the dining room. The plan was to give Rick a ten-minute start. By the look of things everything was going to plan. They avoided their usual breakfast table and sat directly behind Mr. Underwood and Mrs. Edwards instead.

"This plan of yours is quite ingenious," Underwood said. "I'm sure you would have made a great military man."

"I'll tell you about the wars I've been in some day."

"You've fought in the wars?" Mr. Underwood said, surprised. "Which ones? Korea, Vietnam, Iraq?"

"I've had fights in all those countries, and lots more besides."

"How exciting," Mrs. Edwards crooned. "Did you get injured?'

Rick turned his head to one side then pressed down on his nose with his forefinger. The curvature of a broken nose stood out prominently. "What do you think of that." He said proudly.

"Goodness," she cried." Did it hurt?"

"Not as much as it did the other bloke."

"Remind me to show you the scar where someone hit me over the head with a bottle." Rick said to Mr. Underwood, who got up to leave the table.

"They are not the type of wars I was talking about," Underwood replied.

Mrs. Edwards was shocked. "Someone did that?"

"I wouldn't worry about him if I was you. They're still caring for him real well in the hospital."

"Shall we go?" Underwood said, sounding irked.

"By the way," Rick said, just as they were about to leave. "You and the missus haven't been looking very well lately."

"What do you mean," Underwood asked.

"A little pale under the eyes. You definitely look off color."

Mrs. Edwards, took a small make-up mirror out of her handbag and scrutinized the white of her eyes.

"I think you are right," she said. "I look dreadful."

Underwood put his hand to his belly then burped gently. "I think it's the meals."

"Here, take some of these." Rick grabbed his hand then placed a number of capsules into his palm. Underwood stared at the familiar capsules.

"Our vitamin capsules? How on earth did you get hold of them?"

"You could say I have my own supply. Don't say a word to anyone, but the amount of vitamins they dish out here is not enough for people like you and me. Call this an extra supplement. It will make you feel a lot better."

"I must say the vitamins have recently made me feel a little perked up," Mrs. Edwards said.

"A little extra dosage should bring you right to the top."

Underwood stared at the capsules. He was genuinely surprised at Rick's gesture.

"That's very generous of you. I'd never have imagined you would be so thoughtful."

"And here is a couple for the misses." Rick handed a number of capsules to Mrs. Edwards.

She grabbed Rick's hand and shook it. "Thank you. Thank you very much. We really appreciate it."

They both popped a couple of capsules into their mouths, and washed them down with orange juice.

"I think I'll go to my quarters and formulate a plan. Make some notes, things like that... ehm... Mr....ehm.?"

"Just call me Rick."

Underwood coughed. "Ehm..yes..of course...Rick." Underwood offered a polite smile, then turned and marched out of the room with Mrs. Edwards following quickly behind. His friends watched in silence, then erupted into a cheer.

Chris shook his head in dismay. "You're going to get us thrown out of here."

Rick popped a pill into his mouth. "Don't be silly."

Much to Rick's surprise Underwood used tactics carried out with military precision to get the idea to work. Instead of confronting Mrs. Quinten directly he worked his way around it in such a way as to give her the impression it was her idea. He began by inviting Mrs. Quinten to lunch in his room. At first it was difficult to get her to take the bait, since running the home took all of her time. Only when Underwood mentioned something vague about how Mount Merrian could be put on the map as one of the best homes, not only in the state but in the entire country, did she agree. Underwood was careful not to say too much, just that he was playing around with the notion of asking the mayor, along with various local council members, to some sort of reception in the home. He left her to fill in the gaps on how to set it up and execute the plan; her plan. They talked for more than an hour, plotting a strategy; Quinten's strategy. Underwood dropped the hints and she dutifully picked them up and worked them into the grand design. Underwood guaranteed that this would put Mount Merrian on the map and make her a national celebrity.

At the end of it all Mrs. Quinten felt exalted. She left Underwood's room with a feeling that she was once again captain of the ship.

Within a week, invitations were sent out to the mayor, city council, and prominent politicians around the state. Days later, the official reply cards started to trickle in. By the end of the week they were all returned, without a single refusal.

As the big day drew closer, the atmosphere lifted to exceptional proportions. The only people who seemed oblivious to it all were Chalky, who still lived in a world of puzzles and simple prizes, and those suffering Alzheimer's.

The house was cleaned from top to bottom while the gardeners worked overtime in getting everything into shape. Mrs. Quinten toured the grounds and house with Wesley at her side, spotting anything that needed to be changed, painted over or removed.

The only problem was in the kitchen. Zacharia was completely stressed out. He had never cooked for mayors or councilors before. Trying to decide on what suitable dishes to serve for the occasion was a nightmare. He spent hours rummaging through cook books studying recipes from Siberia to

Honolulu. The list was endless but the choice was impossible. Only after consulting Rick he knew what to do.

On the day of the reception the house was buzzing. When Rick, Harlan, and Chris pushing David entered Mrs. Quinten's office she gasped at the sight of them all dressed in identical black oversized suits.

"I don't believe it. You actually look like gentlemen."

David started to rock, and tried to say something.

"Ff..ff..uuu.." Chris quickly placed his hand over his mouth.

"A nephew of one of the boys owns a business in the city," Rick said. "He took our measurements and fitted us up."

"On credit," Harlan said. "In fact he wanted to fit up the entire home."

"How kind," Mrs. Quinten replied.

"Yes it was. No doubt about that. He's the undertaker. When we kick the bucket he collects. He just adds the price of the suit to the bill."

Mrs. Quinten looked dismayed.

"Look on the bright side," Rick said, "at least we know what we're going to be buried in."

"Oh!" She muttered, and stormed out of the office.

At seven sharp a silver stretch limousine followed by two Pontiac Bonnavilles, an Oldsmobile Eighty-Eight, and a Buick La Sabre cruised up the driveway. As they pulled up to the front of the mansion, Mrs. Quinten and her staff, followed by Underwood, dressed in his military uniform and escorted by Mrs. Edwards, marched out to meet the oncoming VIPs. Chris, David, Rick, followed up behind by Harlan with an Indian band around his head and beads plaited into his long ponytails.

The chauffeur opened the door and the mayor and his beautiful wife stepped out. Quinten, Mrs. Edwards and Mr. Underwood stared at them in shock. Rick and the others just smiled. The mayor was dressed in a hippie outfit, with a sheepskin coat, wearing a long wig, and smoking a large joint.

The mayor held up the joint. "Oh it's all right. It's not real. We just thought we'd get into the mood."

The rest of the members of the council got out of their automobiles. They were also all dressed in hippy regalia.

"Lucky for us you organized a fancy dress," Rick said to Quinten, "otherwise I would have looked like a jerk in this outfit. Why didn't you dress up?'

Mrs. Quinten pulled away from Rick and turned to Underwood.

"Why didn't you tell me? I feel like a fool."

"I didn't know," he said, sounding confused.

"Really? I suppose that uniform and all those medals or just for fun."

"I always dress for formal occasions. I had nothing to do with it."

The mayor walked right past Mrs. Quinten and went straight to Rick. "And you must be Rick Macken. I recognize you from TV. I'm very very proud to meet you. I hope you don't mind us arriving like this."

"I hope you don't mind us dressed like coffin bearers."

"Of course not," he said and laughed. "Blues Brothers, right?"

"On the nose," Rick said, as they all suddenly produced a Blues Brothers hat from behind their backs, placed them on their heads then Rick guided them into the house, totally ignoring Mrs. Quinten, and leaving Harlan, Chris, and David to welcome the rest of the guests.

"I'll get some of the boys to crank up the old record player." Rick said, as they headed towards the leisure room. "Then we can really get into the mood of things."

Outside, Harlan chatted to the mayor's wife.

"My daughter Heather has all your records," she said.

"What an honor. I didn't think kids would listen to old-timers like me. I thought we were the generation who belonged in a museum."

"Not true. To many people you're a hero and the kind of person they would love to be. They adore you."

"Did you bring her along?"

She pointed back to the limousine with the door half open. "She's a little bashful," she said, then peered into the darkened limousine. "Don't be silly. Come and out and meet him."

All eyes turned and locked onto the beautiful apparition stepping out of the limousine.

The mayors daughter was dressed in a beautiful native American Indian white buckskin dress like her mother, with triangular turquoise patches on the front and back with beaded hanging straps. She wore a head band with turquoise beads that seemed to melt into her flowing blond hair. A loose black brassiere strap slipped from her tanned shoulder. She quickly pulled it back up. Harlan judged her to be about twenty-five, although she projected the innocence of a teenager.

"I used to tell her that years ago, in our time, women never wore bra's. In fact we burnt them. But they don't do that sort of thing nowadays."

"Maybe we should revive a few old traditions." Harlan said. Heather blushed. He took them both by the arm then headed into the house.

As soon as Rick, the mayor, and the rest of the entourage entered the leisure room they were confronted by Drewberry, dressed in elegant tie and tails, now acting as an elaborate barman.

"May I offer you a drink sir," he said in his Scottish accent.

The Mayor studied the assortment laid out neatly behind Drewberry. "What have you got?"

"Much to my delight nearly every alcoholic beverage on God's wonderful planet."

"A bourbon would do just fine."

"Of course sir. Coming right up."

In the corner Eva placed a record on a very old turntable.

"That's a little outdated isn't it?" The Mayor said.

"We don't have the funds for anything modern here," Rick said, lowering his voice.

"I can't imagine how. Mrs. Quinten has received enough to cover for things like that."

"We're not really complaining," Rick said. "But can just about manage with the little we have."

The mayor sipped his bourbon. The old record player was one of a number of dilapidated props they picked up in town during the last few weeks, and had placed at strategic points around the house.

Returning from his regular smoke in the garden, Steve, dressed as a hippy, headed for Rick and the mayor with a large joint in his mouth. He was more stoned than Rick had ever seen him. He stumbled towards them with bloodshot eyes and sagging head. Rick swallowed hard.

"When's the party going to rock Rick?" Steve asked in a slurred voice.

The mayor turned to meet Steve nearly head on. The only thing he seemed to notice was Steve's joint.

"Steve my friend, this is the mayor of our beautiful little town," Rick said clearly enough so Steve would get the message and clear off. He didn't. The mayor took the joint from Steve and studied it closely.

"Oh, Christ," Rick groaned. "Not that." Rick could see the entire plan going up in smoke. The mayor would have them all in jail once he realized it wasn't a fake. One percent tobacco and ninety-nine percent home-grown California marijuana of the highest quality. Not only that; after the police searched the house and analyzed the vitamin capsules, they would be looking at a fifteen-year sentence, and if that didn't happen he was sure Underwood would get his old army buddies together and organize a firing squad.

The mayor held up the joint. "Would you look at this!"

Rick buried his head in his hands and moaned, then turned to meet Harlan coming in the door with two beautiful women.

"Hey, Rick. Have you met the mayor's wife and daughter." Harlan announced. "Aren't they something?"

Rick was suddenly speechless at the sight of the apparition, then turned back to see the mayor running his nose along the huge joint as if it were a Cuban cigar.

"Christ." Rick moaned. "We're finished."

"This is one of the finest examples I have ever seen," the mayor said. "We've been practicing the entire week to achieve something like this, yet here you are, some of the oldest citizens of our community, turning it into an art form." He sniffed the smoke. "Quality tobacco." He called councilor George Moony over. "Hey George, take a look at this."

George rushed over. "Wow. That's real monster. I don't believe it," he said. "How did you do it? Absolutely incredible."

The mayor patted Steve on the back. "You're a genius."

"Why couldn't we make something like that?" George asked.

"It's all in the fingers." Steve said. "The trick is to make an even bed along the length of the skin."

"Skin?" The mayor said.

"You know, the paper man."

"Oh yes of course, skin."

"Then with experienced foreplay you apply pressure all along the length with your thumbs and forefingers, turning in the skin as you go along."

"Ok. I get it. Amazing," George said.

"Once you got the little sucker in there it's just a question of keeping the pressure in balance and rolling the skin over itself."

"I got more stuff up in my room. If you want you can come up and practice a few."

"Really? That would be great."

Outside, few noticed the UPS delivery van pulling up to the house. The driver got out and began to unload large boxes from the truck. Joe ran out the door to greet him, since he received the playboy from his niece, he had made it a habit to confront everyone delivering post or parcels.

"Is that for me?"

The driver studied the delivery docket. "Are you Chalky?"

"No. He's inside."

"All this is for Mr. Chalky." The driver said, pointing to the boxes packet high in the back of the truck.

"Wait here and I'll get some help," Joe said, and hobbled back inside.

He quickly returned with Wesley and two of the male cleaning staff.

Wesley studied the delivery slip. "It's for Chalky all right." He grabbed the heaviest looking box and began to carry it into the house. The rest followed suit. They placed the boxes in the middle of the dining room. Joe appeared with Chalky, still clutching his crossword puzzle as if his life depended on it.

In the dining room Fred looked at one of the boxes and read the label aloud. "Fairweather Puzzles? He always does Fairweather Puzzles. That's where he won his badge."

Like an excited little boy Chalky flipped over the lapel on his jacket to reveal his Mickey Mouse button.

"It sure ain't no button this time, that's for sure." Wesley said as he tore off the envelope attached to the largest box. He ripped it open and read it slowly, then handed it to Fred.

Fred carefully read the letter. "I don't believe it. He's won."

"What?" Joe asked. "What did he win?"

"He won." Fred went on screaming. "The son of a bitch won the goddamn jackpot."

Chalky threw down the crossword puzzle and started to dismantle the boxes. Everyone stood back. They had never seen him move so quickly. Like a wild man he ripped the cardboard boxes to pieces.

"Quick, get Bobbie," Fred shouted to Joe. "He's going to love this." Joe rushed out of the room in search for Bobbie.

The mayor sat next to Steve on the floor of his room inhaling deeply on an extra-long joint. He held his breath, increasing the effect of the marijuana. George sat across from them, practicing a medium sized joint.

"I always wanted to be a hippy," the mayor said, still trying to hold his breath. "All that peace and love and commune shit. Wake up with a different woman every morning." He finally exhaled, then handed the joint back to Steve.

"It must be a real pain being the mayor," Steve said.

"You wouldn't believe the amount of meetings I have to attend every week. Boring as hell. I would have loved to have been a musician, touring the country, playing to huge crowds, staying in the best hotels, inviting the groupies back to your rooms."

"Sounds more like a president's job to me," Steve replied. He handed the joint back again.

"You think that's for me? I've often thought of running for office."

"As far as I can see you seem to have all the right ideas."

"Maybe you're right. Maybe I should give it some serious thought," he smiled then lay flat out next to the window, and puffed long on Steve's incredible joint.

"What do you think?" George asked, holding a joint he rolled that sagged at both ends.

"It's not bad for a beginner, but don't give up the day job." Steve replied.

There was a knock on the door then Burt and Jack hobbled in.

"Hey you guys." Steve shouted. "Come on in and meet the mayor."

The mayor looked up. "Well I'll be damned," he shouted. "If it ain't Burt Banner and Jack Hammer."

"The very same," Burt said.

The mayor tried to climb to his feet to shake their hands. "I have every song you boys ever wrote."

"Well how about that," Jack said. "We finally found a fan."

Further down the hall Rick had the mayor's wife pinned up against the wall of his bedroom. Her panties lay on the floor and his trousers were down around his knees. He ran his hands up the back of her blouse and quickly unbuttoned her bra.

"Aaahhh," she sighed. "Thank you so much. Now I can breathe."

Rick cupped her breasts in his hands and smiled. "Are these yours?"

She grabbed his naked buttocks and pulled him closer. "At my age? Don't be silly."

"The wonder of silicon." Rick replied, panting.

"Harder. Harder," she cried. Rick increased his speed and thrust. The mayor's wife moaned in ecstasy. In less than a minute Rick started to slow down. His legs began to give way.

"I'm beat," he moaned. "I can't keep it up any longer."

She pulled him up. "Don't slow down. Harder, harder," she screamed. She locked her arms around him and somehow managed to keep him on his feet and in motion. Rick reached down to the bowl on the table next to them that contained a number of vitamin pills. He grabbed them all. He swallowed them as quickly as he could. She dragged him towards the bed and threw him down as if he weighed nothing. There was a wild look in her eyes.

"Are you ready?" She asked.

"If I kick the bucket now I'll die a happy man. So let's rock and roll darlin'."

When Bobbie rushed into the leisure room he stopped dead when they saw what was before them. Chalky and Fred had unpacked a brand new Gibson Les Paul guitar and were now working on the drum kit. The snare, hi-hat and gleaming chrome-plated supports lay at his feet.

"Come on Bobbie," Fred shouted. "We're back in business. Chalky hit the goddamn jackpot."

Bobbie punched the air with his fist. "Yahooooo!" He screamed.

"Never lose faith." Fred bellowed. "That's the key my friend. Never lose faith. I knew he'd hit the jackpot one of these days."

Bobbie and Fred unpacked a Marshall valve amplifier while others around them unwrapped the rest of the drum kit. Chalky unpacked a Fender Telecaster bass guitar and handed it to Fred.

"Is this for me?" He gasped. Chalky nodded. "Yours", Chalky said in a near whisper as tears began to roll down his cheeks.

In Rick's room the tide was turned. He was now on top of the mayor's wife up and was pumping hard.

"This is great." She yelled. "This is fantastic. I never knew it could be so good." She screamed even louder, reaching her climax.

"Hang on in there honey. The volcano's going to blow!" Rick screamed.

Outside in the garden Harlan walked hand in hand down a path with Heather.

"....so about that time I more or less gave up playing to larger crowds and roamed the country on my bike for a while. When I heard that Rick was in the process of setting this up I decided this was where I wanted to be."

"And here you are," Heather said, then stopped and took his other hand. Harlan looked into her bright blue eyes.

"And here you are," he replied, and kissed her tenderly.

Just down the corridor from Rick, CJ had councilor Mannon by the hand and guiding him towards her room. CJ opened the door, grabbed him by his shirt and pulled him in.

In the dining room they had all the amplifiers and equipment connected.

"Let's do the ZZ Top number," Fred said, and called out the beat, "One two, one two three four." Suddenly the revived band broke into the riveting rhythm of "La Grange" from ZZ Top. Bobbie stood in the middle of the leisure room laying out the rythim on his guitar. Fred, sitting behind the brand new drum set, skillfully tapped put the beat lightly on the edge of the snare drum. Bobby began to sing.

Rumour sprendin' a-'round in that Texas town
'bout that shack outside La Grange
and you know what I'm talkin' about.
Just let me know if you wanna go
to that home out on the range.
They gotta lotta nice girls.

Have mercy.
A haw, haw, haw, haw, a haw.
A haw, haw, haw.......

Chalky, plucked the bass guitar while swinging left to right to the beat. Within no time, everyone started to move and sway to the addictive rhythm of the music.

The sound of the band echoed throughout the entire house. The leisure room quickly emptied and everybody poured into the dining room. Steve and the mayor returned the same time Rick appeared with the mayor's wife.

"Now this is what it's all about." Rick shouted. He took the mayor's wife by the hand and started to dance with her. Like a chain reaction everybody began to dance. Mrs. Quinten rushed over to the mayor.

"I'm so sorry, Mr. Mayor. They know they are not allowed to do this. I'll put an end to it immediately."

David rocked violently in his chair, struggling to blurt out a curse. Chris quickly gagged him with his hand and wheeled him to another part of the room.

"It's all right," the mayor said. "You don't have to do that. It's quite a home you've got here, Mrs. Quinten. You must have the time of your life."

Underwood grabbed Rick by the shoulder. "This was not part of the plan."

"Relax, enjoy yourself." Rick said. "Everybody's having a good time. That's what it's all about."

Underwood turned to Steve, who had the last remnants of a joint between his fingers. "You know it's against the rules to smoke in the house."

Steve inhaled deeply and blew the smoke into Underwood's face. Underwood began to choke. The Mayor clapped him repeatedly on the back.

"Are you all right? Maybe you should sit down and take it easy."

Guided by Mrs. Edwards, Underwood staggered over to a chair and sat down.

"I don't know what is going on," Quinten said in a bewildered voice to the mayor.

"You should," he replied, "you organized it. This is what I'd call a party."

He tried to take her by the hand for a dance. "You want to hit the floor?"

Mrs. Quinten quickly pulled her hand away. "I do not dance," she hissed. The mayor turned his attention to nurse Sadie and began to dance with her instead.

Upstairs councilor Mannon came screaming out of CJ's room wearing a short bathroom towel wrapped around his waist.

"Somebody help," he shouted. "I think she's had a heart attack."

A nurse and a male attendant on the same floor rushed into a medical room and grabbed a trolley with a defibrillator and various monitors.

They stormed into CJ's room. Her eyes were open and she lay half naked and motionless on the bed. The nurse quickly checked her pupils with a small torchlight and then her pulse.

"Nothing," she said.

"Okay, stand back," the attendant said as he grabbed the defibrillator and started to charge it up.

Suddenly three old musicians Colton, Blake and Jose, rushed into the room.

"What are you doing?" Colton asked.

"She's had a heart attack." He said as he was about to place the defibrillator on her chest.

"Wait." Colton shouted in panic. "Not just yet. Just give her a minute."

"I'm sorry we have to do this now. Otherwise we won't be able to revive her."

"Then you will kill her. Just wait," he pleaded.

The councilor pushed him out of the way. "Let them do their work. I could be facing prison for this."

Blake and Jose grabbed the attendant. "He's right, you will kill her," Blake shouted, as he and Jose held on to each arm. The nurse tried to pull the men off the attendant.

Suddenly CJ spasmed. The councilor jumped back in fright. Her body went rigid and she took a deep breath, then relaxed. She closed her eyes, opened them again then stared at everyone in the room and smiled.

"CJ." The councilor shouted. "You're alive."

"Of course I am daaarling," she crooned. "You were wonderful."

"I don't understand." The councilor said.

"Well that's why she's called CJ." Blake said. "Comatose Joan. Everybody in the music business knows about Comatose Joan. Happens every time."

"You better stick to musicians CJ." Colton told her. "You're scaring the shit out of these folk. You'll be singing with the angles if you get zapped with one of those things," he said, pointing to the defibrillator.

"Come on lads." Blake said. "I hear some decent music downstairs."

Harlan and Heather stood by the pool. Heather let go of his hand then removed her moccasins. Harlan loosened his belt. Heather's tunic dropped to the ground. She had large pear-shaped breasts with dark brown nipples that stood out stiff in the cool evening air. Harlan's pants dropped to the ground. They both removed their underwear at the same time, and dived into the pool. When they came up for air they were both clasping onto one another and kissing frantically. They twisted and turned in the water and gradually made their way to the edge.

As they approached the edge Heather took hold of the ladder and turned over on her back. Harlan mounted her in the water as she held on with both hands onto the glistening chrome steel of the pool ladder.

Inside the band played on before other musicians took over the instruments and softened the tone with a jazz session. Since there was now no chance in getting everyone down to dinner, Zacharia improvised by turning the tables into a self-service. He laid out dishes from just about every country that made its name in fine cuisine by creating islands of dishes from China, Indonesia, Japan, Italy, Greece, Mexico, and France and placing flags and the name of each country at each. For desert he made up an unusual variant of the only American dish on the menu: Brownies served with custard and ice cream.

An hour after the deserts Mrs. Quinten went to her room complaining of feeling dizzy. The mayor, along with two of the councilors, went up to Steve's room to practice his joint rolling while Rick spent most of his time telling his life story to the mayor's wife.

Now fully clothed, and their hair dripping wet, Harlan and Heather sat out on the verandah watching the stars. She laid her head on Harlan's shoulder.

"That was beautiful." She said. "You were great."

"You're not too bad yourself." Harlan replied.

"Can I see you again?" Heather asked.

"Maybe you should have a word with your daddy about that."

"I don't think he'll mind. He's a very broadminded person you know. Every year we go with the whole family to naturist camping sites. There is not a lot out there that can shock my daddy."

"Well how about that," Harlan said in a near whisper, and they kissed.

Two councilors and a few residents joined the mayor in Steve's smoke filled bedroom. Steve opened up a biscuit tin he took from under the bed and handed everyone a medium sized joint.

"These are some I made earlier."

"Steve," Burt said. "You'd better open a window."

"It is open," Steve replied, ignoring the buildup of smoke in the room.

Downstairs, the band was replaced with some ancient heavy-metal rockers who turned the volume right up. All the windows in the house rattled and vibrated to the sound of the beat.

In another room further down the corridor Colton, Blake and Jose were putting together their own little feast. They sat around a small table covered with food they took from Zacharias' kitchen. Colton held one part of the defibrillator horizontally as Blake placed slices of bacon onto the flat pad.

"Ok Jose. Start her up." Jose pressed a button on the main unit and the defibrillator's whine started to increase to a high pitch.

Colton placed the second part of the defibrillator on top of the bacon.

"Stand back." He shouted.

Jose and Blake took a step back as Colton pressed the button. There was a loud crack. The bacon sizzled. Colton tipped the pads of the defibrillator, and the instantly fried bacon fell onto the plate.

"Now that's what I call fast food." Colton said.

Henry and Mildred Furlong had lived next to Mount Merrian for more than fifty years, and were now used to the old rockers wandering around the grounds. It was nearly dark when Henry who was in his garden shed, heard a scream and then a burst of female laughter. Mildred sat on the back porch knitting. Henry appeared at the door of the shed.

"Sounds as if it came from the O'Malley mansion," he said, then went down to the back of the garden to get a better look. In the distance he heard another scream.

Out of sight behind some large bushes, the mayors daughter lay face down on the grass. Harlan lay on top of her. He put his hand over the mayors' daughters' mouth. "Keep it down." He said.

"Don't stop," she moaned. "I'm not there yet,"

Harlan started pounding into her from the rear. "Harder," she cried. Harlan doubled his pace. She let out another scream.

"Did you hear that Mildred?"

Mildred put away her knitting. "They were going to have a party over there but that doesn't sound like a party to me. That was some girl screaming."

Henry put on his glasses and saw the smoke coming out of Steve's room on the second floor.

"Dial 911 Mildred. The O'Malley house is on fire."

"Oh my goodness," Mildred shouted, and rushed back into the house.

In the dining room the heavy metal group finished playing. Chalky, Bobbie, and Fred took up their instruments again and began to play a Thin Lizzy number, Jailbreak. Rick and the mayor's wife, along with most of the residents, danced to the music. Halfway through the song the fire alarm suddenly went off, triggered by the smoke coming from Steve's room. The sound of the alarm seemed to fit in with the song. Everyone in the leisure room cheered, thinking it was part of the act. After only a minute they heard the sound of sirens above the sound of the music. Flashing blue and red lights penetrated the windows from outside and danced off the walls. The crowd stared in awe and cheered at the spectacle. The dining room was transformed into an incredible discotheque.

"This is better than the fourth of July," Chalky cried.

Without warning, the windows were smashed by jets of water blasting through and showering the room. Light fittings blew up and sparks flew in all directions. Suddenly the jets of water hit the amplifiers, and everything exploded. Firemen in full gear charged into the dining room carrying hatchets and hoses and blasted guitars, drum set, and drowning the terrified band members and party guests in a shower of water. Many rushed screaming out of the room, while others tried to find cover behind overturned tables and chairs.

In his room upstairs and only vaguely aware of the commotion, Steve got up off the floor and helped the mayor to his feet. "Must have set off the alarm," Steve said. "Got to get rid of all this smoke." They threw their joints out the window and frantically tried to disperse the smoke by fanning with blankets and cushions. Suddenly, hard jets of water hit them through the open window and knocked them over. At the same time three firemen wearing oxygen masks broke down Steve's door.

"Isn't that the Mayor?" Steve heard one of them say as he tried to pull himself up off the floor.

Thirty minutes later they were all herded out onto the grounds while the fire brigade searched in vain for the suspected fire. Rick, soaking wet, stood next to Chalky who was trembling and staring gaunt eyed at the firemen going about their work.

"I think I blew it." Rick said, shaking his head. "I knew I should have stayed in New York."

The police were not surprised when the results of the blood tests came in from the mayor, the councilors and Steve. What did surprise them was the presence of amphetamines in the blood of everyone else who resided in the home. Rick's blood contained such a high amount the doctors hospitalized him for two days. He was released from hospital the same time the mayor, councilors, and Steve were released from jail.

In the weeks that followed the frenzy of media coverage around Mound Merrian dominated all other world events. Local and international newspaper headlines confronted the residents with a fate worse than death.
"MAYOR AND COUNCIL REMOVED FROM OFFICE."
"FOUNDATION FUND MOUNT MERRIAN BLOCKED."
"MOUNT MERRIAN IN SERIOUS FINANCIAL DIFFICULTY."
"OLD MUSICIANS THREATENED WITH EXPULSION."

One month later Mount Merrian was not closed, but the damage from the water was extensive. Most of the residents remained in the mansion while the leisure and dining rooms were still being refurbished. Meals were served in makeshift tents in the garden. Mrs. Edwards and Mr. Underwood moved out the day after the incident while Mrs. Orland was hospitalized for severe mental shock. The only difference to the outside of the mansion was the large 'For Sale' sign attached to the front railings.

Rick sat in a small wicker chair in the back of the garden surrounded by all the residents.

"Thank you all for coming," he said, trying not to look anyone in the eye, "but as you can see things are going downhill fast folks, and I don't know what to do about it."

No one moved or said a word. The mood was somber. Harlan sat in a white plastic garden chair staring into nothing. Steve lay flat on the grass with his eyes closed. Chris and David sat next to one another at the front of the crowd staring at the ground.

"It's all my fault." Steve said, his eyes still closed.

Rick shook his head. "Don't be ridiculous. It was my fault. It was my bloody idea and as usual it went right up the Swanee." Rick spotted Charles Drewberry carrying a sheet of paper coming out of the house and heading towards them.

"Anyway, Charles is going to fill us in on what's going to happen with us."

Dressed in his pinstriped suit, Charles walked across the lawn towards the crowd. They all stared at him expectantly as he approached Rick.

"What did they say at the council meeting?" Rick asked.

"As you might have expected. They have replaced the entire city council, who have been charged for using the funds for their own personal use. That pot of money we made from the charity concert is nearly empty. Mrs. Quinten has been relieved of her duties and criminal proceedings have been lodged against her for supplying amphetamines to the residents. Young Wesley has agreed to testify against her in return for immunity from prosecution."

"Good old Wesley," Rick said.

"What about a new place for us?" Chris asked.

"There won't be any," Charles replied. The new council has decided that as soon as the last of the funds are exhausted we have to move out. That should be in about two months. They said by that time we should all have found another place to stay."

"It's not fair." Eva said. "We don't have anywhere else to go."

"At least they didn't press charges." Harlan replied.

"Okay, but that still puts us back on the street." Rick said.

"Maybe we should call Kronin," Drewberry said.

"I rang his office every other day for the last month." Rick replied. "He's not taking any of my calls. There's not a lot we can do. The only option is to go back to where we all came from. I could always go back to the streets, although David would have to go to a nursing home."

"You wouldn't last six months on the streets," Eva replied. "And what about the rest of us? Most of us gave up everything to come here," she said, as tears started to roll down her cheeks. "Any of us who had money either gave it away to charities or passed it on to family and friends. Those who came out of retirement homes like me left for a very good reason. I don't think no one is looking forward to going back. We've got nowhere to go."

A few shook their heads in agreement.

"It's all my fault." Steve said once again, and then there was silence.

"Don't give yourself all the blame Steve, leave a little bit for me." Rick said, and suddenly pulled himself upright. "Just sitting here staring at the grass and moaning isn't going to change a thing. Maybe it's time we stood up and did something for ourselves. I know my ideas are not worth shit but we're all musicians, right? So why don't we give our own benefit concert." They all looked at him in disbelief. "If we have everything under our own control nobody can touch us. We could take care of our own finances, and hire and fire our own staff. No directors or trust-management bullshit pulling the strings. We could run the place as a collective. Everyone can have a say in everything we do, so I won't have to take the blame for everything."

"It's an idea." Eva said, drying her eyes. "But I don't think it will work. It sounds just too complicated."

"You think running a place like this is complicated?" Rick said. "Many of us have had their own businesses and ran them successfully. We've had staff, organized and ran our own concerts and companies. We could break it all down so everyone is just doing a little bit and no one is taking the weight of it all on their shoulders. This would be a piece of cake."

Chris laughed. "A benefit concert? Don't be ridiculous."

"Piece of cake," Rick said again. "The only thing we have to do is get a couple of bands together and give a concert.

"A couple of bands?" Chris said, nearly choking. "Chalky and the boys are the only complete band here. The others would never draw a concert crowd. And besides, we haven't got an instrument left to play on, or the money to buy new gear."

Rick was more than certain. "I think we can do it."

"I think Alzheimer's is setting in Rick." Chris said shaking his head. "You're trying to re-live your youth. The time you thought you could do everything, and you even messed up that as well."

"All right, we all make mistakes, but I don't give up as quickly as you, that's for sure." Rick replied. Chris turned his head away from Rick and gazed at the ground. Everyone in the garden felt the tension between the two of them. The mood among the group had never been so dark. They all remained silent.

Rick stared at David who sat absolutely motionless in his wheelchair. Rick could see him twitching slightly. He lowered his head to get a better look at him. There seemed to be a sparkle in his eye; a fire. He did not seem to have the defeatist attitude the others had. There was half a smile on David's face.

Rick jumped up. "David thinks we can do it," he shouted. David shook violently in his wheelchair and suddenly let out a loud grunt, followed by a clear shout; "Yeeesss, dooo iiiit." They all looked on in shock at David. He tried to get up out of the wheelchair. Rick caught his arm and helped him to his feet. David struggled to stay standing as he shook his good arm from left to right. "Plaaaay." David screamed. "Plaaaay."

"Yes my boy," Rick screamed. "You know we can do it. The weakest of us all yet he's got more guts than all of us put together."

Fred jumped to his feet. "What are we waiting for, let's go for it."

Suddenly they all cheered. "Where would we get the money to stage it?" Harlan shouted above the noise of the crowd.

"The last of the funds," Rick replied. "In a couple of months from now it's going to be used up anyway." The crowd simmered down to listen.

"Where would we stage it?" Charles asked. "Maybe we could we get the Superdome again?"

"Can't afford it." Chris said. "And even if we could it would eat up all the money we could earn from the concert."

Then Rick's face lit up. "What about our own back yard? We've got plenty of room out there. The damn place is probably bigger than Woodstock."

Drewberry cut in. "Easier said than done. What about lights, sound, stage, instruments?"

"We'll stage it in the afternoon," Rick said. "then we won't need lights and all the fancy stuff. We could build a small stage for ourselves, and maybe we can borrow some instruments and equipment from the sound shop in town. I'm sure they'd lend us something."

"Sure," Chris said, sounding unconvinced. "What about publicity?"

"I think I could add a helping hand to that," Drewberry said. "I still have contacts, and all it ever took before was a few simple telephone calls. I'm sure I still know how to pick up a phone."

"How much do you think we could raise?" Rick asked Charles.

Drewberry stood up and began to pace back and forth. Everyone went silent, expectant. This was the Drewberry they knew. He did all his serious thinking on his feet, and by the time he finished he would have it worked out to the finest detail.

"You have to realize," Drewberry announced, "that most of the kids who came to the original benefit concert came to see the bands who were playing. Not us. We would probably be lucky to attract six to eight thousand people. Not a great deal but since we are desperate we could perhaps raise up to two hundred thousand dollars charging twenty-five dollars a head. Television rights about the same. Doing our own catering could raise another ten thousand. We would have to rent extra toilet facilities and security. I think we could probably end up with about three hundred thousand dollars."

Harlan smiled. "Add that to our pensions and we might be able to stay at least twelve months."

"And then have another concert next year, "Rick said, and jumped up out of his chair. He began waving his arms. "Come on people. What are we waiting for? We've got work to do."

The mood switched instantly. Nearly everyone had a smile and started discussing with each other what they could do to help. Only Chris remained sitting quietly in his chair, gently shaking his head in disapproval.

Chapter twenty-nine

The following day Rick spent most of his time talking to the staff about the situation. He was not sure they would stay. Most of them, even Wesley, decided to stay on for free until after the concert. After that it was a question of economics. They knew they could never hope for the same salary Quinten paid, and they all had mortgages to pay and families to feed; so staying on after the concert would be too much of a financial burden. Wesley and all the nursing staff promised to help them find new staff when the time came.

As the days passed, preparations got underway for the concert. In the garden at the rear of the mansion a group of residents extended and enlarged the verandah to create a small stage. In Quinten's old office Harlan sat next to the Xerox machine watching photocopies roll out onto the tray.

Rick appeared in the doorway. "How's the printing department coming along?"

"Not bad. This is easier than I thought. Take a look."

Harlan proudly held up a page. The text was written with a shaky hand using a thick felt-tip pen.

THE GREATEST BANDS STILL ALIVE
THE MOUNT MERRIAN CONCERT
AUGUST 15
Tickets only $25

"Looks great," he said, giving him a thumbs up, then moved on.

The renovated leisure room had been turned into a multipurpose office and conference room. Chris and David sat in the middle at a table piled high with fliers and envelopes.

Charles had confiscated Quinten's desk and had it dominantly positioned against the wall to the right of the room, Facing out, it gave him a bird's eye view of all the goings on in the leisure room.

"Strange," Rick said to Charles, "this looks like your old office in London."

There were three old-fashioned telephones on his desk.

"Found these in the cellar," Charles said. "Just enough to keep me occupied." Suddenly one of the telephones rang.

"Charles Drewberry," he said with a definite air of authority. Thank you for calling back. I would like to speak to the chief editor of Rolling Stone magazine. I said Drewberry, Charles Drewberry. I was the agent to every top band except the Beatles. Yes... that Drewberry. Thank you, I'll hold." Drewberry looked up at Rick. "You would expect people writing about the industry would know about the industry."

"Maybe you just got the receptionist." Rick said.

"No doubt," Drewberry replied, and sighed deeply.

Rick moved on to Joe Riley who sat a small table, writing a letter. His granddaughter's centerfold was spread out in front of him.

"I'm writing to my granddaughter Tracy." Joe told Rick. "I'm going to ask her if she can help us out with the promotion. She's got lots of connections."

"I bet she has," Rick replied. "She's more than welcome to come and help. We could do with a pair of hands like hers."

Joe laughed. "You dirty old man Ricky. I know what you're thinking."

"Well don't write in your letter okay, you'll get me into trouble," he said, tapping Joe on the back. Joe, forever smiling, returned to his writing.

In the center of the room Chris had just finished stuffing Harlan's fliers into envelopes. He took a roll of stamps and started to tear them off one by one. David sat next to him with his tongue sticking out. Chris ran a stamp over David's tongue, then pasted it to the envelope. With his tongue hanging out, David managed a smile as Rick strolled past them behind Chris, who didn't notice him at all. Charles was now busy with another call. Everything was going better than Rick expected.

Steve came in from the garden. "The boys are doing a great job with the stage out there," he told Rick. "How many bands do you think we can put together?"

"It's not as bad as we thought. I've rounded up lead singers from at least three top bands," Rick replied, "and we've got enough session musicians from the house to group together. With a little luck I think we could end up with at least five good bands."

"You think this is going to work? Some of these people are really old, not like you or me." Steve said.

"I don't think anyone could carry a session as long as they used to." Rick replied. "Probably half an hour at most. That will give us about two and a half hours of music. After that I think we'll have to spend some time hooked up to some equipment in a hospital to recuperate."

They strolled out into the garden and watched a number of residents working on different jobs. Some carried floor boards towards the makeshift stage, while others placed fairy lights and Christmas decorations on trees and bushes in the garden. Every object they could find in the house that could be put to use for the concert was used. Small table lamps and flashlights were taped along the front of the stage to light up the bands. Large armchairs and sofas were placed at the back of the stage so the musicians could rest before and after the performance.

Suddenly, the scream of a fire engine siren came from the other side of the house. From all corners of the garden everybody dropped what they were doing and rushed towards the front of the mansion.

"I can't see any fire or smoke." Rick shouted to Steve as they both ran after the crowd. A large fire engine pulled up to the house with lights flashing and sirens wailing, followed by an equally large rental truck. All along the front of the house men and women, curious of the spectacle, opened windows and stood on balconies as they watched firemen jump off the fire engine and head towards the truck. Rick recognized the fire chief coming towards him; the same one who destroyed their party. He removed his helmet and waved to the anxious men and women running out of the mansion.

"It's all right folks. No need to panic. We're just here on unofficial business." He shook Ricks hand and guided him towards the rental truck were his men were unloading boxes of every size and shape.

"We heard about your fundraising concert," he told Rick, "and I realize the insurance company is going to take some time to pay for the damage we caused. So to make sure the concert is a success we decided to present you with these in advance of the settlement." The boxes were opened up to reveal amplifiers, large speakers, guitars, saxophones, and other instruments. The entire front of the house shouted and cheered.

Fred, Chalky and other elderly musicians rushed over and grabbed the new shining instruments. One old musician picked up a saxophone while another grabbed up a trumpet and started to play. The sound was terrible.

"I think they're just a little out of practice." Rick said.

"I'm sure they'll get it together in time for the concert," The fire chief commented.

"I wouldn't put money on it." Rick replied.

During the following week, every soul in Mount Merrian seemed to be practicing chords or learning the words to long-forgotten songs. The house was alive again, and pulsing with a new energy. Harlan spent the week driving around on his Harley Davidson handing out fliers in all the surrounding towns.

After Charles had contacted the national and international music magazines he concentrated on the newspapers. Throughout the week he called just about every newspaper in the country. Some were interested, many were not. In the end he found it difficult to judge the response. Worse than that he found it impossible to judge the turnout. He had sold the television rights for the price he wanted, but spent three valuable days bargaining for it. The controversy surrounding their party with the mayor was not easily forgotten, resulting in them being shunned by the national stations. The only deal he could make and the closest he got to a national broadcast was with twenty-two local stations spread throughout the country. The concept was to link up live between two and three in the afternoon, making it a semi-national broadcast. It was not the worst deal in the world, and certainly not the best, but it was the only deal he could get, and it drained him. Charles also tried to contract national ticket vendors to sell tickets to the concert throughout the country, but they all refused. The damage caused by the scandal made all deals impossible.

Chapter thirty

On the morning of the concert, breakfast in the dining room was very different to any other day. Zacharia had laid out a full English breakfast: fried bacon and eggs, black and white pudding, fried sausages, baked beans and fried tomatoes.

"English breakfast to get engine going and keep strength up. Isn't that right mister Rick." He shouted over to Rick, who sat in the corner of the dining room in front of his untouched breakfast. He stared down at the front gate and began to count heads. Twelve people stood at the closed gate. He smiled and nodded gently at Zacharia, then checked the clock on the wall. It was nine in the morning and things were not looking good. He could feel it in his bones; the turnout was going to be a disaster. At a normal concert, even one like this, there should have been thousands or at least hundreds lined up outside the gates by now. Another couple of people strolled up to the gates; bringing the headcount up to fourteen. What the hell was going on out there? Didn't they know that some of the greatest musicians in the world were here and going to give them a fabulous concert at a price they could afford? His heart sank.

At nine-thirty, when Rick had finally finished his breakfast, the crowd had doubled. Now there were at least twenty-five. He could feel his stomach turn over and it was not because of Zacharias' cooking. Things were looking desperate. He finished his coffee and went to look for Charles Drewberry.

Since early morning local television technicians had been setting up their equipment. Television cables ran from the stage along the back of the house and around to the front where one outside broadcasting van uploaded the signal to a geo-stationary satellite above the equator, then down again to the various local stations situated throughout the country. Just like in the Superdome, Drewberry had a central telephone room installed in the leisure room where people watching the broadcast could call in to make donations. Fourteen old men and women sat around telephones with pen and paper in hand, waiting anxiously for the phones to ring. This was one part of the concept Rick had no faith in. Less than a year ago people were being asked to give money to help set up the home. Now, they were being asked to help keep it on its feet. Everyone in the world had heard about the pot-smoking, drug-addicted elderly residents and their corrupt retirement home. No way would they would donate money a second time.

Rick could feel a familiar twinge at the back of his throat. He needed a shot of whiskey to settle his nerves. The urge to reach for the small bottle lodged in his inside jacket pocket was strong, but he knew he couldn't. If he started now it would be difficult to stop, and however bad the day was right now whiskey would only make it worse. He decided to keep it until the end of the day then he would drown his sorrows, pack the few remaining possessions he had, then head back to New York.

Charles had been smart enough to get in contact with Jimmy Olding, a seventeen-year-old local internet whiz kid who set up a website for the concert and were donations could be made online worldwide through PayPal. He also tapped into the television feed in the van, making it possible to stream the whole concert live to the Internet.

Rick watched the gates swing open at ten-thirty. He was surprised to see that the crowd had grown to roughly two hundred. Never enough to save the house but it did give him a sense of satisfaction. At an improvised booth next to the gate,

Rick watched CJ as she and a couple of other residents manned the entrance.

"Come on in darlings. Don't be shy." CJ said to two students dressed in moderate hippy outfits.

"Two tickets please," The first boy said, placing his money on the counter.

"Thank you very much." CJ said with a broad smile. "That will be fifty dollars. And if you're good boys maybe I'll give you a private tour of the house later."

"Wow, that would be great." The second boy replied.

"Fifty dollars is a lot of money for boys like you. I'll have to give you your money's worth. Here's your tickets. Go on and enjoy yourselves. I'll see you later," she shouted to the boys as they headed into the grounds.

CJ did not notice Rick watching her from the house. But he relaxed. At least they were in their early twenties. They couldn't afford another scandal. Without any rush or obvious excitement he had seen at the last benefit concert, people walked slowly through the grounds towards the back of the house and the stage. Rick was not only surprised to see people his own age or slightly younger entering the grounds, but there were many teenagers among them, even families with children.

At midday at least another two hundred had passed the gate while another twenty or thirty people were waiting to get in. Back around to the front of the house Rick kept his eye on the gate. Six to eight thousand people Charles had said. But right now he didn't think that more than four hundred had turned up. Chris came out of the front of the house and joined him.

"Did you see how many people are out back?" Rick asked.

"It could be better," Chris replied.

"It couldn't be worse," Rick said, shaking his head. "Another Rick Macken fuck up. Maybe I should start listening to you after all."

"Do you think that would help?"

"Probably not. I'd end up in the nut house alongside Preston. I'll end up there anyway because we are not going to make a penny today. We've spent all the little cash we had putting this together so we're finished. I think we'll be all out of here by the end of the week."

"What will you do?" Chris asked.

"I've already decided. I was going to head back to my old haunt but I think I'll move to San Francisco. Not so cold and no hurricanes. And you?"

"I think I can go back to the hospital. Luckily I still have my furniture. All I need now is somewhere to put it."

Suddenly, a couple of coaches pulled up to the gates and people began pouring out of them. A large sign on the coach read 'Baltimore'. Shortly after, more coaches pulled up from Pittsburgh, New York, Philadelphia, and as far South as Atlanta. Within an hour the grounds were packed, and the line of busses and automobiles turning up at the gates never ceased.

Much to Zacharias' astonishment, his hamburger tent at the rear of the grounds was doing great business. More of a surprise were the groups of people with guitars, tambourines, and fiddles forming little islands where they played folk, rock, and modern pop songs. The atmosphere throughout the entire garden was one of a huge family get-together as people entertained one another. Young musicians listened to old, while the old took the time to listen to and appreciate the young. Ancient friends met up once again to review past exploits and tell them to crowds who listened with envy. In every part of the garden a little miracle was happening and Rick, while changing into another set of clothing for the concert watched it with utter exhilaration from his room on the second floor. At nine this morning he felt his life sinking into another hell. Right now he was looking out onto a Garden of Eden.

At precisely two o'clock Charles Drewberry stepped nervously out onto the stage from behind the curtain made from drapes sewn together from the dining room. He tapped the microphone which cracked and boomed across the gardens, then suddenly turned away to aggressively clear his throat. Rick, standing in the wings, thought he was going to have a heart attack. Finally, he stepped up close to the microphone.

"Ladies and gentlemen, welcome to the grounds of Mount Merrian."

The crowd roared and cheered. When they finally settled down Charles seemed more nervous than ever. "Not unlike the Woodstock concert so many years ago you are about to witness history in the making. You are about to observe the gathering of some of the most influential rock bands of the last century. You may have thought that many of them were long dead or disappeared into total obscurity, but have we got some surprises for you. Ladies and gentlemen, welcome..." Charles said, raising his voice. "..welcome to the greatest concert ever staged on God's great earth."

Suddenly the music erupted from behind him. In the wings, Harlan and Steve pulled on a chord each side of the stage and the curtains opened up. Chalky, Fred, and Bobbie started the concert with one of their first hits; "Bear Tree Rock."

"From the heart of Texas. Please welcome the one and only... Bear Tree...." The crowd erupted.

Drewberry quickly walked off the stage. The sound was tight and dynamic. The little islands of music broke up as people were drawn to the stage by the riveting beat.

Since they did not have towers of speakers to shower the grounds in sound, they had placed smaller speakers, borrowed from everyone who would lend them, in bushes and trees throughout the garden. Instead of a massive booming sound, it turned out to be very local, and very clear. They danced and sang along to the music. Chalky, Bobbie, and Fred played seven of their most memorable hits which lasted for little more then half an hour. When they finished the curtains closed to the wild applause.

Charles Drewberry took to the stage once again, and less nervous then his first appearance

"I would like to welcome all the viewers on television and the internet to our concert. As you know our humble home has suffered from poor publicity and we do not attempt to deny any of the stories you might have heard, however, we plan to take over the management of the house and make sure nothing like that ever happens again."

Charles finished by calling out the bank account number where donations could be sent. He then called out the number of the phone room so people could make their contributions directly with their credit cards.

In the leisure room telephones began to blaze. People were calling from all over the country to send their contributions. Their only worry was the length of the broadcast; it was only an hour. After that the donations would definitely ease off. The question was by how much.

Jeffrey Baxter, who managed the small electronics shop in the nearby town, now running the operations at the call center, was called over to one of the operators, Jim Broadmoor, an old resident.

"I think you better take this call," Jim told Jeffrey, "it's serious."

"Police?"

"No, it's worse than that." He handed Jeffrey the headset.

"Hello? Can I help you?" Jeffrey did not recognize the voice on the other end of the line, but he quickly grabbed a pen and paper.

"When?" he asked. "Where? And your name is?" Jeffrey scribbled everything down in a rapid tempo. "Thank you for calling. We really appreciate it." He handed the headset back to

Jim, then turned around to find the room deadly quiet. Everybody had put their calls on hold and waited anxiously to hear what was going on. Jeffrey ripped the note out of the pad and went out the room without saying another word. He had to find Rick, and quick.

"And now for the big moment you have all been waiting for." Charles announced to the crowd from the stage. "Playing for the first time in nearly thirty years, please welcome....." The curtains opened and the sound of the crowd erupted in cheers and clapping as Rick's old band was revealed, totally drowning out Charles's introduction. For the first time in nearly thirty years Rick stood on stage with Farno on guitar, Chad on drums, and David. Television and radio commentators were on their feet shouting out the names of the reunited band members. Rick quickly grabbed the microphone from Charles and shouted, "This is a little number from a few mates of mine."

Farno hit the guitar, let the note hang then Chad came in on the drums followed by the rest of the band. David sat in his wheelchair with a guitar strapped to him. He hit the chords hard with his good hand while Chris, kneeling next to him, played the chords on the frets. As if it was an assault on their elderly years and increasing frailty the band began to blast out 'Together'. He composed after he came to the house since the words stuck in his mind and kept haunting him. When Farno contacted him after the house made the headlines he told him about the planned concert. They agreed to come, just once, to help David, not him, to prevent him from being sent to a home. Rick gave him the lyrics and Farno did the rest. The moment they rehearsed he knew it would become one of those numbers that would stay in the memory of everyone who heard it. This was another classic, and the world was going to take note. Rick darted across the stage.

"Here is to the misfits, wandering through the night
lost in streets and alleys
drinking in the full moonlight

Here is to the loners, so easy to recognize
this one's for all of us
'cause time is on our side

And I'll raise my glass to you, my friend
let's drink until we're stoned

We are all alone together but together we are not alone
We are all alone together but together we are not alone

      Chad played the drums with a force equivalent to that of a twenty-year-old. Farno, a cigarette dangling precariously on the edge of his lips, picked the chords on his well-worn guitar with rejuvenated energy. When they finished the crowd went wild. Even when they were famous as a band, Rick had never seen an audience react to a new number such as this. He felt uplifted, proud and humbled all at the same time.
      Then Farno played the chords to one of their old numbers, and as if he had never been away Rick's back went rigid; his legs shot him across the stage, just like the old days, and wearing a long trench coat borrowed from one of the television reporters, he waved his long arms wide and punched the air with his index finger. This is what he missed. Thirty years ago there was only one band that mattered, and they were it. Now he felt the blood rushing through his veins, absorbing all the energy from the crowd as they went crazy to the sound of the music.

      No one in their wildest dreams had ever believed it possible. All around the country the news spread like wildfire. The link-up of local broadcasting companies paid off. As the word spread, millions of people tuned in to witness the unique event. CNN rushed over a camera crew and within twenty minutes had their satellite dish up and running while their reporter hurried around finding people to interview for the historic event. MTV, who signed up for a tape but not for a live broadcast, had three camera crews roaming the grounds and house while another two filmed the event on stage. The idea was to gather enough material for a four-hour marathon broadcast of the Mount Merrian benefit a month after the concert.

In the wings Charles noticed Jeffrey waiting impatiently with the note in his hands. Jeffrey handed him the note and he read it.

"When did this come in?" Charles asked.

"Twenty minutes ago." Jeffrey replied.

"Oh my God." Drewberry muttered. Jeffrey did not wait for a response from Charles, he knew there wouldn't be one. He left him looking at the small piece of paper, in shock, and went back to the telephone room.

Rick's set carried on for a quarter of an hour longer than planned. Every time the band wanted to finish the crowd went wild calling them back for more. When they were finally allowed to leave the stage Charles appeared once again and stepped solemnly up to the microphone.

"Ladies and gentlemen. Less than an hour ago, a good friend of ours died at the Ryder Psychiatric Clinic in upstate New York." When Charles called out Preston's name a deep moan rippled through the public for what seemed an eternity.

Rick lowered his head then Eva and Harlan speedily put him down on a chair when they noticed his legs starting to give way. Chris went to his side, and put his arm around his shoulder in an effort to comfort him.

"If it is possible I would like to have a minute's silence." Charles said. The crowd responded immediately. Around the grounds there was a near total silence except for the odd baby crying. Suddenly, Charles could hear people weeping in the audience and behind him among the musicians. He realized he had a decision to make. He turned and saw Rick slumped over David in the wheelchair, both of them obviously in tears. The concert would have to be called off. In all his years in the business he had never encountered anything like this. Members of the audience and many of the musicians broke down and cried like children.

Charles glanced down at the piece of paper with the names of the bands he would have introduced. He had not thought about the next artist or the significance he held in relation to Preston and generations of fans. But suddenly it hit him. Charles looked to his left and saw him waiting in the wings. After the minute silence the crowed started to talk quietly to each other. They turned their focus once again towards Charles, expectant. He put away the paper and straightened his long and commanding posture.

"Ladies and gentlemen." Everybody in the audience grew deadly silent. "Mr. Bruce Springsteen." The crowd seemed to be hit by a second shock wave. The split second Springsteen stepped onto the stage the atmosphere broke like a shattering of glass. The crowd were on the feet clapping; a standing ovation. Bruce had no backing band behind him. He just stood with his guitar in hand and started to strum before the crowd had settled down. When they realized what he was about to play their applause grew even greater. Shouts of praise came from all corners of the audience.

Bruce played one of the songs that had made Preston famous. The song that started out as a social protest for the poor and downtrodden and ended up making him a worldwide hero. A song for the millions who felt he was speaking for them.

Bruce began the ballad quietly and subdued. The crowd started to sing with him. Gradually he began to pick up momentum. The multitude followed. Unexpectedly, a bass guitar came in and picked up the song. The drums followed suit. Bruce turned to see Chad at the drums. In the corner of his eye he saw Farno tuning his guitar. David started to strum a rhythm as Chris picked the chords. They played as if they had always played together.

Bruce built up more momentum, bringing the song to a sweeping finale. The crowd stayed with him. They finished with a blaze of chords, followed by a hard end. The crowd cheered and clapped. The television crews and presenters were also on their feet applauding.

He played another three songs then Robbie joined him on the stage to the applause of the crowd. After Bruce, Robbie sang a set of ten songs. Finally, Eva took to the stage.

"I want to thank you all for making this an unforgettable day. And now I'd like you all to relax and sit down in the grass. Throughout the grounds everybody began to sit down and make themselves comfortable. Eva started to pluck away on her guitar and sang the songs that made her famous. To her surprise, young and old sang with her.

Eva played for half an hour, and was joined by all the musicians on stage for the finale. They sang another ballad made famous by Preston and finished the concert.

Immediately after, they joined all the people in the grounds signing autographs and singing with them.

Even with the forty people who had come to the concert and stayed behind to help, it took four days to clear up the Mount Merrion grounds. Rick checked the bank account for donations nearly every few hours. He had never seen anything like it. By the end of the week there was a little more than fourteen million dollars on the account, and that was only the United States. About the same amount was waiting to be processed from all the countries who had watched the concert on the internet. He knew they would never have to worry about losing the house, in fact they would never have to worry about anything again.

A month after the broadcast and all the excitement, things began return to normal. Wesley and all the regular staff kept their jobs and Zacharia never dished up another goulash. They even decided to take on more staff for the simpler chores around the house. Steve now took normal vitamin pills, but still kept his favorite spot at the back of the garden for a nice quiet smoke. The cellar was converted into a rehearsal room and a forty-eight channel digital studio for anyone who wanted to use it.

For the first time in years Rick felt at home and unconstrained. His little flings with the nurses did not seem important any more since there was no one to caution him or tell him otherwise. Apart from that, life was bliss.

Advertisements in the newspapers for new staff had drawn thousands of responses from all over the United States. It took Charles, Rick, and Chris a week to wade through the letters. Chris made the final selection for those who would be invited for an interview.

When Jenny applied for the job she never believed for one moment she would be asked for an interview. Why should she? From the sixty vacancies she had applied for in the past year, none produced any results. What surprised her most was the personal invitation she received, which sounded as if she got the job already; apart from that, the flight down had been paid for. She just had to fill in the date. It took her three hours to get there by plane but when she saw the house and grounds she knew it was worth it. There was no way she was going to return to nightshifts at the diner ever again.

The end

Made in the USA
Charleston, SC
26 May 2011